Healing Passion

Healing Passion

SYLVIE OUELLETTE

Black Lace novels are sexual fantasies.
In real life, make sure you practise safe sex.

First published in 1995 by
Black Lace
20 Vauxhall Bridge Road
London
SW1V 2SA

Copyright © Sylvie Ouellette 1995

The right of Sylvie Ouellette to be identified as the
Author of this Work has been asserted by her in
accordance with the Copyright, Designs and Patents Act
1988.

Typeset by CentraCet Limited, Cambridge

ISBN 9780753541005

*All characters in this publication are fictitious and any
resemblance to real persons, living or dead, is purely
coincidental.*

This book is sold subject to the condition that it shall not, by way
of trade or otherwise, be lent, resold, hired out or otherwise
circulated without the publisher's prior written consent in any form
of binding or cover other than that in which it is published and
without a similar condition including this condition being imposed
on the subsequent purchaser.

Chapter One

Ten toes were mischievously staring at Judith, almost begging to be pinched, peeping out of the rectangular hole in the mint-coloured sheet like a family of tiny, stumpy puppets. They looked so out of place; her eyes were always coming back to those silent characters, her attention constantly diverted.

On the whole the feet looked rather anonymous; quite rugged but distinctly female, their wrinkled skin tinted a dark yellow by the iodine-based disinfecting lotion. But only the toes seemed to be in a laughing mood this morning.

At the other end of the operating table the patient's face was hidden behind yet another pale green screen, held up by a contraption hanging from the ceiling. The rest of the body was entirely covered under a sterilised sheet, the legs propped up in preparation for the surgery.

From where she was standing Judith could just see the top of the head of Edouard Laurin, the hypnotist sitting next to the patient's head. However, she could hear his voice fill up the room; warm, calming, haunting.

'Your feet no longer belong to you,' he said slowly in a heavy French accent, each word forever echoing in the room. 'We have borrowed them and in a few minutes we will give them back to you, all nice and new.'

Judith couldn't contain a nervous giggle. This was her first day at work and already she was overwhelmed by the unusual nature of the Dorchester Clinic, which offered state of the art cosmetic surgery and treatment to its select, wealthy clientele, in addition to a comfortable stay in a modern, luxurious building overlooking Holland Park.

Today, Lady Austin, rich widow of the late Lord Austin, the shipping magnate, was about to have her feet re-shaped. The woman was a regular patient, having visited the Clinic no less than eight times in the past five years, first to have a face-lift, then a tummy tuck. This had been followed by a long series of various repairs, according to her whims, on a body which would otherwise reveal its real age and probably betray almost five decades of over-indulgence.

This time she had claimed to no longer like the sight of her feet, complaining that she found them very unfashionable as she walked on the sandy beaches of some remote exotic island or strolling along the deck on the yacht of a rich friend.

Judith thought that they simply showed the result of years of torture from endless shopping sprees. Rich feet made to be pampered. No wonder the toes were in such a happy mood.

The cost of the operation and hospital stay would probably be more than the annual salary of the staff who would be looking after this wealthy patient, but that was always the case with the clients of the Dorchester Clinic. Here, money could buy them a new, lovely body, made to order.

The set-up of the operating theatre was impressive to Judith. All the equipment was top of the range, brand new and shining. The sweet smell of honeysuckle filled the air, a nice change from the strong smell of disinfectant that usually floated throughout the corridors of other clinics.

Smooth music was escaping from a loudspeaker, concealed somewhere in the ceiling. The soft orange tint of the ceramic tiles both on the floor and on the walls gave the room a subdued, quiet look, which was pleasantly different from the standard dark green found in older institutions.

The atmosphere was warm and comfortable and, if she closed her eyes even for just a second, Judith could almost believe this was a room at an expensive beauty salon, not a hospital.

It was only a month since she had graduated from nursing school, and she was lucky to have been hired right away. Most of her classmates had applied for the vacancy and had reacted jealously when Judith had been offered the position.

A prestigious clinic, and a matching salary. Not bad for a first job. On top of that everyone here was charming, young and good looking. It seemed as though the Clinic's staff advertised how the clients could expect to look like if they came here. Judith had been told her pretty face and her attractive figure had been a key element in obtaining the job. Nevertheless, she had been hired on a three-month contract and had to prove she was a competent nurse.

Today, for the first time, she would assist on a procedure where the patient was not anaesthetised but hypnotised. As Lady Austin was being put under, Judith somehow felt Edouard's voice transport her as well. She was finding it difficult to concentrate on setting up the instruments in preparation for the surgery.

The tinkling sound of the metal seemed louder than usual, although it couldn't quite bury the words that were still coming to her ears, the way Edouard slowly pronounced each word, the R's rolling like a cascade in his throat.

'You shall remain in this state, relaxed and comfortable until I tell you otherwise,' he continued. Judith breathed a sigh of relief. Lady Austin was now in a trance, but thankfully she was herself still wide awake.

'I think we are ready, Nurse Stanton.' She was startled when he spoke again, this time in a more lively tone. It took Judith a few seconds to realise he was now talking to her.

Peering in his direction, she saw a smiling face appear over the pale green screen, topped by a matching green surgeon's hat. Two blue eyes were looking at her, eyes so pale, so washed out they seemed unreal, like the eyes of ancient porcelain dolls. Edouard wasn't much older than her but the unusual tint of his eyes gave him a certain authoritative look.

Judith felt herself blush, ridiculously, like a teenager under the gaze of a handsome teacher. She dropped a scalpel and the noise it made as it hit the ceramic floor brought her back to reality.

'The Doctors should be here in just a minute ...' The remainder of her sentence was lost in a ruffle of noise as the operating team entered the room.

Like a magical ballet three peoplè, all gowned, coiffed and masked in matching green, proceeded around the table and its patient, speaking only a few words, their movements precise and decisive, like robots.

As the powerful lamps were switched on above the operating table, the rest of the large operating theatre disappeared in the dark, the strong light swallowing the whole of the room, save for the patient and the attending staff. Almost simultaneously the music that had been creating such a comfortable atmosphere seemed to die as well, leaving only silence to accompany this darkness.

Judith came forward to join the team and took her place to the right of Doctor Robert Harvey, the chief surgeon. He turned to face her. She couldn't see his mouth behind his mask but his laughing eyes told her he was smiling.

'You're the new nurse ... Miss Stanton, right? Welcome to the Dorchester Clinic. I hope you enjoy working with us.' His voice was warm and low, his tone velvety, making him sound like a radio announcer on the late-night programme.

His proximity was disturbing. His dark and piercing eyes watched as her trembling fingers tied her mask behind her neck. Judith looked away, unable to stand his gaze without blushing.

'Are we ready?' he asked around. Everyone nodded. 'Let's start then.'

Two other doctors on the opposite side of the operating table, a man and a woman, were assisting him. Judith didn't recognise them but they also acknowledged her presence and silently smiled at her with their eyes. Smiled and stared. Intensely.

Judith suddenly felt uneasy under their gaze. Not so long ago she had faced a series of examiners who wanted to probe her knowledge, forcing her brain to recapture and spit out everything she had learned in nursing school. Those grilling sessions had been difficult but she had passed the final tests with flying colours.

Today, however, the questions in the surgeons' eyes were of a different nature. She had no answer for them, unable to make out what they wanted of her, only that their powerful glare was overwhelming. It was as if they were seeking to get at her very soul; they didn't care for what she knew but rather they wanted to find out who she was. It soon became intolerable and she swallowed a nervous sob.

The atmosphere grew heavy as she looked at them in turn. Was this their way of showing their authority? A new nurse against three experienced surgeons, what did they expect from her? Dressed identically they almost looked threatening; a uniform colour from head to toe, completely concealed, anonymous. Time stood still for a while and so did Judith.

When Doctor Harvey held out his hand in her direction, it took her a few seconds to realise it was his way of asking for the scalpel. The surgeons' eyes were still on her, Harvey's as black as marble beads, the assistants' a matching pair of emeralds. Once she reacted, however, they looked down towards the task at hand and they seemed to forget all about her.

Almost instantly she ceased to be the object of their curiosity. Their hold on her, the spell, was broken. As if they had extracted what they wanted out of her, even if she couldn't make out what it was, they were silently dismissing her.

For the next four hours Judith lived a dream, like a spectator to the operation rather than a participant. Occasionally the surgeons glanced at her, but only briefly, and when they did she could read their silent questions.

She replied swiftly and exactly to each of their demands by handing them the instruments they required. Meanwhile the surgeons worked their art on yet another pair of feet, transforming the rough, tired extremities into delicate jewels any fashion model could envy.

All the while only Edouard's voice would break the clicking sound of the instruments, always soothing and haunting, as it kept the patient under the spell and cast its relaxing effect all around the room.

Now and again she had to wipe the surgeons' foreheads, keeping her eyes on the procedure to anticipate their demands. Her concentration was extreme and she was so busy that it was all over before she knew it.

When instructed by Edouard, Lady Austin began humming an old folk song. This was his way of gradually guiding her out of the trance. During the surgery the patient hadn't uttered a word, oblivious to what was going on in the room.

Judith helped Edouard push the operating table and the patient out of the theatre and into the recovery room. The doors closed behind him and the patient but her work wasn't over, she still had to set the instruments aside for the cleaning staff. She turned around and walked back into the large room. The powerful lamps had been switched off and the room looked just as cosy as before. It even seemed larger, now that the table had been pushed away.

The doctors were exchanging comments following the operation, and paid no attention to her, unlike before the surgery. The smacking sound of latex covered their words as they all pulled off their gloves. In unison, they also took off their hats and masks.

At that moment Judith recognised one of the assistants as Doctor Elizabeth Mason, a loud, feisty brunette she had met at her job interview. Doctor Mason had been very friendly that day, but why hadn't she spoken to Judith at all during the operation? A single word of encouragement could have made a big difference. And although she had remained silent during the whole time the surgery had lasted – as if her mouth was gagged by her surgical mask – her loud voice was now making up for lost time. Pearls of laughter bounced around the room, amplified by the emptiness and the ceramic walls. But even then she didn't have a single word for the new nurse.

The other assistant was a young blond man Judith hadn't been introduced to, but she knew he was Doctor Tom Rogers, one of the orthopaedic surgeons. He looked boyish, almost frail and delicate in his manners. He seemed nice enough, but not very manly, to say the least. His high-pitched, whining voice was very irritating. His sandy hair was wispy like a baby's, straight and squarely cut all in one length just above his ears. A good-looking boy, in a cute sort of way. Nothing to get excited about. Probably a spoilt brat; a mummy's boy.

The two assistants kept chatting together, making their way out of the room. Only Doctor Harvey stayed behind. Judith's heart began to pound when she realised she was alone with him and he was still staring at her, his smile now plainly visible.

All was silence in the operating theatre once the assistants had gone. There was no way Judith could avoid him now. She felt uneasy but somewhat flattered by the way he looked at her; no longer threatening, rather amused, almost friendly. Immediately she felt herself blush again.

This was stupid, what was so embarrassing about being alone with a man? But there was more to it than that, obviously. Without his mask and hat, Robert

Harvey was incredibly handsome. Although he was barely in his thirties, he was already a prestigious surgeon. Tall and dark, he vaguely reminded Judith of those actors cast as doctors on television, so good-looking they're almost unreal. Yet in real life anyone half as decent-looking had failed to materialise once she started nursing school.

He hoisted himself on a high stool and grabbed a piece of slim, clear rubber tubing from the table next to him, slowly studying its length and twisting it with his fingers.

'You work fast,' he commented simply, his voice echoing in the empty room.

Judith didn't reply, unable to find anything to say. Her hands began to shake as she placed each instrument in a basin of green disinfectant solution. Just as when he had first entered the room and looked at her so intensely, the effect he had on her was surprising and quite difficult to manage. Thankfully she had been able to control her hands during the surgery, when it really mattered.

Never taking his eyes off her, Doctor Harvey continued toying with the plastic tubing, slowly wrapping the long piece around his fingers several times before tying it in knots, using only his fingertips.

Judith watched the play of fingers intensely, mesmerised by the sight of his hands and the way they moved. Curiously, the effect was similar to the sound of Edouard's hypnotising voice, or perhaps even more powerful.

During the operation those hands had looked unreal through the latex gloves; like expert and strong tools. Now she could see them for what they really were. The long, slim fingers appeared smooth and caressing, just like the man's voice.

And as she felt his eyes on her, two hot rays surveying her body, Judith suddenly wished, foolishly, that his hands could follow the path of his gaze. To feel his fingers twitching over her bare skin the way they were toying with the rubber tubing would no doubt be extremely enjoyable . . .

She had to force herself to look elsewhere, to take her eyes away from the captivating sight. Her feet were like lead by now but she found the strength to move around, desperately trying to look casual as he kept watching her every move. She turned around, gathered the soiled linen into a heap and dropped it into the basket by the door.

His eyes followed her and were now fixed on her breasts. Judith could feel the weight of his stare. The surgery had been demanding and Judith had felt very hot. Half-moons of sweat had collected under her breasts and were now emphasising their plump roundness. And that's exactly what he was looking at.

Her nipples grew hard despite herself, brushing against the rough, starched cotton of the green gown she was wearing and making her blush further. If he kept looking at her like this for much longer, there was no way he wouldn't notice the effect he had on her.

Then he spoke, but by now Judith was so troubled she couldn't hear words, only the melody of his voice. She looked up, the fire of her embarrassment throbbing on her cheeks. He smiled again. 'Are you always this quiet?'

'N ... no ...' she managed to reply as she turned around, unable to stand this sweet torture any longer. She was angry with herself for reacting this way, yet she was also flattered to have him look at her like this.

She wasn't used to being the subject of so much attention, especially from a man like him. Up until now all the doctors she had worked with, even the most competent, couldn't remember so much as her name.

'So, I'll ask that you be assigned to my team whenever I'm operating,' he concluded. 'I'm sure we'll work well together.'

Judith wasn't quite sure what to make of that, hearing the words but not really understanding their meaning. Did he want her on his team because she was competent, or was it simply because he wanted the opportunity to disrobe her with his glare as often as possible?

Without a word he let himself slide from the stool, in a silent, feline motion. Still without a word he walked away, glancing over his shoulder and smiling at her one more time before disappearing.

Chapter Two

Everything was quiet as Judith glided down the long corridor of the sixth floor, the thick carpet cushioning her steps, her white uniform reduced to a faint shadow in the dimness of the night lights.

She passed a series of pale, solid oak doors, all identical, all numbered in sequence regardless of whether they were patients' rooms or just utility closets. Of course, there were no wards at the Dorchester Clinic, only private rooms.

But in the corridor each door was identical to the next. This was somewhat disconcerting and confusing, and Judith couldn't help feeling lost. If only there were signs to indicate what could be found on the other side of these doors.

In other clinics only the patients' rooms where numbered and there were always signs to differentiate the bathrooms; the treatment rooms had very large doors and the closets narrow ones. And in most places the doors to the patients' rooms and the wards were always kept open.

Curiously, at the Dorchester Clinic, the doors all looked the same, numbered from one to thirty on each of the six floors, and they were all kept closed, making the place look just like a hotel and ensuring maximum privacy for the patients. But whilst this added to their comfort, it didn't make things easy for the staff. Only in time would Judith manage to figure out behind which doors the patients' rooms were.

As she made her way to the end of the corridor the silence seemed to increase, the sounds swallowed before they were even born. She looked down and saw that her feet had become two white stains on the dark carpet. That was something else she had never seen before: this was probably the only clinic in the world to have carpeting in the corridors ...

She stopped by the last door on the right and consulted the chart once again, making sure she was at the right place, then entered the room. Her shoes made a faint squeaky sound as she walked across the hardwood floor to the bed at the far end of the room.

The only source of light was a tiny halogen lamp above the headboard, casting a vaguely greenish glow. Lady Austin was laying comfortably, as if she were in her own bed. Only the bulk of the bandages around her feet looked out of place, the rough bundle a stark contrast to the ivory silk night gown she was wearing.

Judith had to take her patient's blood pressure one more time before going home. Her first day at work had turned out to last longer than she had expected and her back was getting sore, her feet tired. However, in just a few minutes she would finally be allowed to leave.

Lady Austin stirred from her slumber, looked up at the nurse and smiled, still groggy from the medication she had been given.

Judith reached into one of the drawers of the wall unit and took out the leather cuff. She secured it around the naked arm and set the stethoscope in the groove of the woman's elbow. The cuff swelled gently as Judith pressed the pump and the sound in her ears isolated her for a minute. She felt rather than heard a presence behind her. In the circle of light around the bed Doctor Harvey appeared, his white coat cutting a large patch out of the darkness. Obviously, he had also come to check on his patient.

Judith's heart started to beat faster as she recalled their brief conversation in the operating theatre that morning, although now it seemed like years ago. Looking back, he had been very friendly with her, nothing more. It had lasted just a few minutes, yet she had been glued to the floor the whole time as she had felt him examining her. Was it only her imagination, or had he really been trying to guess the contours of her body under her pale green gown?

She couldn't figure it out. Perhaps it was all because of his voice, so sensuous, seductive, that in Judith's mind it had turned small-talk into a flirtatious chat.

Again tonight, as he addressed Lady Austin, he spoke in a low voice which was both captivating and warm. No doubt he was trying to make Lady Austin feel she was more than just another pair of feet to him.

'The bandages should be coming off in a couple of days,' he told her as he came to stand just behind Judith. 'So if everything is in order you'll be able to go home by Friday.'

Once again Judith was so troubled by the sound of his voice that she ceased to understand him. She only knew that she didn't want him to stop talking.

She hadn't seen him at all after the surgery, although she had kept an eye out for him. For a couple of hours after coming out of the operating theatre she had imagined him around every corner, her heart pounding fast whenever she saw a vaguely familiar silhouette across a crowded corridor. And every time she had been mistaken and disappointed – until now. Now he really was there, just a few inches away from her.

Standing between him and the bed, she couldn't dare turn around and look at him, nor even merely divert her eyes in his direction. But what was *he* looking at, peering over her shoulder? Did he come to make sure she took good care of her patient? Or was his visit simply aimed at comforting Lady Austin to help her relax before going to sleep?

He had come in and talked to the patient. Now it seemed he had nothing else to say, and Lady Austin had closed her eyes and was gradually going back to sleep. So what was he still doing here?

Judith grew confused and nervous, unable to read the result of the blood pressure on the tiny meter. She had to pump up the cuff again, clumsily. At that moment she was taken by surprise, almost shocked, when his hands gently lifted her dress. First she felt the faint caress of his fingertips, slowly pulling up her white uniform until her buttocks were exposed, clad in tiny cotton panties.

A wave swept her and she desperately tried to hold in the nervous sob of joy that rose in her throat. Listening to the swishing sound of the blood flow in the stethoscope, somehow she felt it was her own blood she could hear racing through her veins.

She didn't need to look at his face to know that there could be no doubt about his intentions. The only problem was that her own mind was in no condition to function clearly.

She couldn't gather the strength to turn around and look at him. His hands were slowly studying the swell of her behind, like a blind man feeling the dark world around him. Already her skin was replying like an echo to the pulsating warmth of his touch.

Deep within herself, sensations long forgotten surfaced: the first time a boy had lifted her dress, the first hand she had felt caressing her behind. She hadn't been touched in such a long time it seemed . . . But what was she to do? Should she encourage his behaviour, and possibly have to deal with something bolder, or would it be best to tactfully ask him to stop?

Then his fingers found their way inside her panties, ever so easily, as if they belonged there. The same fingers she had marvelled at earlier that day were now teasing the smooth skin of her buttocks, their touch light as a feather. She could never ask him to stop now... Her legs began to tremble in excitement.

'I think we should let Lady Austin sleep now, Doctor,' she managed to whisper. Her hands still trembling, she undid the blood pressure cuff and rolled it up in a bundle before putting it back in the drawer, along with the stethoscope.

'Quite right, nurse,' Doctor Harvey replied in her ear, the warmth of his breath caressing her neck as he slowly pulled his hands out of her panties. 'However, I would like to discuss her chart, if you have a minute.'

'Of course,' said Judith, glancing at her watch. 'I was just about to go home but if you need to speak to me I can spare a moment.' The timing was perfect and she saw it as a good omen, though she was wondering what he really wanted to discuss, if indeed he wanted to talk at all.

She couldn't erase from her mind the way he had looked at her in the operating theatre, and how he had now caressed her so intimately. Surely he would want more than just a friendly chat this time around? There could be no doubt about his intentions. Judith knew she probably wouldn't have the strength to refuse his invitation.

He didn't turn around as they walked out of the room, stepping back into the semi-darkness of the corridor. Instead of turning left and making his way back to the brightly lit nurses' station, he opened the door to the stairwell and started to walk down several flights of steps.

Judith was just a few paces behind him, obediently following his white silhouette all the way down to the basement and then to the door marked 'Doctors' Lounge.' She didn't know what to expect and didn't dare to hope.

'They're all gone at this hour,' Harvey said, opening the door. 'We won't be disturbed.'

Judith hesitated a moment as he ushered her in. The only light came from the open door which revealed the entrance to the doctors' lounge to look like a posh sitting room, with leather furniture, glass tables, cushions everywhere and a large bookcase alongside the far wall. Beyond that it got darker, and it was almost impossible to tell how big the room actually was.

Doctor Harvey stood tall behind Judith, gently pushing her inside, his hands on her shoulders.

'What exactly did you want to discuss with me?' she asked, without turning around. She was excited yet afraid to be discovered in a place where nurses were not allowed to set foot.

'Well, for one, I don't like the way you take your patients' blood pressure. I think you need a quick refresher course.'

Without turning on the lights, he led her to a leather couch at the back of the lounge where he made her sit. Once the door closed behind them the cloudy light filtering through the frosted glass enabled her to make out his profile in the shadow as he sat next to her.

'First, you need good equipment,' he said, taking out a stethoscope from the pocket of his white coat. With his other hand, using only his fingertips, he started to slowly undo the series of buttons at the front of Judith's uniform, stopping half-way down her belly.

Judith felt the cool air of the room flow inside her dress as her skin was gradually exposed, her nipples reacting to the difference of temperature and also in excitement. The doctor was just about to examine her . . .

He placed the flat piece of the stethoscope between her breasts and she was startled by the cold contact. She shivered nervously.

Of course, she knew this 'refresher course' was just a farce and would probably lead to something outside her nurse's duties. At any other time she might have tried to stop him, but tonight it seemed she was no longer in control of her own body. She was also intrigued by the way she had responded to his blatant invitation and so wilfully followed him. Her own desire both amazed and scared her at the same time.

The memory of his eyes on her body had stayed with

her all day, and only served to enhance the desire to be near him again. She felt powerfully attracted to him and although in some remote part of her mind something was telling her this wasn't professional at all, at this moment her body was more than willing to do whatever he would ask of her.

Already she could feel the fire of arousal building up between her legs. So far she had only ever been with men her own age. And although he wasn't much older than her, Doctor Harvey was already a prestigious surgeon. He was her superior, but nevertheless utterly irresistible. She had never been attracted to a man this way before – after all she had only met him that morning – but tonight she was most eager to yield to his charm.

He placed one hand on her lower back whilst the other held the stethoscope gently on her chest. His face was just a few inches from hers; he looked even more handsome in the dark. In a blurry shadow she could see the fine hair of his eyebrows, his thin nose, his dark lips.

Her heart was pounding fast and hard, and Doctor Harvey could certainly hear it. There was no need for words to disclose her arousal, her body spoke loud enough. She felt her face flush and the heat spread down along her neck to her abdomen, then all the way down between her thighs.

After a while he dropped the stethoscope but not his hand and looked at her with an amused smile. Slowly he reached inside her dress, his fingertips gently stroking her breasts through the white lace of her bra.

Judith closed her eyes and let out a faint sigh. His touch was like fire. She felt him coming closer and gently nibble at the corner of her mouth whilst increasing the pressure of his fingers over her erect nipples, sending delicious waves directly to her loins. His lips at the corner of her mouth were smooth and full, and just as warm as his fingers.

Memories of her teenage years came back to her as she placed one hand on his thigh and clumsily slipped the other inside his white coat, caressing his muscular back with trembling fingers. She felt a bit silly, not really knowing what to do. There was always a risk of somebody entering the room, but she didn't want to leave.

His tongue was now on her chin, gradually working its way down. Its wet warmth left a cool trace on her skin, only enhancing the fire that now raged inside her. She knew she had to do something in reply, but what? Surely he would expect more from her than to just remain passive to his caress. Yet as she made a move to unbutton his shirt he stopped her.

'Don't forget I am the teacher tonight, nurse.'

She didn't reply, giving up. Maybe he didn't want her to do anything after all. Perhaps it would be best to just let him take the lead. It was much better this way.

Slowly pushing her down until her back came to rest on the couch, he gently seized her ankles and lifted her legs, bringing them behind him as he sat on the edge of the seat. Then he slipped both his hands inside her dress and began massaging her skin, caressing her breasts, teasing her nipples.

Judith turned her head sideways, pressing her burning cheek against the cool leather. His touch was increasingly warm on her sensitive skin. Those hands again ... She could see them in her mind as well as feel them on her body. Tonight they were operating another kind of magic, something that wouldn't require any fancy instruments, but that would heal in its own, special fashion.

The pins holding her hair up slipped and her straw-coloured mane spilled onto the dark leather. Her own image appeared behind her closed eyelids: a white, virginal figure just waiting to be taken.

She could feel the heat of his body through the thin cotton of her uniform as he gently bent over her, his abdomen pressing against her thighs, and immediately longed to get rid of this cumbersome obstacle. As if reading her mind he brought his hands up, slipping the dress from her shoulders, and his fingertips undid the hook holding her bra fastened at the front.

Her generous breasts jutted out, nipples erect and

pointing to the ceiling, finally freed from the restraint that had held them prisoner. The cool air in the room was not enough to calm the heat of their excitement. And at this moment Judith desperately wanted to feel his naked skin on hers.

'Excuse me, Doctor,' she ventured timidly, 'but could I just unbutton your shirt?'

He laughed softly, surprised by the childish tone of her voice. After all, she was just a new recruit. A competent nurse no doubt, but only fresh out of school.

'Don't move,' he said. 'I'll take care of that myself.'

Standing up, he took his white coat off and threw it over a chair. His shirt followed. The stethoscope had mysteriously disappeared.

The room was dark but Judith's eyes were quickly getting accustomed to it. At least she could see his broad chest, covered with dark, tight curls. This sight doubled her excitement. All her previous boyfriends had been bare-chested, and the thought of losing herself in this velvet carpet suddenly fuelled her desire for the man.

Instead of sitting down again he kneeled on the floor, next to the couch. Instinctively, Judith lifted her hips and in a swift move he pulled down her dress, then gently took off her bra, throwing it aside nonchalantly.

Finally his head came down on her chest and his tongue started dancing on her breasts, at first gently but gradually increasing its eagerness, worrying her nipples. His hands continued to flutter over her body, one on her belly and the other on her thighs.

Judith thought she was going to faint with excitement. She spread her legs slightly, instinctively. Her vulva was so wet that her dew was quickly spilling between her buttocks and the leather of the couch. It felt warm and wet, and its sweet smell gently floated to her flaring nostrils.

All her senses were ablaze. She let out another sigh, slightly louder. She knew this was a dangerous game, anybody could enter the room. However her uniform was now on the floor, she had lost sight of her bra, and her panties were soaked with her warm dew. She didn't really want to leave, at least not just yet.

'This is wild,' she thought. She had never felt this good, not even that time behind the barn with Jon, last spring when she had gone back home during half-term break. She smiled in the dark. Jon was just a boy in comparison, just a naughty boy. He knew nothing of a woman's needs. Doctor Harvey, on the other hand ...

He let out a loud sigh as he got up, looking at her almost naked on the couch; her legs apart, her breasts heaving with every breath, her long blond hair spread over the contrasting brown leather. He bent down slowly, his slim fingers catching the elastic band of her panties and pulling them down.

He was impressive, towering above her, half-naked, his eyes sparkling in the darkness of the room. There was a distinct bulge in his trousers, his organ pushing to get out and meet her.

Judith felt warm and wanted to bask in this warmth, like a lazy kitten on a carpet. She closed her eyes and caressed her breasts with her fingertips, her hands toying with her own nipples for a while, pleasantly surprised by their engorged size, then slowly sliding down on her belly until they came resting on the inside of her thighs.

She looked up at Harvey and smiled. She had never caressed herself in front of a man before. Yet tonight she felt boldly comfortable, she knew he was turned on by the sight of her hands fluttering over her own body. He just stared at her for a moment, the same amused smile still on his lips, until she extended her arms up towards him, arching her back.

He made her stand and then sit in a swivelling armchair, a few feet away from the couch. This time the leather felt ice-cold on her bare skin and she shivered. However, the sweat of her body quickly formed a thin film between her skin and the soft leather, and she could feel her body slip every time she moved, the motion enhanced by the rocking of the chair. She felt hot, very hot, the surface of her skin now alight with the fire of her excitement.

Harvey knelt in front of her. They were closer to the door this time, she could see him better. And she liked the sight of him as he gently parted her legs with his hands and caressed the soft skin of her inner thighs.

Inserting his middle finger in her wet vagina, he slowly caressed the inside wall in a circular motion. 'You are very relaxed,' he commented. 'That's very good. Very good.' His voice had become a mere whisper.

Judith could feel his warm breath on her vulva, sensing his mouth was just a few inches away. She wanted him to kiss her there, to seize his head and direct it towards her flesh, but she didn't dare ask him. Instead, she parted her legs as wide as she could, hoping he would soon reply to her silent invitation.

'You have a nice, clean smell,' he said as his mouth drew close. 'I like nice, clean girls.' His sentence barely finished, his tongue started probing her intricate folds. At the moment he touched her Judith jerked her hips in a spasm of surprise and joy.

Then his tongue went deep inside her as his thumb flickered on her clitoris, his hand gently cupping her curly mound. The sensation was exhilarating, his mouth and hands now concentrating their caresses around this most sensitive area of her body. She liked the way his tongue felt especially, soft and wet and moving about sensually, discovering her slowly, methodically. She knew it wouldn't be long before she would climax right there against his mouth. Already she could only muffle the sounds of pleasure that were coming out of her mouth in a mix of cries and sobs.

His thumb let go of her stiff bud and he lifted her thighs onto his shoulders, pressing his face against her fragrant bush, now licking her with long, gusty laps, grunting noisily as he relished her wetness.

By now Judith had ceased to think, letting her body react instead. Crossing her legs behind his head, she pushed her knees together, forcing his tongue to probe deeper and deeper.

Her behind was now bathed in a mix of his saliva and her lovejuices, her body making slurping sounds as it moved on the chair, slipping and sliding, rocking back and forth and sideways, like a frail boat caught in the storm of their arousal.

Suddenly, she felt an irresistible urge to point her toes, contracting all the muscles in her legs, her calves quickly growing rock-hard, aching under the strain. The wave of the orgasm rose from her knees, crept up along her legs and rapidly reached deep inside her pelvis. She clenched her hands and her fingernails ripped the thin leather of the armrests.

She let out a loud moan as she climaxed, throwing her head back, out of breath and exhausted. Now she felt nothing but utter delight, no longer concerned that somebody could walk in on them. It seemed her pleasure had taken the whole of her body and her mind into another dimension. She didn't feel like she was sitting on a leather chair anymore, but rather floating above it, her skin no longer in contact with anything. In a haze, a blur, she saw Harvey getting up. The smile had disappeared from his lips, but in his eyes now shone a new light, the fire of lust. Unmistakably, his own desire hadn't been appeased; he wasn't done with her yet.

With a fluid movement of the wrists, he undid his belt and dropped his trousers, suddenly standing completely naked in front of her. He stood still for a minute and she admired his tanned skin, his hairy chest. His erect member was so stiff its tip almost reached his navel and the purple head was glistening in the dimness of the room.

As though in a dream, Judith reached out, grabbed the shaft with both hands and squeezed it gently. It was like an iron rod enveloped in a thin layer of soft fabric, the skin fluid and moving under her fingers, the core stiff and unyielding. For a moment she felt him throb in her hands, its velvety hardness radiating warmth and softness.

But almost immediately he seized her wrists, laughing, and forced her to let go. Then he pulled her arms up, as if he didn't want her to touch him but wanted her to remain passive under his domination. Bracing himself on the back of the chair, he raised his knees onto the armrests, then lifted his pelvis to her face and brought her hands down to his buttocks before thrusting his organ into her mouth.

At first its size almost gagged her, yet holding him in her mouth gave her a sensation of power, as if his pleasure now depended on her. Already she could feel a throbbing vein on her tongue as the head began sliding back and forth, along the roof of her mouth, compact and rounded like a small cushion. It was soft and warm, and a few drops of warm fluid escaped from the tiny slitted mouth, tasting sweetly new and pleasant, a bit salty.

She simply let him move in and out of her mouth and let her fingers run all over his bottom. By now she was reacting instinctively, gently scratching his bottom with her fingernails whilst in her mouth her tongue tentatively caressed the ridge of his glans.

'You are new to this,' he remarked. But already I can tell you have potential.' In reply she slipped one of her hands under his balls, hesitantly discovering and caressing them with her fingertips. They were small and firm, like two marble beads tightly held up in his sac which was covered with soft, silky hair.

Against her nose his flat stomach brushed repeatedly and she liked his aroma, a clean, musky scent that was also new, her brain unable to associate this manly perfume to anything she had ever smelled before.

In her mouth his plum seemed to grow bigger, tiny drops of fluid now freely flowing out of the slit-like tip. She found it most arousing to get him to react to the caress of her tongue and began sucking at him eagerly. She brought both her hands to take hold of his shaft and this time he didn't try to stop her.

He was right, she had never done this before. She was supposed to be a nice girl and in the small village she came from, nice girls saved themselves for their husbands. The thought almost made her laugh. None of the boys she knew would ever ask their wife to do something like this!

She was amazed to discover the extent to which she could have a man's pleasure at her mercy. Grabbing his shaft tightly, she began to suck the swollen head forcefully, feeling a strange hunger within her, compelling her to suck on further as her breath grew shallow. She felt powerful, holding his cock in her mouth, stiff and velvety. As it throbbed on her tongue she felt another rush of warmth between her legs; she was ready for more.

So was Harvey. Breathing fast, he let go of the back of the chair to stroke her hair, moaning loudly from the pleasant embrace of her eager mouth. She could feel him pulsating on her tongue, whilst she sucked and licked the purple head, somehow wishing she could swallow it completely. As she reached out to caress his balls again she realised they were now withdrawing inside him and wondered if he was about to climax. The thought of receiving his seed in her mouth was both exciting and frightening.

But then he suddenly withdrew. For Judith this was totally unexpected, and somewhat disappointing for she was anxious to discover more of him and to find out whether her mouth could bring him to the peak of pleasure. For a minute she thought she might have done something wrong but his smile reassured her.

'You learn quickly,' he commented, laboriously getting off the chair. 'You deserve top marks for enthusiasm.'

Again he stood naked before her. With her eyes she caressed his muscular figure, his flat stomach, his narrow hips, his firm thighs. He was indeed very attractive and probably the best teacher any woman could wish for. And right now he was with her. She longed to feel him inside her, she wanted to be taken by a man who knew what he was doing, not by some post-pubescent stable boy.

He went down on his knees and grabbed her hips, pulling her towards him. Very slowly, he entered her. Still slower, he began thrusting back and forth. Judith found these unhurried thrusts most pleasurable, so different from the quick, jerky stabs she had endured with her inexperienced boyfriends in the past. She moaned gently as she felt him fill her repeatedly.

'I won't come until you do,' Harvey said. It sounded like a promise.

'It shouldn't be very long,' she admitted.

Already she could feel the surge of another orgasm building up inside her, his hardness rekindling the reaction his mouth had triggered earlier. He slipped his wrists under her legs, the backs of her thighs slipping down along his forearms to comfortably nestle in the groove of his elbows.

His motion then started to gain momentum, accompanied once again by the swaying movement of the chair. Her climax came back very rapidly and suddenly, almost violently. She couldn't help the cry that came out of her mouth, she didn't care if the whole world could hear.

'Totally uninhibited,' he whispered, almost to himself 'It's nice to see a woman enjoying herself to the limit.' His thrust grew fast and powerful. He bent forward and grabbed her breast in his mouth. His suction was strong and he briefly took the nipple between his teeth. Judith screamed again, enjoying the slightly painful sensation. Then he let go with a groan and threw his head back, his mouth wide open. Cries were coming out of his throat in tandem with every jab of his member; stronger, louder, echoing through the room.

An ultimate sob came out as he climaxed and he fell on top of her, lifeless, as if his pleasure had taken all of his energy away. For a while his head rested on her breasts, his breath gently brushing her nipple as it came out from both his mouth and his nose.

His hair had the sweet smell of summer. Judith ran her fingers down his cheek and kissed his forehead.

'Thank you,' she whispered.

He slowly looked up at her and smiled. 'The pleasure was all mine, nurse.'

He remained motionless whilst the fire within Judith's body slowly subsided. She was exhausted, but happy. She could have stayed like this forever, holding his warm body in her arms silently. But after only a few seconds he got up and staggered towards the bathroom.

'I think I need a shower,' he said drowsily, looking at her over his shoulder. 'I hope we shall have the opportunity to work together again soon. Once again, welcome to the Dorchester Clinic.' He disappeared behind the door. Soon she could hear the sound of the water running in the shower.

She got up and picked her clothes off the floor, her legs now barely supporting her. Her first day at the Clinic had been a revelation, in more ways than one. It was nothing like the places she had been sent to during her training years.

But as her brain began functioning again she realised that what had just happened was beyond belief. She was amazed at her own reaction, how easily she had let him seduce her. But how could she have refused?

She looked around, suddenly worried. This was not professional at all, especially on her very first day at work! If anybody had walked in on them she could have lost her job. She couldn't let herself fall prey to a doctor, no matter how good looking he was. She couldn't take such a chance.

She sat down again, her flesh still warm from his touch, her body weak from the pleasure that had just rocked her. This would be the first, and the last time. It would have to be.

Chapter Three

Judith opened her sports bag and pulled her towel out. Still panting from her jogging session, she felt relaxed and alive, ready to start her second day at work. She was also pleased with herself and how she had managed to find her way through the busy streets of south-west London.

The nurses' locker room was deserted in the early morning. Judith's locker was in the middle of the last row, quite far from the main door but close to the sitting room. It was one of about 60 tall metal boxes, all painted pink, all bearing a golden sign with the occupant's name.

Sitting on the wooden bench, she peeled off her damp T-shirt and leggings and placed them in a plastic bag. It was a good idea to run to work. She could take a shower before starting her shift, washing away the dirt that collected on her skin as she ran through Hammersmith. Arriving early also meant she would have time to recover from the strain of the five-mile run.

She slowly walked around the corner and entered the shower room. The white ceramic tile floor was cool and refreshing under her aching feet. This was one large, communal room, not individual stalls like she was used to at her health club. But this morning Judith had the whole place to herself and could choose any of the nine showers alongside the far wall. She picked one somewhere in the middle and turned the tiny tap.

The water came out of the shower head in a powerful jet, immediately drenching her from head to toe, massaging her sore legs, calming the fire that still throbbed on her cheeks. She dribbled a small puddle of shampoo into the palm of her hand and combed it through her wet hair, working it into a rich lather. Its papaya fragrance was also refreshing and soothing, the thick foam sliding down like white fat snakes along her neck and over her breasts, gathering at the bushy mound at the base of her abdomen.

Her fingers followed, covered with soap, as she slowly reached down between her legs, letting her fingertips lovingly slide against the soft, sinewy folds of her vulva. In a fraction of a second, her clitoris responded stiffly, rearing its tiny head under the soapy caress.

Judith sighed. In her mind the images of the previous evening were emerging once again, images that had haunted her sleep through the night. Despite the guilt she felt after he left, she now longed for Harvey to come back and again take her to the ultimate peak of pleasure. Given a chance, she would not remain passive next time . . . If there was a next time.

In her mind she had everything worked out. It would be just perfect if they could meet outside working hours so nobody would find out about it. But this was very risky, they would have to be very discreet.

That also meant they would be having an affair! Her, Judith Stanton, nursing school graduate, having an affair with Doctor Robert Harvey, the prestigious surgeon! Unbelievable!

Yet she knew he might have many lovers among the staff. She wasn't stupid enough to think she was the only nurse ever to have been taken to the doctors' lounge. But she would gladly share him if in return he could keep her satisfied.

Would he want her again? He seemed pleased with

her the previous night, but was it due solely to the thrill of a new conquest?

She tenderly traced the path his tongue had followed on her silken flesh, inserting two fingers inside her vagina, stroking her clitoris with her thumb. Her pussy contracted and readily sucked at her fingers, her body gently yielding to the arousal that had been kept constant within her since the previous night.

He seemed just right for her, instinctively knowing how to pleasure her, how to make her body react in ways she had never even suspected. But then there was the danger of being discovered. Could she risk her job for a few minutes of pleasure, however intense it might be?

This was a difficult decision. She would have to fight her desire if ever he came near her again whilst on duty. At the same time she could still feel him inside her, and would be prepared to do anything to be in his arms again. Such a contradiction. She didn't need that; she hated facing dilemmas.

Right now, however, there was nothing she could do about it, but let her mind wander and the recollection increase her excitement.

Her fingertips began dancing on her vulva with a life of their own. Already their pace was quickening, and Judith reached deep inside her, stroking the very centre of her bushy treasure as she felt her climax approaching.

'I bet she's thinking about Harvey!' an unexpected voice clamoured behind her.

Judith turned around suddenly, surprised to realise she was not alone in the nurses' locker room after all.

The shower room was steamy from the hot water gushing out of the wall, but she could clearly see two white silhouettes, two of her colleagues staring at her naughtily.

Her right hand was still clutched to her vulva, fingers engulfed in the throbbing tunnel, whilst her other hand was paused on her swollen breasts. She suddenly felt ashamed and turned around to face the wall again, quickly bringing both hands to her head and pretending to be washing her hair. How long had they been standing there? What had they seen?

'Nice addition to our staff,' the girl behind her continued in a loud voice. 'I wonder if she's had her initiation yet...'

The other nurse burst out laughing. 'From what I heard she's already had Harvey, which is not a bad start for a first day.' They both laughed hoarsely, almost grunting.

Judith didn't reply, desperately wanting them to go away, to leave her alone. She was also upset about their talk. Who were they? And how did they know about her and Doctor Harvey? She continued to rinse her hair, hoping they would soon disappear.

But instead she heard them giggling again as they approached her. A small hand grabbed the tap and turned it to increase the flow of hot water. Judith suddenly felt trapped and turned around to leave but the taller girl pushed her against the wall. Her mind raced furiously and now that they were closer she remembered them from the previous morning.

Tania and Jo, two nurses on the night shift; they were probably finishing work at this hour. Right now they seemed to be enjoying themselves tremendously, holding Judith against the wet ceramic wall, preventing her from going anywhere.

'What do you want?' she asked, becoming suddenly annoyed with their behaviour and a bit frightened. 'Let me go.'

The other two kept on giggling, still pinning her against the wall. Tania was dark and beautiful, with long, straight jet-black hair and piercing eyes. Tall and slim, she held Judith's arm in a grip of iron, her slim fingers clenched around Judith's soft skin.

'Let you go?' she said sarcastically. 'But my dear, we've only just met. It would be a bit rude not to offer to get to know you better at this point. Right, Jo?'

Jo was shorter, pale, blond and voluptuous. Very pretty, but she looked a bit artificial, probably because of all the make-up she wore. The two women were night and day, yet both seemed cruel, each in her own way.

Judith wished for them to disappear or at least let go of her. The hot water coming from the shower nozzle was creating a lot of steam and their uniforms were getting splashed. Surely they wouldn't want to remain here much longer. But they seemed to take pleasure out of tormenting poor Judith. Obviously they knew exactly what to do to annoy her.

'So what did you think of Harvey?' Jo began. 'Isn't he something else? Did you like to feel his hands on you? I know I do ... Did you like him caressing your breasts?' She slowly ran her fingers around Judith's breasts, cupping them in turn, teasing the nipples which reacted like traitors by jutting out.

'Good,' Tania said, staring down at the swelling globes. 'I see we can get something out of you, my pretty. We were really looking forward to welcoming you, in our own special way.' She kissed Judith on the cheek, forcefully, almost violently, her thin lips quickly working their way down until they reached her mouth.

Meanwhile Jo kept teasing Judith's breasts, caressing them gently, almost lovingly, her fingertips delicately playing with the droplets of water that were still pearling on the white skin.

Judith was petrified. The women were caressing her against her will, but surprisingly she couldn't help being aroused by their behaviour. Never in her life had she felt the caress of a woman's touch, although she suspected it would not be very different than being touched by a man. And somehow her anger was offset by her curiosity.

'You have wonderful breasts, my love,' Jo whispered in her ear. 'Would you let us taste them? Your nipples look delicious. Let's see how much they can take.' She reached up to grab the shower head and redirect the flow of the shower onto Judith's nipples. The water fell like a boiling rain of needles, pinching and bouncing off her chest. Judith gasped under the sweet torture. Tania and Jo laughed again.

'Do you think we'll get to her eventually?' Tania asked before taking a hold of Judith's mouth and invading it with her tongue. Jo continued whispering in her victim's ear.

'Nice tongue, isn't it? Don't you like the way it possesses you with its pleasant roughness? Don't you wish you could feel that tongue elsewhere on your body?' She continued caressing Judith's breasts for a moment. 'Here? I know you'd like it.' Her hand swiftly slid down Judith's belly until the fingers disappeared under the bushy mound. 'Or here? She is a good licker, she knows exactly what to do to make you come quickly. Or slowly, if that's what you prefer. Today, however, you are in no position to tell us what you like. We're in charge.'

Judith couldn't reply. Her knees now buckling under her, rapidly growing weak. Tania's mouth was glued to hers, caressing Judith's lips with her tongue in a snake-like movement. Jo kept talking the whole time in Judith's ear, only slightly louder than the noise of the splashing water.

'How often did Harvey make you come? Did he lick you first before he took you with his delightful rod, or was it the other way around? I can't begin to tell you how often I've climaxed under his tongue. He's so skilful ... But you know, Tania here is just as good, if not better ...'

Both women reached down simultaneously and their fingers assaulted Judith's throbbing vulva, stretching the wet tunnel to the limit, creating a painful but pleasurable sensation as they slowly moved around inside, discovering the softness of the smooth prison walls. Judith felt herself yielding under their touch.

She was aroused despite her anger, reacting to the caresses of her tormentors beyond reason. She couldn't figure out whether it was solely due to their touch or because of the images that were forming in her head as she listened to Jo's litany. Perhaps it was a combination of both, compounded by her memories of the previous night.

Tania was very strong and domineering, her mouth still in control of the new recruit. 'Let her suck your tongue,' Jo advised in a sultry voice. 'Then you can better imagine what it will be like when she starts to lick your gorgeous clitoris . . .' At this point Judith realised she was actually replying to the tall girl's kisses, their tongues twirling around each other, their lips sealed in a passionate embrace. Her anger was quickly vanishing, giving her mounting arousal even more room to flow.

By now she was held up only through the strength of the girls pinning her to the wall. She was still somewhat incensed, but she was also close to climax. This combination of anger and arousal was something she had never felt before and the latter was quickly increasing as a result.

She couldn't decide whether she loved or hated it, nor if she wanted them to stop or continue. Her breath became laborious, her heart pounding furiously as her legs became weaker and weaker.

They let her go slightly and she slid down along the wall until she came to sit on the tiled floor. The water now fell just a few inches away, but not on her body, which was a relief. Jo knelt behind her, hoisting her head and wet tresses onto her lap, grabbing both breasts in a tight grip, holding her so that she couldn't escape. But by now Judith was beyond thinking of escaping. Although she couldn't approve of their cavalier approach, her excitement was such that she had to yield to their attack despite herself

Jo bent forward until she came to take Judith nipples in her mouth. 'They are so big, so luscious,' she said. She stopped talking only briefly to give them a quick, slurpy suck. Meanwhile Tania was kneeling between Judith's legs, her mouth quickly aiming for the stiff bud that was eagerly expecting its reward.

'Wait,' Jo said. 'Have a taste of these first.' Tania smiled wickedly and approached her target. Her fingers, long and slim, quickly surrounded the heavy breasts whilst she pinched a nipple between her lips. The feeling was so strong that Judith couldn't help cry out in pain.

'Don't you like it?' Jo asked. 'It's a most marvellous pair of lips. When I tell her she'll begin to lick and suck your clit like you've never been sucked before. Believe me, not a man on this planet can tease a woman the way she does. That's why she got her job here, by the way.'

The two women were now working on her breasts, hunched over her like hungry vultures. Judith couldn't move, either because they were restraining her with their bodies, or more probably because she was simply hoping they would soon fulfil their promise to make her achieve her climax.

Tania's mouth was swiftly grazing on her nipples, alternating between the two erect peaks, fast and furious. Ever so often her teeth would brush them as well, sending a bolt of pleasure and pain through Judith's abdomen, all the way down to between her legs, all the while still increasing her arousal.

Jo was using only her tongue, caressing the whole of the breasts with long, deliberately slow licks. Every so often Judith would feel their cheeks brush against her tender skin, so much softer and more pleasant than a man's rough skin. Even their hands were more gentle despite the way they were caressing her. At this moment she realised that perhaps a woman would know better how to pleasure another woman . . .

Judith began to sob, more in pleasure than in outrage now. Her tormentors were skilful, but she was still somewhat concerned about the power they seemed to hold over her.

'Now,' Jo ordered, before bending down to take hold of Judith's nipples once more.

And Tania went down, her mouth switching targets, going from Judith's breasts to her vulva in a flash. Immediately her thin lips grabbed the swollen clitoris like a steel clamp, making it react and become even stiffer.

Judith screamed. The sensation was intense and painful, like a bite, but it also sent a simultaneous wave of pleasure through her whole body, making her tremble uncontrollably. A second later, Tania released her grip completely. Judith was somewhat relieved, but her body was terribly disappointed. She moaned loudly. Jo burst out laughing.

'What did you think of that?' she asked loudly. 'Didn't I tell you she was good? Now would you like her to make you come? Would you?'

Judith started crying. She was exhausted, she needed release, she wanted her attackers to pleasure her yet she was too ashamed of her desires to ask them.

'That's enough!' another voice shouted.

Tania and Jo looked up suddenly. Judith continued crying. At the entrance of the shower room stood Mrs Cox, the Clinic's nursing supervisor, a woman in her late thirties, quite tall and curvaceous, with dark wavy hair. Extremely beautiful, she looked like a movie star from the 1940s, her skin pale and her lips a luscious red. But despite her classic beauty, she was also stern and very strict.

Although she generally spoke in a low voice, her words were almost always orders, as they were right now. Judith had heard from a colleague that despite this severe attitude the woman was nonetheless respected and even liked by all the nursing staff. However this morning she seemed most angry at what was going on.

Their uniforms soaking, Tania and Jo stood up sheepishly. Laying motionless on the ceramic tiles, the water bouncing off the floor just a few inches from her shoulder, Judith looked at them through her tears. Both women looked like lustful vampires, two vague silhouettes lost in a cloud of steam, their erect nipples nevertheless clearly visible through the wet fabric of their uniforms. For a split second, Judith couldn't help feeling attracted by the sight of their swollen breasts. If only Mrs Cox hadn't come in, she might have been given the opportunity to caress them as well ...

'You both know the procedure regarding new members of staff,' Mrs Cox told the two girls. 'I do hope you can restrain yourselves in the future. Meet me in my office before you come on duty this evening. Now go.'

The two dripping figures disappeared outside the steamy room.

Judith stood up slowly, slightly relieved, but her body still aroused and angry at not having obtained release. Mrs Cox walked towards her and turned off the flow of water.

'I'm sorry about this,' she said dryly. 'I hope they didn't hurt you. They will be punished, if that's any consolation to you.'

Judith continued sobbing, more in frustration than in relief

'Did you come?' Mrs Cox asked still in the same tone. Judith looked up in amazement. Why was she asking her that? The question was direct, matter-of-fact, but so out of place that Judith lost her speech for a moment. However, the tone of voice commanded a reply

'N . . . n . . . o,' she stammered.

Mrs Cox walked to her with determination and quickly slipped her arm around the nurse's naked waist, holding her tightly, her other hand sliding down between Judith's legs.

Judith was too surprised to say anything. The woman's touch was not too gentle, a bit forceful, but pleasant. Already she could feel her arousal mounting again. Quickly, the expert fingertips teased the swollen clitoris into madness, rapidly sliding back and forth on the wet vulva, once again transforming Judith into a wanton puppet.

She slipped her arms around the woman's neck and shyly nestled her head in its curve. Her pleasure grew, increasing powerfully until it burst within her, and was finally allowed to overflow. Her climax was long and strong, like a tidal wave. Judith moaned softly as her head fell on Mrs Cox's shoulder, her tears quickly absorbed by the thin fabric of the supervisor's uniform.

'There,' Mrs Cox said as she released her embrace

around the naked waist. 'Now get to work, you have patients to attend to.' She turned around and disappeared, leaving a fulfilled, but very puzzled Judith alone in the locker room.

Chapter Four

Judith's arms were so weak she was barely able to lift her raincoat to hang it on the rack. Leaning against the wall, she took her shoes off without untying the shoelaces, prying each one off with the other foot, too tired to bend over.

She kicked them away in a remote corner and each banged the wall with a thump. They bounced back in different directions, her left shoe disappearing under the telephone table whilst the right one found its niche behind the umbrella bin.

She looked at them and sighed. Brand new shoes, but they wouldn't last long if she didn't take better care of them. Not to worry, now that she had a job she could afford a new pair every month. Besides, this pair wasn't of the greatest quality, to say the least. The thick leather didn't want to yield and adapt to the shape of her feet, making her heels sore after just a few hours.

Under her sore feet the carpet of the entrance hall was much softer and she wriggled her toes a couple of times. That felt better, but what she needed most right now was simply to put her feet up.

Walking to her room, she mechanically undid the clip that held her hair up and her blond mane fell all over her shoulders in a cascade of pale curls, bouncing around her neck, free at last. That was also quite a relief, she hated having to tie her hair up.

For some strange reason her handbag was heavier than when she had left that morning. She had taken it up the three flights of stairs to the flat half-dragging, half-carrying it. Tomorrow morning before leaving for work she would have to go through it and take out all the useless stuff that constantly found its way in there.

As she passed the door to the kitchen she noticed there was somebody in there. Already she knew it wasn't Brenda, her flatmate, but probably one of the many boyfriends that constantly streamed through the flat, in one day, out the next. Judith glanced in furtively, not really wanting to meet this one.

The man was half-hidden behind the open door of the refrigerator, his head tilted back as he drank milk straight from the bottle. A stream of thin, pale drops trickled down along his neck and his bare chest. He didn't seem to notice her. Judith made a mental note to take her coffee black the next morning and kept walking.

She turned her head slightly and took one last look as she opened her bedroom door, only to see him right before he disappeared inside Brenda's room. Only then did she realise he was completely naked. All she saw was his back, broad and muscular, and a tight pair of buttocks, round and firm. No-one she knew; obviously a new guy on Brenda's list.

She entered her own bedroom and sighed as she shut the door behind her, throwing her bag in a corner before collapsing face down on the bed. Another hard day at work, only half-way through the week, and she was already exhausted.

Hours of walking through corridors, meeting staff, getting to know the set up, in addition to helping out in the operating theatre. Hopefully it would get better once she knew everybody and where everything was.

She slowly turned onto her back and laboriously stood up. As she flicked the switch of the lamp on her bedside table the faint light cast a blue glow around the small room. With a tired sigh she started to unbutton her uniform, the white cotton amazingly still crisp under her fingertips. She would have to buy more of these when she went shopping for shoes.

The rules of the clinic stipulated all the nurses had to be dressed in white from head to toe, even their underwear, but they didn't have to wear the traditional cap. Apparently it looked more professional yet less medical; just like in America, the realm of cosmetic surgery. In fact, many of the clinic's guidelines were modelled on American institutions, to give the patients an impression of Hollywoodesque glamour and to make the nursing staff look more like beauticians.

Judith stared at her half-naked reflection in the mirror as her dress fell to the floor. She barely recognised herself, but was quite pleased with the image she presented.

Her bra was brand new, a thin lacy garment with a metal wire, and fastened between her breasts, pushing them up and emphasising their perkiness, letting the brown circles of her nipples shyly show through. She was wearing matching panties, deliciously soft and lacy as well and revealing, ever so slightly, the small mound of her blond curls. Her suspender belt completed the outfit and held up sheer white stockings, although she wasn't required to wear stockings if she didn't want to. Nevertheless, Judith had tried wearing them for the first time today and definitely felt prettier that way. White suited her, something she never would have thought, considering the milkiness of her bare skin.

Suddenly she didn't want to undress any further; she wanted to simply look at that pretty girl who stared back in the mirror. Was this the girl Robert Harvey had caressed just a few evenings ago? The same girl who had been submitted to sweet torture in the shower room the previous morning? Judith now felt different, somehow she even looked different...

Again today she had been rather uncomfortable at work. Everyone she had been introduced to had stared at her perhaps a little longer than was really necessary, their eyes travelling up and down and quickly sizing her from head to toe, seemingly studying her body with a barely disguised interest.

Maybe this was just her imagination running wild. She had to admit everyone had been very friendly and welcoming, even if at times it had puzzled her. Perhaps they seemed too friendly. That scared her, yet excited her at the same time.

She had started her new job in a most unusual fashion, her sensuality being awakened and even challenged at the very outset. Now she was thinking clearly, she could see the situation for what it really was. What had happened with Robert Harvey, and then with Tania and Jo, was just a coincidence. They were probably the kind of people who enjoyed sex and got a kick out of impressing the new nurses. All she had to do in future was avoid them. But would she have the strength?

Tania and Jo were not really a problem, unless she had to work a night shift. That would come sooner or later, but she would deal with it in due time. Robert Harvey was another story. She hadn't seen him at all today, but she was bound to work with him again sooner or later. What then? Would he try seducing her again? Hopefully, yes... Or not... She didn't know anymore.

As for Mrs Cox, there was nothing to worry about. The supervisor had probably simply sensed her need to be pleasured that morning in the shower room. She had given the young nurse the release she needed, that was all. Yet Judith couldn't shake the weird feeling that had seized her and still lingered as a result. The woman had been so cold, almost clinical, in the way she had pleasured her. It was almost as if it was part of her job. Strangely, Judith somehow longed to experience this again, as if the woman's rough caresses had only left her yearning for more.

She looked in the mirror one more time. She realised she was very attractive, but also quite inexperienced when it came to physical pleasure. Even as a teenager, the few young men she had gone out with were almost scared of touching her, afraid of rejection. Those who did were out to get her like a trophy, interested solely in their own pleasure, never hers.

She needed a man, a real one, like Harvey. Or did she? Her body yearned to be taken to the heights of pleasure, to experience new sensations, to discover fulfilment. Her flesh was aching to know how much there was to take.

Across the hall sounds were coming from Brenda's room, the same, familiar sounds Judith could hear almost every night: moans and grunts. She sighed. Brenda was insatiable, having in her bed one man after the other, unable to spend even one night on her own it seemed. Judith was somewhat annoyed about that. Yet at times she couldn't help but feel aroused by the loud lovemaking. It got to the point where she couldn't figure out whether she was fed up with Brenda's loud cries, or if she was simply jealous of always being alone.

She lay back on the bed and closed her eyes, imagining she was the one being taken right now. The warmth of her man's body enveloped her in a comforting embrace, like a fluffy cloud. Involuntarily she began to writhe on the duvet, her arousal coming alive within her, her fingers gradually initiating their dance on her warm skin.

And in her mind he appeared, tall, beautiful, powerful. An imaginary lover, incredibly handsome, wanting nothing but to pleasure her, a slave to her desires. As usual he didn't have a face, or rather he had many looks. Sometimes dark, sometimes fair, always perfect in his male beauty. Of course, his muscles were taut and his skin warm and soft. But most of all he was hers, and hers alone, only one of the many men who had visited her like this, as she lay alone in her bed.

Laughter rose in Brenda's room. Whatever they were up to, they seemed to be enjoying themselves. Suddenly Judith was no longer annoyed or upset: now she understood. She realised that she and Brenda indeed had something in common, they were sisters in their quest for fulfilment.

Judith was now guiding her invisible lover's hands over her lace-covered breasts, pressing him to caress them gently, to softly toy with her nipples, making him graze them with his fingernails, worrying them until they became so stiff they practically pierced the delicate fabric. Her nipples were so much more sensitive when being teased through the lace ...

Next she showed him how to caress the underside of her breasts, having him cup them gently but without ever ceasing his ministrations on the erect peaks. His touch on her was exquisite, as always, and she moaned gently through pursed lips.

Her vulva replied readily and immediately she brought his hand down to briefly feel her wetness. She didn't let him slide his hands under her panties, not just yet. He had to touch her through the fabric first. Just like her nipples, her tiny shaft wanted to be teased indirectly, gently scratched into submission.

She moaned and pressed her legs together, the tender skin above the edge of her white stockings pushing against his fingers, squeezing his hand into a soft embrace, holding him prisoner. His thumb kept moving nonetheless, at first lightly discovering her warmth, but quickly growing insistent on her swollen clitoris, rubbing it forcefully along its length, crushing her still-clothed flesh. He caught the whole of her soaked pussy with his hand, pushing at her entrance through the gusset of her panties, his fingertips desperately trying to pierce through and directly touch her wetness. His palm kept massaging her mound, grinding down on it, stopping only short of her throbbing clitoris.

His face now lightly rested on her chest, his tongue gliding inside the cup of her bra, laboriously pushing the fabric down to uncover an engorged nipple. First he took it between his pursed lips and pinched it delicately, deliciously toying with it until it grew long and firm. Then he gently seized it with his teeth, letting their sharp edge lightly graze its stiffness whilst his tongue hovered over it like a butterfly.

Judith grunted, echoing the sounds coming from Brenda's room. She opened her eyes and stared at the ceiling for a moment, suddenly wondering what it would be like to press her naked body against the rough and cold stucco surface, to feel each prickly bump softly scrape against the warm skin of her breasts, her hips, even the moist folds of her vulva ... Yet at the same time she felt much more comfortable laying on the thick duvet, her body enveloped in warmth and softness. And, of course, that was the way it should be; no-one would ever think of using something rough to generate pain in order to achieve pleasure.

After a while she lifted her head and looked at her reflection in the mirror once again. Of course, she was alone. As usual, her imaginary lover had disappeared from the moment she had opened her eyes. All she could see was a wanton creature laying half-naked over a thick duvet, one breast uncovered, a stiff nipple caught between her pink nails, the other hand hidden between her legs.

In the blue light of the lamp her skin looked even whiter and perfectly silky, the smooth curve of her thighs amazingly pleasing. The more she looked in the mirror, the more she became aroused by the sight of her own image, as if she was watching another woman, beautifully sexy. So that's what they had seen, those who had so casually approached and caressed her ...

She sat up and squarely faced the mirror, her stockinged feet landing flat on the floor. As she undid the clasp that held her bra fastened at the front, her breasts jutted out, round and swollen, pushing the lacy fabric away, revealing stiff nipples pointing up and protruding proudly. She wriggled her shoulders lasciviously, watching the straps gently glide down along her arms until they encircled her wrists. She was surprised by how warm such a slim piece of elastic could feel, knowing that this warmth could only have been imparted by her own burning skin.

Then she swiftly tossed her head forward, her blond

locks landing right on top of her swollen breasts. She grabbed them with both hands and pushed them together, rubbing and enveloping them with her hair, pinching her nipples between her thumb and forefinger though the silken strands.

Her hair felt coarse on her tender skin, but she rather enjoyed the slightly prickly sensation. She caressed her breasts with her hair in a slow kneading motion, all the while watching herself in the mirror. Her skin grew hot in her hands, and that warmth radiated through her body, following a delicious path right down to her throbbing pussy.

Her parted legs revealed a soaked patch at the crotch. The flimsy fabric wasn't thick enough to stop the flow of her dew as her arousal kept mounting. She briefly let go of her breasts to unfasten her stockings so she could pull her panties down, suddenly wanting to see her own wet bush.

Her fingers fumbled impatiently as she undid each of the clasps. She didn't even bother taking her suspender belt or her stockings off. Her hips jerked up and she pulled her soaked panties down, revealing the golden hairs of her mound now dark and curly with wetness, clinging together and adorned with pearly drops of her own moisture. Her stiff clitoris stood out, swollen and glistening like the rest of her dark pink folds. She licked her lips nervously.

If only she really had a man with her... She would make him kneel in front of her right now, his hands tied behind his back, and bid him to lick at her folds endlessly. He would be her slave, he would have to do anything she would ask, or else...

She reached down and gently brushed her clitoris with the tip of her middle finger. It was hard as steel, smooth and slick. Her own touch made her tremble, as if her fingers were charged with electricity. She closed her eyes again and imagined her finger was her lover's tongue. She knew he would soon grunt with desire for her fragrant bush, licking it in long strokes, wanting to taste all of her. His tongue would then find its way deep within her, discovering her silken tunnel, losing itself in its throbbing warmth.

Judith looked up again, watching her fingers disappear inside her, her flesh sucking them in greedily. She could almost see her stiff bud contracting under the strength of her rising climax.

She wanted to watch herself come, but the wave of pleasure that began to shake her made that difficult; she was almost forced to close her eyes, yet she managed to keep watching, a voyeur to her own climax, and her pleasure was even more intense. She saw the muscles in her legs tensing rapidly, her knees shaking under the strain. Only when she saw her wet vulva contract forcefully under her fingertips did she allow herself to let go, collapsing on the bed in a soft thump as her pleasure swept through her.

Turning onto her side she pulled a corner of the duvet over her midriff. She didn't have the strength to take her stockings off, that could wait. Her body was still reeling from the wave that had just shaken her, leaving her completely drained. Even sliding under the duvet seemed like too much of an effort right now.

Across the hall, she heard Brenda yell with pleasure. Her lips twitched in a faint smile as she fell into a dreamless slumber.

Chapter Five

Mike Randall. Judith couldn't believe her eyes. The Olympic athlete turned movie star was lying just a few inches from her, his left leg in an enormous plaster cast from the ankle to the hip. She put the chart down on the bedside table and looked at him more closely before pulling the blanket over him.

He was gorgeous. Still sedated, his breath was regular, with occasional sighs coming out from between his parted, luscious lips. His right leg was slightly bent, the thigh firm and covered in fine golden hairs, the calf perfectly sculpted.

Nothing but the thin straps of a black G-string around his hips held up the distended pouch that muzzled his genitals. Fine pubic hair, strands of silk, escaped from under the hem. His abdomen was flat and ridged like a washing board, emphasising the square definition of his chest. The body was uniformly tanned, taut and inviting.

Images flashed though Judith's head: the Olympic Games, three years ago. His muscular body crossing the finish line triumphantly; his maleness blatantly encased in the tight, dark blue lycra running shorts, finishing first in the 400 metre hurdle race, the sweat of his effort glistening on his arms and chest.

Upon his return home he had been plagued by hordes

of women hysterically throwing themselves at him, some of them completely naked, stupidly claiming they wanted to have his baby. He was everyone's idol, his smile could have melted a statue. Afterwards he had become a popular movie star, unashamed of filming steamy bed scenes, showing off his firm flesh, flexing his muscles, often stealing the show from his female partners, the glamorous actresses who would have waived their fees just to be his partner in bed, albeit for the benefit of a camera.

And now he was asleep, almost naked, right in front of Judith. She had been assigned as his nurse for today, to help him recover from the surgery, his leg having been repaired following a motorbike accident. The surgeons would make sure there would be no scarring, for it could jeopardise his career. As his nurse, Judith would make sure he wanted for nothing.

She checked the orders on his chart and took his blood pressure. He had a manly aroma about him which was musky and inviting. It was probably one of those upmarket men's colognes he had advertised on television. As she set the stethoscope on the pulse point, she let her fingertips slightly caress the hard muscles of his biceps, tracing the edge of the groove at the junction of his elbow.

He opened his eyes slightly and looked up at her. 'Hi,' he whispered with a sleepy smile. His famous smile, rich and inviting. Judith felt a sudden rush of warmth invade her.

'Hi,' she replied, returning his smile.

He looked at her hand, still paused on his arm.

'I like your touch. Will you take good care of me?'

'Of course.'

'Promise?'

'Promise.'

He closed his eyes and tilted his head the other way. Judith dropped the stethoscope but her fingers continued their journey for a while, feeling the curve of his biceps, the rounded shoulder, then stopping at the base of his neck. His skin was warm and soft as velvet.

His regular breathing told her he was sleeping again. Sweet temptation grew. The medication he had been given was very strong, chances are he wouldn't remember any of this when he woke up, or at most he would think it was all a dream. What harm would there be in letting her hand wander?

Judith became more daring and cautiously slipped her hand under the thin blanket, following the sliding path of his bare chest. He didn't even twitch.

His skin was supple over the hard muscle, the nipple large, readily contracting under her touch. She lightly caressed him with the palm of her hand, letting his warmth radiate up her wrist. Her fingertips followed the underside of his pectoral muscle, the ridge deep and hard, and then switched to caress the other one. On that side his nipple was already hard, yet seemed to pucker further still under her fingertips.

She kept her eyes on him the whole time, looking out for signs that he was coming out of his slumber, but she was happy not to see any indication that he could feel what she was doing. Her heart was pounding fast and she bit her lip nervously. This was dangerous, he could wake up at any moment.

Not being able to see what she was touching was also a strong incentive to keep going, but it made her feel very naughty to caress his sleeping body without his knowledge.

Yet this was an opportunity too good to pass on. Already her fingertips had resumed their journey down his abdomen, bobbing up and down along the peaks and valleys of his finely ridged stomach. She stopped when she felt the beginning of a long line of silky hairs she knew would lead down to the thick bush right above his genitals.

This was getting a little too far, she thought. She began pulling out her hand, caressing him just as slowly on the way back. At that moment she realised she wanted him. Such a body.

She sighed. He probably had enough women to deal with, what would he want with her? Besides, right now he was her patient, it wouldn't be right to think of him in any other terms. With regret, she turned around and left the room to attend to her other patients.

'I'm sorry to hear you are leaving tomorrow,' came the voice behind the peach-coloured curtain.

Judith had silently stepped in the room, but stopped when she recognised Edouard Laurin's heavy accent. Lady Austin's bed was hidden behind the drape, yet the light coming from the window was casting the patient's and Edouard's shadows on it. From where she stood, Judith could see them like a Chinese puppet theatre: two silhouettes, one lying on the bed, propped up by pillows, the other standing next to it.

She had to check up on Lady Austin, apply some medicated lotion to her feet and give her another dose of painkillers. Yet the fact that they had pulled the curtain told her they might not want to be disturbed. She hesitated a moment. Should she let them know she was in the room with them or just quietly make her way out? Would her squeaky shoes betray her presence?

'I'm sorry I didn't get to see more of you,' Lady Austin said in a childish tone. 'I remember last time I was here, you couldn't get enough of me.'

'My dear,' he replied, 'believe me when I say I am just as sorry as you are. But you are not leaving just yet and I am here now, *n'est-ce pas*?'

Judith was just about to turn around and leave discretely, but froze in her steps when she saw him bending down to kiss the woman. She was astonished, yet there could be no doubt about what was going on behind the curtain. She distinctly saw their tongues coming out of their mouths to touch in a sensuous caress, their lips never quite coming into contact. At the same time his hands pulled down the blanket, and then ran across Lady

Austin's chest. Judith was mesmerised by the sight of it all, it looked so unreal.

'Undress for me,' Lady Austin whined again, sounding like a spoilt child.

Judith watched as his shadow stood up again and he started to quickly undress. First he took off what Judith concluded must have been his white coat which he wore even though he wasn't a doctor. With a swift move of the wrist he then managed to get rid of his tie and started to unbutton his shirt.

Simultaneously Judith also saw her patient pulling up her gown above her head. The woman's breasts, reshaped or false as they might have been, pointed up perkily, like a teenager's, her nipples stiff and eager.

A second later Edouard dropped his trousers. The shadow of his naked body was very impressive; his erect cock standing up, a long and thick rod. The image on the curtain were so clear that Judith could make out the ridge of the head, an enormous, swollen plum.

She ran her tongue across her dry lips. Although she had seen him quite often in the operating theatre, she had never realised what a nice body he had. His shoulders were broad and square, his buttocks rounded and pert. His shaft seemed powerful, pointing towards the ceiling, animated with a life of its own.

And as she watched, Judith's vulva came alive as well, exuding a warm, honey-like dew, suddenly hungry to feel Edouard's length enter and fill it. She felt like a voyeur, watching two faceless, naked bodies. She didn't know what to do, torn between the temptation to stay and be a witness to their coupling – the need to follow orders and attend to her patient – and her wish to simply do the decent thing and leave them alone.

Her thoughts were interrupted when she felt a presence behind her. Mrs Cox had also entered the room.

Silently, she took a hold of Judith's arm and swiftly led her out of the room whilst sighs and moans began to rise from behind the curtain. The nurse followed without a word, horribly ashamed.

They stopped in the corridor just a couple of feet from the door. How long had Mrs Cox been there? Did she realise Judith had been watching the couple? If she did, this could only mean trouble.

'You are very likely to be a witness to scenes like this,' Mrs Cox told the blushing nurse. 'Never intervene unless you are invited to do so. After you've been here a few weeks, you will have a different perspective on such situations. In the meantime, just go about your duties and come back to your patient in a few minutes.'

She turned around and walked back towards the nurses' station. Judith's heart was pounding, the supervisor's words still echoing in her head. Luckily, the corridor was deserted and hopefully nobody would ever find out that Judith Stanton, the new nurse, was a voyeur.

She was on the verge of tears. She hadn't meant for this to happen, it was just a case of being in the wrong place at the wrong time. Surely they couldn't fire her for that? Yet at the same time she had taken some kind of wicked pleasure out of watching them . . .

Things were happening too fast. Everywhere around her there seemed to be wantonness beyond control. Somehow Judith felt left out, she wanted to be part of this whirl of passion, her body was aching to experience new sensations, to merge with all these gorgeous, desirable sources of pleasure. Doctor Harvey, Tania and Jo, Edouard, and even Mrs Cox. The effect they had on her was overwhelming. She was being teased in a cruel way, like a child left looking at a window full of toys but never being allowed to play with them.

She briefly ran her hand across her chest, feeling her nipples hardening under her uniform. She could also feel her panties soaked with her warm dew, like they had been so often since she had started to work at the Clinic, just a few days ago.

This was too much to take. She had been in a perpetual state of arousal, but only seldom been satisfied. Right now she craved the touch of another body. Her desire was so powerful it was sending shivers down her spine. She leant against the wall, her mind numb.

Suddenly Edouard appeared in front of her, a broad smile on his face. '*Ma chère*,' he crooned, 'were you in there watching us? That would be naughty...' He quickly looked around; they were alone in the corridor. Coming closer, he raised his hand and casually stroked Judith's breasts, feeling their heavy weight in turn, gently tweaking the erect nipples through her uniform. She sobbed and shuddered, unable to resist his touch, unwilling to push him away.

'I see you enjoyed it,' he continued in a whisper, his accent getting heavier, sexier. 'I wish we could spend more time together, but right now I have to visit other patients.' His right hand continued stroking her breasts whilst his left hand quickly snaked its way under her dress and inside her panties, never stopping its search until the fingers finally lost themselves inside her wet, gaping vulva.

His smile got even broader. 'I can smell your desire,' he continued, his face now just a few inches from hers. 'Soon, *mon amour*, very soon...' He let his lips lightly brush her cheek, then suddenly let go of her and quickly walked away, leaving her even more puzzled.

As he disappeared around the corner, Judith leant back against the wall, as if awakening from a dream, wondering if all this had really just happened or if her mind was going crazy with lust.

Lady Austin was sitting upright in her bed, noisily nibbling on chocolates. The thin blanket covering her chest was tucked underneath her armpits.

'Would you like one?' she said with her mouth full as she pushed the box towards Judith. 'They're Belgian, the finest. I find the Continentals are such refined people. In any case, they make lovely chocolates.' The tip of her pink tongue slightly came out of her mouth to lick her finger.

Still shaking from her encounter in the corridor, Judith

pushed the medication trolley aside and lifted the blanket to have a look at her patient's feet. Tiny red lines betrayed the fact that there had been surgery, however they would disappear in just a few weeks. Already the feet looked younger; the skin seemed soft and plump, and the blue veins had disappeared.

'Aren't they adorable?' Lady Austin asked, wriggling her toes. 'I know a boutique in Madrid where they make lovely sandals. I think I'll drop by sometime next week.'

Spreading the feet thickly with medicated lotion, Judith carefully massaged the skin, making sure the heavy cream penetrated even between the toes. Lady Austin lay back and let out a sigh.

'What a nice touch you have,' she commented softly. 'I wish you had been here a few years ago when I had my breasts done.'

She pulled down the blanket and uncovered her bare breasts. Judith was startled by their sight. They looked even better than the shadow she had observed on the curtain just a few moments earlier. Firm and round, the two globes were pale and milky, the nipples dark and puckered, pointing at the ceiling, proud and sophisticated.

'Just like they were when I was twenty,' Lady Austin continued. 'They're all mine, you know. I refused to have implants. Just make them look good, I asked. Doctor Harvey works wonders on me. He's quite expensive, but worth every penny.'

Judith's fingers continued finding their way between the patient's toes, clumsily, almost mechanically, for she wasn't paying attention to what she was doing anymore. Now she couldn't keep her eyes off those breasts, inviting, compelling. Never before had she been so disturbed just looking at a woman's chest.

Lady Austin was slowly caressing them, as if she wanted to make sure they were real. 'I told him to pretend he was a sculptor, and to make them as he liked, something he would be attracted to.' She looked up at Judith and winked.

'It worked.' she confided. 'He can't keep his hands off them when I come here now.' She paused to stare at her nurse's hands.

'Would you like to touch them?' she asked in a childish tone. 'Please?' Her voice was the same that had been talking to Edouard earlier, as if issuing some form of invitation. 'I'd like you to touch them. I know you'd like it . . .'

'I don't think this would be very proper, Lady Austin,' Judith said in a trembling voice. She could almost picture Edouard's hands on them. No wonder he couldn't resist their sight. Judith was tempted to touch them as well, just to see what it would be like to feel the nipples contract under her fingertips, but could she ever bring herself to willingly fondle another woman's breasts? A woman who was her patient? 'Not very proper,' she repeated. 'After all, you are my patient . . .'

'What does it matter,' the woman whined. 'Wouldn't you like to join me in bed? Edouard was here just a few minutes ago. His caresses were exquisite, but right now I want a woman with me.'

Judith didn't reply. Now there was no doubt Edouard had ended up in bed with his patient. In fact, she could still smell him on the blankets. Not only was that highly unethical but now Lady Austin wanted Judith to join her in bed as well! How strange. How tempting.

She looked at the breasts once again. Judith couldn't understand this new attraction and arousal she felt by the sight of a woman's body. She licked her dry lips as a wild image flashed through her head. She saw herself reaching out towards the firm mounds. Somehow she could feel their fluid weight in the palm of her hands. She closed her eyes and willed the thought away. There was no way she could let herself do that, she had to fight it.

She flipped the blanket back over the woman's feet and quickly pushed her trolley out of the room, almost running away from temptation.

* * *

'We hope to see you again soon,' Mrs Cox said with a smile.

'So do I,' Lady Austin replied. 'I have enjoyed my stay like never before. Your staff have been most pleasant, as usual, especially the new nurse. She has such a sweet, innocent look about her, although she seems bit a hesitant when it comes to dispensing special care . . .'

'We can assure you this will change when you come back. She has only just joined our staff. We hope to make her one of our best nurses.'

The chauffeur closed the door and got in the car. Mrs Cox stood silently as she watched the dark Bentley drive down the tree-lined street before disappearing around the corner.

She had mixed feelings about Judith. She fondly remembered their moment together in the shower room, but masturbating girls was not her style. Although she found the young nurse's innocent look most attractive, the plans she had for her would surely change all that. With a shrug, she turned around and went back inside.

Chapter Six

*T*he lecture hall was buzzing with the noise from several simultaneous conversations. Judith entered hesitantly through a door at the back and quickly picked the nearest empty chair, in the last row. She sank into the deep seat, almost out of breath, her heart still pounding.

She was nearing the end of her shift – and the end of her second week – and she was so tired it was hard to believe she could still walk. Yet she practically had to run through the corridors, desperately looking for directions. It would have looked rather bad had she arrived late, but she had made it with just a few minutes to spare.

The meeting was just about to begin. A few latecomers were still arriving, red-faced and puffing, quickly finding chairs amongst the two hundred or so people who were already seated. These sessions were held on the last Friday of each month and attendance was mandatory. Only one nurse remained at each station and would be given a transcript of the discussion.

Her colleagues had been rather vague about the usual content of these meetings, so Judith didn't know what to expect, although she suspected they were probably on the whole rather boring.

Yet the atmosphere was charged with electricity,

people laughing and waving at each other from across the room, giddy and excited like a bunch of school children. The front row seats were occupied by people dressed in street clothes, members of staff who were off duty but had to attend the lecture anyway, colourful dots in the sea of white uniforms. The rest of the staff seemed segregated, doctors on the right hand side, nurses in the middle, kitchen and cleaning staff on the left.

A tall man walked to the lectern and started shuffling a bunch of papers.

Judith recognised Doctor Alan Marshall, founder and Director of the Clinic. He was a handsome man of about fifty and was therefore quite a bit older than the rest of the staff. Standing tall and proud, he looked very distinguished but somewhat snobbish; like a businessman rather than a doctor. His tanned face offered a sharp contrast to the silver threads of his hair. Judith still remembered the first thought to cross her mind when she had been introduced to him: he was the man with the expensive haircut.

His lips were dark and thin, seemingly unable to smile; his jaw square, stern and unforgiving; his nose perfectly shaped. The white coat he was wearing didn't suit him, he would look better in dark clothes. In fact, a dark aura seemed to follow him, making him look attractively calm, yet sending disturbing vibrations, giving the impression of imminent threat. On the whole, he seemed an utterly cold man, with the cruel beauty of a vampire.

Judith cast her gaze around the room, looking for familiar faces. From where she sat she could only see the back of their heads but she recognised the brown locks of Elizabeth Mason's thick mane, alongside Doctor Rogers's pale head. These two were almost always together, inseparable, like a kid brother endlessly following his older sister.

Robert Harvey was sitting at the far end of the front row, engaged in a deep conversation with another surgeon whom Judith didn't know. The seat he had taken was at a diagonal extreme from where she was sitting, away from her body but still very close in her mind. After all, it was only a few evenings ago that they had shared that moment in the Doctors' Lounge. Yet somehow it seemed like a lifetime already. Her hopes of being with him again were quickly evaporating, but without any bad feelings or regrets.

Her heart jumped in her chest when she noticed Tania and Jo sitting a few seats apart in the front row. Perhaps she still hadn't recovered, or come to terms with the unusual treatment they had put her through. Their faces haunted her every time she stepped into the shower room, wondering if they would ever come back, in some sort of frightened anticipation. But today they were just two women sitting in a large crowd, anonymous and completely harmless. At that moment Judith remembered she was scheduled to work a few night shifts the week after next. That would mean working with them. Could she cope with that?

They would have to do their rounds together, strolling along the dark corridors or doing the inventories in the isolated stock rooms. She would be at their mercy, in more ways than one. The thought of having to spend even one night working with either one of them also conjured up fear and, curiously, sweet expectation.

Doctor Marshall coughed and silence fell across the room. He began talking and everyone kept still, drinking in each of his words as if they were Gospel. Judith was rather surprised to see the effect he had on his audience, for what he had to say was in fact rather insignificant.

There was an update following several complaints about the lack of parking space around the clinic, announcements about the new fire drills and emergency evacuation procedures, and a brief discussion on possible plans to extend one of the wings and take on more patients. Utterly boring.

'We had only one addition to our staff this month,' Doctor Marshall continued, 'in case you haven't already met her...' He paused briefly and looked around the room several times. 'Miss Stanton,' he called out, 'could you please stand so that everyone can see you?'

Judith suddenly felt her face flush. She had to stand up and show off in front of all these people, one of the things she hated most. She sank in her seat even further, hoping in vain that everyone would conclude she wasn't in the audience.

But already some of her colleagues had spotted her and were gesturing to her to stand up. In the second row Mrs Cox stood up and turned around, staring straight at her above the audience, silently ordering her to do as she was told. Judith lowered her eyes in embarrassment and slowly stood up.

Murmurs of appreciation travelled around the room, and she felt like some piece of art on display. 'There you are,' Doctor Marshall announced. 'Please let us welcome you to our clinic. We hope you enjoy working with us.'

Judith wanted to disappear a thousand miles away. She could feel their eyes on her, and this time it wasn't just her imagination. She looked up and stared at the audience briefly. Most faces stared back, some curious, others indifferent.

Far away in the corner Robert Harvey looked at her and winked. Judith suddenly felt better, realising he had not forgotten her after all. Tania and Jo were already looking elsewhere, completely uninterested. She sat back, her heart still pounding. The rest of Doctor Marshall's speech became utterly insignificant to her, and, no longer paying attention, she didn't try to understand what he meant.

'Because Miss Stanton has not finished her probationary period with us,' he continued, 'I shall not discuss in detail the issue of our Special Care Programme, which she doesn't know about yet, but I shall only say it is going very well and as usual we have received very good comments.'

There followed a short question period but Judith was no longer listening; her ears were still throbbing with the rush of blood that had flowed to her face and was only now slowly returning to her shaking limbs.

It hadn't been so bad after all. Everyone had looked at her with various degrees of interest, but once Doctor Marshall had resumed talking they had seemed to forget all about her instantly.

The talk ended shortly after and Judith quickly made her way out of the lecture hall, not wanting to talk to anybody. She couldn't wait to get home.

'Step on, step off,' the voice yelled at the front of the class. 'And on, and off.'

The music was loud but entertaining. In the overheated room, sweating bodies moved in unison, stepping on and off their square plastic boxes, their arms rhythmically rising above their heads in a complicated pattern.

In the back row, Judith was trying to concentrate on the choreography. Her thighs and buttocks were on fire. Her lips were dry and droplets of sweat left a burning sensation on her cheeks as they rolled down her face. Another fifteen minutes before cooling down. If she concentrated on breathing deeply, she knew she could keep up with the rest of the class.

As usual, her leotard was rather uncomfortable, the strip between her legs constantly moving back and forth, a most delicious torture on her swollen folds. As she kept moving the pressure seemed only to increase, and so did her arousal.

'Oh no . . . Not now,' she thought to herself, 'not again.' She had to resist. Unless she kept her mind on what her feet were doing, she knew she would have an orgasm again. The timing couldn't be worse. She remembered the last time she had climaxed during the aerobics workout. Luckily, everyone else in the class was huffing and puffing in loud, moaning sounds. With any chance nobody guessed the real reason behind her sighs.

Again today everything was against her, from the tight, rounded buttocks of the man in front of her, to the obvious, large nipples of the aerobics instructor. Some of her classmates were not wearing much, which didn't help either. Everywhere she looked the muscular, sweaty bodies were arousing her senses, coupled with the brushing touch of her leotard on her stiff clitoris.

'OK,' the voice yelled again. 'Cool down.'

The tempo of the music changed and Judith collapsed to the floor, legs wide apart, stretching the muscles inside her legs. She was relieved it was finally over, but her flesh was protesting. Too bad, she thought.

Some people were already rushing out of the room, not taking the time to stretch and cool down. This was the moment Judith liked best, feeling her limbs graciously lengthening as her heartbeat slowly returned to normal, the sweat of her effort gently trickling down her back, soothingly cool and tickling.

Turning her torso sideways to stretch the side of her ribcage, she noticed the man who was sitting on the floor next to her. Slim and blond, his body was toned and well-defined, chiselled but without the bulk of muscles that usually attracted her. He looked almost aristocratic, his movements slow and elegant. Catching her eye, he blushed and turned his head the other way.

Judith was somewhat puzzled at first, but realised the reason for his uneasiness when she glanced down between his legs. He wore tight lycra running shorts, the kind that leave nothing to the imagination. And judging by the stiff, erect cock that distended the elastic fabric, his imagination had also been running wild during the aerobics session. His legs were extended remarkably wide, like a ballet dancer, and his genitals practically rested on the floor, as if the fabric of his shorts couldn't hold them up.

So Judith wasn't the only one who got aroused during exercise. The thought both comforted and intrigued her. She was slightly amused and decided to wickedly make the most of the situation. Extending her arms behind her back, she pulled hard, stretching the muscles in her chest and hoping he would notice the way her breasts were thus emphasised.

He stared at her with a bewildered look. Her heart pounding, she issued a silent invitation by demurely licking her lips, looking at him through half-shut eyes. He finally smiled and she saw his cock throb slightly through his shorts. Encouraged by this reply, her movements became exaggerated and deliberately slow. She knew he was watching her intensely now and, curiously, at this moment she liked nothing better than showing off.

Quickly glancing around the classroom, she noticed quite a few people had already left. In fact, only she and her handsome neighbour were still on the floor, stretching and subtly examining each other. The others were standing by the door, chatting and paying absolutely no attention to Judith and her companion.

The music was now softer, relaxing, but her mind began working frantically. She closed her eyes for a minute and quickly assessed the situation. Just a few inches from her was a man with a gorgeous body, a man who was obviously enthralled by the sight of her, and for the past few days she had herself been in a near-constant state of arousal. Right now there was a handsome body within her reach, a body which no doubt wanted her as well. Would she dare make the most of it?

Thinking fast, she assumed it was up to her to make the first move. Would he respond to her invitation? The anticipation sent a shiver through her abdomen; there was no way of knowing if he would want anything to do with her, but she had to find out.

The last few people were coming out of the equipment room, having replaced the plastic boxes where they belonged. Yet they seemed in no hurry to leave the gym. Judith knew she had to do something before her prey escaped, but what? There was no way she could do anything until everybody had left.

The instructor was standing near the audio system, sorting out her tapes. She finally turned off the music, took the tape out and waved at Judith before making her way out of the room. Soon after, the last few people who had been waiting by the door followed her out. By now there were just a couple of women still in the equipment room, but they were probably about to come out any minute.

In a mental gamble Judith decided it was stupid to wait any longer and got up slowly, gathering her towel, her water bottle, her plastic box. Without looking behind her, she slowly walked towards the equipment room, letting the last person out before going in. With any luck he would join her soon enough, if indeed he was interested. Otherwise, she would just leave it at that.

Just as she was hoping, he came up behind her almost immediately and she felt the warmth of his breath on her neck. His body exuded a sweet aroma, musky and attractive despite the effort he had just put into the workout. She reached out to put her box on top of the others. His arm brushed hers, warm and smooth, as he stepped forward to help her. Now the game was afoot, and there would be no looking back.

Without turning around, her heart pounding with excitement, she extended her hand behind her until she came to lightly touch his cock with her fingertips. At the same time, she heard the main door of the gym close shut. They were alone now.

She felt him hard as steel in her hand, and still getting harder. Immediately she wanted him inside her. She closed her eyes and tilted her head back. In a brief flash she saw herself being taken, impaled on this delightful shaft. Somehow she could already feel his thick phallus stretching her, she knew his thrusts would be powerful and strong. She wanted him *now*.

Still standing behind her, he got bigger in her hands. She felt his fingers on her body, finding their way to her breasts, quickly zeroing in on her erect nipples, kneading the soft mounds in a rough, frenetic caress. She turned around and grabbed his mouth in hers, roughly, releasing the fury of her arousal. The taste of sweat was still on his lips, salty and bitter.

Grabbing hold of her hips he swiftly hoisted her onto a stack of floor mattresses as if she had been feather-light. She marvelled at his strength as she quickly fondled and surveyed the hard muscles of his shoulders and upper back.

Raising both his hands to her cleavage, he ripped her leotard apart without hesitation and she screamed gleefully, her excitement rapidly increasing as her breasts were exposed. For a second he stared at her naked breasts, as if mesmerised by their sight then lowered his head to take them in his mouth. He was rough with them, his mouth travelling incessantly between the stiff nipples, sucking them violently and even grazing at them with his teeth.

But Judith liked each of his love-bites, and found his rough treatment even more arousing. In reply she dug her fingernails into his skin, letting out a loud moan of painful pleasure.

Their sweaty bodies melted onto each other, his enormous cock pushing forcefully against her clothed vulva. His arms around her waist held her tight, his hands pulling down the back of her leotard and kneading her sweaty skin.

She buried her face into his wet hair, pleasantly surprised by its spicy scent. She liked the way their moist bodies brushed each other in a raw friction. Soon, hopefully, they would be naked and she could feel all of him.

Already his hands were fretting over her crotch, unable to get at her flesh. Under her leotard she was wearing a pair of exercise shorts, which came up to her waist. He had to fight the fabric to get to her pussy, at first trying to pull down the shorts from under the leotard but to no avail, thus becoming more and more impatient. Next, he fitfully tried to get at it by running his hand up her leg underneath the shorts but his success was still limited.

All the while he kept caressing her breasts with his mouth, forcefully, grunting like an animal between each sucking bite, his hands desperately trying to find a way to get to her flesh. Their coupling was noisy and almost violent. Judith was already moaning with pleasure, the strap of her leotard between her legs digging deep into her vulva, squeezing her clitoris in exquisite torture as she wrapped her legs around her new lover's waist. With a sigh of impatience, he let go of her breasts for a moment and quickly glanced around the room.

She felt a cold chill run down her spine when she saw him reach for a large pair of scissors on the shelf behind her and immediately tried to push him away in a panic.

'What are you doing?' she screamed in anger. Suddenly worried, she tried to make him let go of her, but he was stronger and no match for her tiny arms. Because his hips were pressed against her there was no way she could reach his groin and hit him there, and her fingernails digging in his skin only seemed to excite him even more. His face buried between her breasts made it impossible for her to slap him. All she could do was pound his muscular back with her tiny fists, still trying to push him away.

But his arms around her waist held her tighter, preventing her from escaping. They struggled for a minute, she wanting to get off and him not willing to let her go. The pile of mattresses upon which she sat collapsed under her and she fell to the floor, taking him down with her.

She ended up on her back, with him on top of her, his legs straddling her naked chest, the bulge of his erection just a few inches from her mouth. He seized both her wrists in one hand and pinned her arms against the floor up above her head. She felt trapped, yet amazingly excited.

'What's the matter, love?' he said with an amused, lustful look in his eyes. 'Don't you trust me?'

'I don't even know you!' she screamed. And suddenly, the reality of what she was doing hit her: she was just about to have sex with a complete stranger, in the equipment room of a health club. The thought seemed preposterous, but very arousing at the same time. For the longest time it had been a fantasy of hers to be taken by a complete stranger, almost by force, by someone she had never met before and would perhaps never see again.

On either side of her chest his tanned, hairy thighs

offered a stark contrast to the fluid softness of her breasts. Her globes were falling on either side of her chest under the pull of gravity. They lightly brushed against the rough skin of his knees, which touched her armpits. She could already see faint, pink marks on them, her skin delicately throbbing in reply to his rugged caresses.

Putting the scissors aside, he took her breasts in his free hand and tortured them skilfully, worrying her nipples until she moaned with desire despite herself.

'Let me do it my way...' his tone became softer, yet still slightly threatening. 'I promise you won't regret it.' Slowly he let go of her wrists and she stopped trying to fight him off.

Once again she was torn between anger and pleasure. Of course, she wanted him, but what exactly did he want to do with her? Once again, it was up to her to decide.

In reply she quickly pulled his shorts down and eased his member out. She marvelled at the sight of the thick shaft, never before had she seen one so big. The purplish head was enormous and luscious. This suddenly eased her last worries and she took him in her mouth, quickly running her tongue along the slit of the swollen plum.

She tasted him only briefly as he almost immediately pulled out and pushed her breasts together, using them to envelop his cock, slowly gliding back and forth inside the soft cleavage. With each of his thrusts the swollen head found its way inside Judith's mouth, her lips quickly closing around it in a strong suction before releasing it again. Tiny drops of clear fluid seeped at the mouth and she felt his buttocks contract on her stomach. She increased the strength of her suction, now wishing to make him lose control and abandon himself in her mouth. But instead he pulled away even further to escape this burning embrace.

'Not yet,' he said as he moved down along her belly.

Kneeling between her parted legs, he took tke gusset of her leotard and pushed it to one side, contemplating the large, wet patch her vulva had cast on the pale blue fabric of her shorts. Judith remained motionless, paralysed by arousing anticipation.

Pinching the fabric delicately between his index and forefinger, he took the scissors and made a small cut in the shorts, then inserted the lower blade in the small hole.

Judith shuddered as she felt him at work. Very slowly, he cut the hole bigger, moving the scissors around expertly, as Judith writhed with pleasure under the icy assault. She was no longer angry, reassured that he wouldn't hurt her, almost amused by his resourcefulness.

Putting the scissors aside once more, he inserted his fingers inside the opening and tore it to make it bigger. As she glanced down Judith could see her wet, curly bush appearing out of the hole, encasing the red, swollen lips glistening with the dew that was drenching them.

Bending down, he caught the whole of her throbbing pussy in his mouth. She moaned under the invasion as his tongue foraged around, quickly discovering each of the intricacies of her vulva. She grabbed both her breasts and caressed them roughly, duplicating the treatment she had just received from his mouth.

With each of her breaths she let out a sigh, feeling the wave of an oncoming orgasm quickly building up inside her.

'Fuck me,' she whined, surprising even herself. 'Fuck me now!'

He responded without hesitation and impaled her quickly, thrusting forcefully as she contracted the muscles of her pelvis under him. Just as she had imagined, she could now feel him stretching her to the limit, in a perfect, almost painful but pleasant fit.

Although she was pleased to hold his thickness inside her, it still wasn't enough for her. She wanted to come. She wanted to come now. Sliding her hand between their bodies she began to tease her clitoris herself, rubbing its shaft up and down, pressing on it with her fingertips. He pushed up from the inside, squeezing the swollen flesh only tighter between her fingers and his hardness. She wasn't used to being touched so intensely, but this made her response even more violent. Her climax was sudden and powerful, and she let out a loud sob. Meanwhile the stranger inside her continued his in-and-out motion, clearly amused by the wanton creature that writhed underneath him.

'How often ... do you go for ... strangers ... in gymnasiums?' he asked laboriously between each of his thrusts. She was amused that he wanted to carry on a conversation at this point, but felt happy to answer his question.

'Believe it or not,' she replied slowly, 'it's my first time.'

'You are ... incredibly ... beautiful,' he managed to say. 'I can tell ... you were made ... for pleasure.' She didn't reply this time. More than a compliment, this was a revelation about herself, something she had never thought about before.

She felt her arousal mounting again as he continued to impale her. Back home she had had a few physical encounters with occasional boyfriends, but never had she felt this urge to be pleasured over and over again, her body alight with a passion she couldn't seem to quell.

The change had seemed to start the moment she had started working at the Clinic. From that day she had begun to feel constantly aroused, always yearning to give and receive pleasure. Even now, the gorgeous cock in her vagina would soon make her reach her peak once again. This was the moment she liked best, as she felt the fire grow out of control before the explosion. She moaned.

He withdrew and turned around to take her in his mouth again. She moved onto her side, towards the luscious phallus that appeared in front of her, stiff and glistening with her juices. She tasted her own dew as she took him in her mouth, caressing him with her tongue, hungrily sucking the swollen head as if it were a ripe fruit.

His mouth on her vulva was like a spider, slowly rediscovering her, this time only just brushing her swollen folds with the tip of his tongue. His hands ripped her shorts completely, freeing her rounded bottom and surveying it roughly, groping and kneading her smooth skin.

She bent her knees and crossed her legs up behind his neck, holding him prisoner, forcing him to delve harder into her wet pussy. Soon after she felt a hard, pinching blow on her buttocks and she immediately sensed she was being hit with a metallic object. Without looking up she also realised there was now somebody else in the equipment room, standing just a few inches from them. Somebody who was watching them closely.

'Do you like sucking the little wanton, Jimmy? Do you like her sucking you?' a voice croaked.

'Jimmy' didn't reply. If indeed it was his name, Judith knew he wouldn't let go of her pussy to talk to this newcomer. She tested him by lowering her legs and releasing his head. She was proven right as he kept on licking her.

The notion of having a spectator aroused her even more and increased her eagerness. She grabbed Jimmy's thick shaft and roughly squeezed it with both hands, working on it frantically in an up and down motion, holding the swollen head fast in her mouth.

She recognised the clicking sound of metal from what probably was a set of keys. In a slow movement of the wrist, their lone spectator was using it to hit her behind methodically, at first merely brushing her tender skin, but steadily increasing the freguency and the force of each blow.

The keys were cold and rough, their serrated edge sending needles of excitement through her buttocks, like mild electrical shocks. Gradually, she felt Jimmy's mouth moving away and the keys getting closer and closer to her aching bud.

Jimmy pulled away completely and turned her onto her back, holding her legs apart. Looking up, she recognised Bert, an aerobics instructor. He was also wearing running shorts and sporting an enormous erection. However the look in his eyes was only mildly appreciative and he didn't seem tempted to touch her.

She remained motionless as he kneeled between her legs and smiled wickedly. Without a word he began swinging the heavy set of keys in a triangular path, nonchalantly, from one thigh to the next, then on to her engorged vulva.

'I don't care much for pussy,' he finally said in an arrogant tone, 'but I can't resist the sight of a pretty woman such as yourself. If you'd be kind enough to suck my friend Jimmy off, I promise I'll make you come.'

Panting with desire, Judith was too weak say anything; her mind numb but her body very much alive and yearning for more stimulation. Jimmy was now kneeling next to her, kneading her heavy breasts, pinching her nipples forcefully. She quickly grabbed hold of his shaft once again and greedily sucked him into her mouth.

At the same time the keys hit her bud directly, sending a shock wave of pleasure through her belly. She moaned.

'You like it rough, don't you?' Bert asked in a low voice before lowering his hand again.

Judith moaned louder in reply to each stroke. Never before had her tender folds been treated so roughly. Yet the pain quickly gave rise to pleasure, growing more and more intense with each blow, the sensation so powerful she thought she was going to faint with excitement.

He encircled her swollen vulva with his thumb and forefinger, holding it into a wet, musky bundle, making her stiff clitoris stick out, throbbing and glistening. Dropping the keys, he slapped her flesh with his bare hand. At first it was just a series of friendly taps, but he kept teasing her treasure expertly, each slap sending waves of pleasure that quickly merged into a strong, mind-blowing orgasm.

All the while, she kept on torturing Jimmy, echoing the treatment she was receiving despite herself, often letting her teeth graze the purplish head, sucking him so hard he was also moaning in pleasure and in pain. He reached his climax as she did, spilling his honey inside her mouth. She received him with a loud moan, her pleasure enhanced by the taste of his seed on her lips.

Judith was too weak to get up, and slightly dizzy. She lay on her belly, her moist skin stuck to the floor mattress, a witness to the heat of the passion that had transported her some time earlier. Reaching out in front of her, she grabbed the shapeless bundle of her torn leotard and cut up shorts and brought it to her face. They were soaked with her sweat, fragrant with the animal smell of her excitement. Turning onto her back, she blinked as the light coming from the ceiling assaulted her sleepy eyes.

Jimmy and Bert were gone. She couldn't remember when or why they had left, but the treatment they had given her body was unforgettable. Her vulva was still aching, swollen and occasionally throbbing. Her bottom and her breasts showed large, red marks; her skin was raised and still burning. She didn't feel any pain, but her whole body was now numb. She didn't care, she was fulfilled.

Lying completely naked on her back, in the equipment room of a health club, she could hardly recognise herself now; a wanton creature, willing to submit to strangers, keen to be violated, albeit in the most delightful way.

What else lay ahead for her? She didn't feel any shame, only amazement at what she had just done, and the overwhelming desire to do it all over again and again. Her whole body had become a slave to pleasure, and somehow she was wickedly happy about that. She wanted to explore all possibilities, yearning to learn more, yet she wasn't sure how to.

It had all happened so suddenly, so recently. Was this just a phase she was going through? Somehow she didn't think so, and she also felt her job had a strong influence on her lustful behaviour.

In a brief flash she remembered Mrs Cox, and how the supervisor had released her in the shower room. The woman had been very straightforward that time, asking her bluntly if she had come, as if it had been of the utmost importance.

Her vulva clenched violently at the recollection, her dew once again oozing out of her. She had to go and see her superior again. Deep within her was this powerful feeling that there was some sort of connection between the Dorchester Clinic and the unexpected awakening of her senses. She had to find out why her body had become so lustful, and somehow she knew that Mrs Cox had the answer.

Chapter Seven

Judith wanted to take her gown off. Never before had she felt so constricted, so uncomfortable, and the atmosphere in the operating theatre was warmer than usual this morning. She had dressed in a hurry, not realising that the mint-coloured garments stacked in the sterilisation cupboard were all of different sizes and she had picked one that was too small for her. Now the seam under her armpits was digging into her skin and the fabric was crushing her breasts, chafing her sensitive nipples. But it was too late to go back and change, she had work to do.

On the operating table, the naked girl smiled at her sleepily. 'You look nice in green,' she mumbled. 'Just like in the films . . .'

Judith smiled at the patient and pushed the girl's left breast up to put the stethoscope underneath it. The smooth skin fell back under the fluid weight of the breast and gently touched her fingers. Simultaneously, she noticed the coffee-coloured nipple contract and felt a tingling sensation tease at her crotch.

Lisa Baxter was twenty years old, a hip and modern girl, with skin soft as velvet. Three months earlier her father had died and left her a generous inheritance. Like any other girl of her generation, Lisa had everything figured out: now that daddy was no more, there was no reason why she shouldn't have that nose job she had been wanting for so long, even though she was probably the only person on the planet who thought her nose was anything but pretty.

Just a few years younger than Judith, her body had the fresh look of youth with round, perky breasts, a slim, inviting waist and a soft, pale mound of curls which most probably hid a lovely clitoris. Her hair was hidden under a pink cap but a few straight strands the colour of straw stuck out behind her right ear. Her skin tone was even, tanned to a pale brown but without any marks from a bathing costume.

This was a girl who probably liked to lie in the sun covered only with lotion, Judith thought. She felt tempted to run her hands all over that smooth skin, glancing at the brown nipple again and suddenly longing to take it in her mouth, to discover its smoky taste.

She pulled the stethoscope from underneath the girl's breast and placed it higher up on her chest, half-way between the two globes. Lowering her wrist, she let the cuff of her gown gently brush against the girl's breast without realising it. Once she saw what she had done, however, she felt herself blush and nervously pulled her hand away.

Lisa closed her eyes and sighed, and Judith was startled by this reaction, then realised it was probably more from the effect of the sedative she had received than from the caress of Judith's cuff.

Replacing the stethoscope in the pocket of her gown, Judith let her eyes wander some more over the naked figure. She imagined her own body was probably not much different from this one, albeit paler and milky. But did her skin look just as soft and inviting? The only way to find out would be to reach out and touch . . .

She shut her eyes for a second, ashamed at the images that were now forming in her head. Not again . . . Why was she feeling like this? Her own desire scared her now. How could she ever be attracted to another woman?

Why was it that every inch of exposed skin sent her mind racing and her flesh come alive? Would she ever be able to chase these thoughts and feelings away? What was happening to her? She had to fight it.

She took a deep breath and looked at Lisa again. Reluctantly, she pulled the thick, mint-coloured sheet on top of the lovely body, then turned to Doctor Wilson, the anaesthetist.

'She's comfortable, you may begin,' she said.

The rubber mask came to cover the pretty face. 'Take a long, deep breath,' he said to the girl.

Doctor Wilson was a man of a few words and soft manners. Like the rest of the staff, he was also terribly attractive. But right now Judith could only think of the nude body she had just covered. She had seen lots of naked, beautiful women before, but she had never felt attracted like this. This wasn't like her, something had happened to her. She was different now, and she had to find out why.

'Did you like it?' asked Mrs Cox. 'Do you wish I hadn't shown up to rescue you from them?'

'I don't know,' Judith replied slowly, carefully weighing each word. 'At first I was angry with them. But then I couldn't help feeling attracted.'

'Attracted by what?'

Judith blushed and stared at the floor. 'When they got up,' she continued hesitantly, 'I could see their nipples through their uniform...'

Silence fell. She sat still in the leather chair, her feet flat on the floor, her heart pounding with embarrassment and anticipation. Mrs Cox kept pacing in front of her. Every time she came near, Judith felt tempted to reach out and touch her bare arm, on the underside, right below the hem of the short sleeve, right where the pale skin looked baby-soft.

She had come hoping to find a listening ear. Instead, Mrs Cox was rather cold, almost cruel, as she forced

Judith to reveal more, to relive every moment of the past couple of weeks, recounting every lustful detail.

'Do you like the sight of erect nipples?' the woman continued.

'I never really thought about it until I came to work here,' she confessed, 'but now it seems I always have naked bodies on my mind.' She paused for a few seconds, trying to make some sense out of the mess of thoughts in her mind. 'You see, it all started when I came to work in this clinic. Since then I have been having these thought all the time . . .' her voice broke.

Mrs Cox stopped pacing just a few inches from her and looked down at her intensely. 'What kind of thoughts?' Her voice was a hoarse whisper.

Judith wrung her hands nervously. 'Thoughts of others . . .' she muttered.

'Could you be a little more specific?' Mrs Cox said as she bent down towards a blushing Judith, putting her hands on the armrests.

'There was Lady Austin.' Judith began, lowering her head.

'What about her?'

'She asked me to touch her breasts . . .'

'Did you?'

Judith couldn't reply. Her heart kept pounding against her chest, her face flushed as she recalled her patient's invitation, feeling the heat rapidly spilling down her neck.

'Did you touch them?' Mrs Cox repeated louder.

'No,' Judith whispered, almost to herself.

Mrs Cox began pacing again. 'How were her nipples? Describe them to me.'

Judith closed her eyes and took a deep breath. Their sight rose in her mind, and she remembered how she had been surprisingly aroused.

'They were dark and puckered.' She stopped, unable to say more, her throat tightening under the heat of the fire that blazed within her. Mrs Cox didn't say anything, as if expecting Judith to tell her more, her silence pressing for a reply.

'I could almost imagine them becoming harder under my fingertips, stiff and pointing,' she managed to say in a whisper.

'Did it arouse you, or were you already aroused?'

'I don't remember...'

'I don't believe you. You had been watching her with Edouard, surely your pussy must have been soaked.'

Judith looked up in dismay, once again stunned by the casual tone of the supervisor's voice as she spoke such words. It seemed she was almost doing it on purpose, either to shock or to excite the embarrassed nurse.

'Would you have liked to suck them?'

'No,' Judith protested.

'What about Lisa Baxter? What do you think of her?'

'She's very pretty...' Judith began.

'Isn't she?' Mrs Cox continued, her tone suddenly turning sarcastic. 'Very nice body. Does she turn you on?'

'I don't know.'

'Of course you do, she has skin just like velvet. Wouldn't you like to wrap your body around hers, to feel her young, warm flesh on yours?'

'Maybe...' Judith hesitated.

'Imagine, for a minute, that you are in bed with her. What would you do to her? Suck her nipples? Lick her clit? Would you like her to do the same to you?'

Judith couldn't reply. The conversation was having a powerful effect on her, making her arousal bloom as she recalled the moment she had touched the girl before her operation, how indeed she would have liked to caress the youthful flesh. Sensing her confusion, Mrs Cox insisted.

'Would you like her to suck your nipples? What about your clit? Do you want her to lick your pussy, to suck your clit? Tell me Judy, are you wet yet?' She paused and bent down again, her face just a few inches from

Judith's. Her voice became low and sultry. 'Would you like *me* to suck you?'

Judith couldn't stand to look at her. Yes, she did, she wanted the woman to pleasure her, to torture her flesh into submission, like she had done in the shower room. Only she would never dare ask her.

'Since you're not replying I can only assume you don't want me to,' Mrs Cox said dryly. 'But we're not finished. I want to hear what else you have to say. You told me you were aroused by women now, but do you still like men?'

'Yes,' Judith replied softly.

'Then tell me about the last time you were fucked,' she said, sitting down behind the desk. 'I want to hear every detail.'

The equipment room at the gym, two days ago. Judith tried to describe the scene but only succeeded to blush further.

'I had it with a man at the gym, a man I had never seen before,' she confessed, twisting in her seat, feeling her vulva contract deliciously as she remembered her encounter with Jimmy and Bert.

'And?'

'That's it.'

'That's all?'

'Well, what else can I tell you?' She was on the verge of tears, she couldn't stand this much longer. Mrs Cox was obviously waiting to hear more, but Judith didn't know how to.

'I'm afraid it's not good enough,' Mrs Cox said. 'You came here asking me to help you but so far I have failed to understand where the problem lies. You're holding back, and I can't let you out of this room until you have told me everything. At this point I have no choice but to ask you to take your clothes off.'

Judith stared at her in disbelief. Take her clothes off, right here in the office?

'You heard me,' Mrs Cox insisted. 'Get up and undress for me. That will make things much easier for both of us.'

Her whole body swept by a hot wave, Judith got up slowly, looking the woman in the face, and began to unbutton her uniform. Her hands were strangely steady as they worked their way down. The dress glided off her shoulders and fell to the floor with a soft thump. She kicked it away with her foot, shivering nervously as the cool air from the ventilation system assaulted her bare skin.

Across the desk, Mrs Cox licked her lips nervously. The young nurse now stood in her underwear, her nipples erect and pushing at the lace of her bra, her panties heavy with the warm dew that was soaking them.

Still hesitant but deliberately slow, Judith clutched her fingers around the clasp of the bra between her breasts.

'Now talk to me,' Mrs Cox ordered in a commanding tone.

'I didn't know him,' Judith began as she unhooked her bra. 'He was lovely and I could tell he was turned on . . .'

'What made you think that? Be specific.'

'I could see his penis hard under his shorts.'

'Did he have a big cock? Describe it.'

'It was quite long and thick, very thick,' she continued, pulling her panties down. She closed her eyes, unable to look at her superior, lest the woman would notice the desire in her eyes. 'I wanted to feel him inside me, stretching me.'

'That's much better,' Mrs Cox told a naked Judith as the wet panties fell to the floor. 'You have to say it out loud, I want to hear it all and so do you.'

Encouraged and aroused, Judith described the encounter in greater detail, telling how rough Jimmy's mouth had been with her breasts, what he had done with the scissors, what Bert had done with the keys. Mrs Cox started fidgeting in her chair at the mention of the rough treatment, the scissors and the keys.

'Did it excite you to feel cold metal on your skin?' she asked, standing up and slowly walking towards Judith.

'Yes,' Judith admitted. 'I have to admit I liked it.' She

watched the woman come forward and stop just a few paces in front of her. The shape of erect nipples now showed through the uniform, and Judith realised she had succeeded in arousing the woman.

Yet there was something unusual about those breasts, as if both nipples had an unusually distorted shape. There was no doubt that they were erect and pushing against the fabric of the woman's bra and uniform. However, it was impossible to figure out their shape; the fabric was too thick. Flat, rounded shapes were strongly visible, but that was all, unfortunately. There was no way to guess what the colour of those nipples was either.

Judith was intrigued and desperately wishing the woman would now take her clothes off as well.

'Are you aroused now?' Mrs Cox asked, suddenly walking away.

'Yes,' Judith confessed in a whisper.

'Then sit down and spread your legs,' she ordered, 'I want to see your pussy.'

Judith did as she was told, ready to do anything in the hope of having the woman come back towards her. She spread her legs wide, her hands gliding along the inside of her legs until her fingertips came to grab and gently pull apart the swollen love-lips.

Already she could feel her dew escaping and quickly gathering between her buttocks and the chair. Its sweet scent also rose, unmistakably. She looked at Mrs Cox and smiled demurely, hoping to see some kind of favourable reaction on her part. But the lack of response disappointed her. It was worse than Judith could have imagined; Mrs Cox stood back even further, and walked back to the chair behind her desk.

'I'm not too sure where your problem lies,' the woman advised, 'so I'll need a second opinion.' With a steady hand she pressed a button on the corner of her desk and, before Judith could ask what exactly she had in mind, a door opened behind the young nurse.

Turning her head slightly, Judith felt her blood freeze in her veins as she recognised Doctor Marshall, the

Director of the Clinic, entering the room. Her clothes were on the floor, quite a few feet away from her. She instinctively crossed her legs and covered her breasts with her hands.

'Don't be such a baby, Judith!' Mrs Cox snapped. 'Doctor Marshall has seen thousands of naked women in his career. Spread your legs this instant, he will want to examine you.'

Putting both hands flat on her desk, Mrs Cox turned to the man as he came to stand in front of Judith and began talking about the young nurse as if she wasn't there.

'What we have here is a young healthy female with an overactive libido,' she explained. 'I have not been able to establish whether there is something wrong with her or if indeed she is normal. I was hoping you could shed some light on the subject.'

'That can be quite tricky,' he acknowledged. 'You are right Mrs Cox. But I'll need to know more.'

He stood tall in front of Judith and briefly glanced at her with a look of disdain, his lips slightly twisted at the corners. His eyes looked down but he didn't lower his face. In fact, his nose seemed to turn up even further. Under the bright light coming from the ceiling his silver hair shone strangely, almost metallic. His blue eyes had a similar gleam, indifferent, even hostile.

Judith felt his icy glare survey her body and she couldn't help the shiver that shook her.

'Her nipples are hard,' he coldly stated after a while. 'Is she aroused?'

'Perpetually, it seems,' Mrs Cox advised. 'She claims to be constantly disturbed by thoughts of naked bodies and she is attracted to both men and women at this stage.'

'Is that so?' he said sarcastically. 'That doesn't tell us much, though.' He finally looked at Judith's face. 'Spread your legs, nurse,' he ordered. 'Let's see what kind of pussy you have.'

Judith slightly parted her legs and felt a sob rise in her throat. Now there were two pairs of eyes examining her. Although she wasn't too concerned about showing off in front of Mrs Cox anymore, it was all very different now that Doctor Marshall was here.

She saw him lick his lips at the very moment her pussy appeared. Obviously, he wasn't insensitive either, and the thought gave Judith some comfort. After all, he was a man, just like any other.

He leant on the edge of the desk and bent forward slightly, staring at Judith's wet bush. With a sharp slap on the inside of her thigh he forced her to spread her legs wider, all the while still examining her with eyes of steel, clinically. After a moment he turned to Mrs Cox and nodded silently.

The supervisor turned to Judith. 'You need release now,' she advised. 'Let's see you masturbate.'

Whereas up until now Judith had been embarrassed, she now felt utterly mortified and yet somewhat disappointed as well. What they were asking her to do wouldn't have been so bad if their attitude hadn't been so clinical. But Mrs Cox was right, she needed release; her flesh was aching to be pleasured.

Only she would have liked Mrs Cox to do that herself, of course, and she hadn't counted on anybody else being there with them. However, both Mrs Cox and Doctor Marshall were staring at her in such a way that she knew she had no option but to obey.

Her hand hesitantly snaked up along her thigh and two fingers gradually disappeared inside her throbbing tunnel whilst her thumb began flickering over her clitoris. Despite the charged atmosphere in the room the effect was almost immediate. The reaction of her body erased her concerns from her mind and in a matter of seconds she was on the verge of reaching her peak. Tilting her head back, she moaned gently.

It seemed ages since she had last given herself pleasure, for recently she had realised this was in no way comparable to having somebody else do it to her. Yet having her superiors watching her was a novelty, a wonderful and exciting experience. If she obeyed, maybe she would get a reward.

As her arousal mounted she became more daring, eager to reach her climax. She rubbed her clitoris hard and fast, already feeling pleasure build up inside her. Once she got to this point, she usually liked to come quickly, unable to hold out any longer. Today was no exception.

She gave a wailing scream as she climaxed, totally unconcerned, but rather pleased with having an audience. Panting but happy, she opened her eyes and demurely smiled at Mrs Cox and Doctor Marshall. What would they ask of her next?

'Thank you,' Doctor Marshall said, suddenly walking towards the door. 'I don't think your problem is very serious and I'm sure there's nothing to worry about. I'm afraid that's all the time I have for you.'

Mrs Cox reached down, picked up Judith's discarded clothes from the floor and practically threw them at her.

'Now I need you to take Major Johnson to Physiotherapy,' she said dryly. 'He has an appointment at two o'clock. You should hurry or else he'll be late.' She followed Doctor Marshall out of the office, closing the door behind her.

Judith was left all alone, still rocked by the vanishing strength of her orgasm. She stood up slowly and began to dress. Once again she was baffled. They were dismissing her! Having just spent an hour discussing her most intimate moments, undressing for them and even masturbating in front of them, was that all the effect it had?!

She had achieved absolutely nothing by coming here today. None of her questions had been answered. If anything it made everything even more complicated. Instead of finding out why her body craved constant pleasure, or at least how to control her urges, she had fallen into some kind of trap by yielding to her arousal once again.

And what about Mrs Cox and Doctor Marshall? For a while Judith had thought she had managed to arouse her supervisor, but things had not turned out the way she had planned, to say the least. In fact, it was quite the opposite.

The situation was most upsetting, and left Judith more puzzled than ever, even angry at herself and her superiors. This was the first time she had been rejected like this, and it wasn't for lack of trying. Initially she had come to Mrs Cox's office just to talk, but the woman's behaviour had led her to think she actually desired the young nurse.

However, it seemed Mrs Cox had a powerful sense of restraint. She could have kept Judith in there after Doctor Marshall had left, and possibly continued their conversation, maybe even touched her. There was no doubt the woman was aroused, but obviously not enough to engage in anything more than a useless, cruel interrogation.

And although Judith had never thought she would eventually need the woman to hold her again, the fact that Mrs Cox seemed unimpressed only fuelled the young nurse's peculiar hunger to try seducing her superior.

She felt wicked, confused by this sudden desire to get the woman to pleasure her, by the need to play some kind of game, a game she had never even played with men. Yet she didn't want to fight her impulses anymore.

Just like the other day, in the gym, when she had foolishly set out to seduce Jimmy, she knew that if she could get Mrs Cox, the result could only mean intense pleasure, in ways she couldn't even imagine. She could already feel it. It would be her way of turning the tables on her superior, a revenge on what had taken place just now.

There had to be a way of getting to the woman, to tempt her enough that she wouldn't be able to resist coming close to the young nurse and caress the waiting flesh. Judith felt resolute that someday she would find a way to get to her, only on Judith's own terms.

All she had to do was to find a way to break through Mrs Cox's defences, to offer herself in such a way that the woman wouldn't be able to resist.

Chapter Eight

The wheelchair purred softly as it rolled along the corridor. Major Johnson was sitting comfortably in the leather seat, content to be driven by such a lovely nurse. The dashing young army officer had injured his knee during a manoeuvre and now needed some physiotherapy following the surgery.

Steering the chair around the corner Judith stared down his neck, through the large opening of his T-shirt, examining the sinewy line of his shoulders. Ever since she had been a little girl she had been impressed by strong, taut bodies, attracted by the smooth skin that usually tightly wrapped the hard muscles. When her femininity had blossomed, the men who had begun appearing in her fantasies were always superb machines, strong and fit.

The man in the wheelchair was just like them, but he was no fantasy. He was close enough to touch. Her hands clenched around the handles of the wheelchair, her knuckles rapidly turning white as she backed up into the lift. The doors closed and she reached down to lock the wheels.

Being alone with him in such an enclosed space suddenly made Judith feel powerful. After the unusual session in Mrs Cox's office just a few moments earlier, she needed to be in charge for a change; she wanted to call the shots. And right now Major Johnson would be a perfect victim. Too bad she had to keep her hands on the handles of the wheelchair, his skin seemed to be calling at her to touch it.

Judith let her imagination drift for a moment, wondering what would happen if she were daring enough to slip her hand under his T-shirt, to awake in his body a desire for her, to impose her will on him, to get him to do whatever she would ask.

Standing silently behind the wheelchair, she looked at him from above. Slowly she reached forward to push the button on the panel next to the door, and moved back almost immediately when she noticed she had been pressing her body against his back for a moment. For a fraction of a second, she had felt the heat of his skin against her abdomen. She hadn't done it on purpose, but now she was glad she had.

But this was a stupid, silly little game. How dare she touch a patient like this? Major Johnson didn't seem to mind however; he didn't make any effort to move away from her.

Judith was almost surprised he had not reacted to such a close contact. Or had he only slightly noticed her belly pushing at his back, her breasts brushing the back of his head? If he had, there surely was no sign to betray his reaction. Judith was annoyed. How can a man not react? Wasn't she tempting enough for him?

She let her gaze travel down the front of his body, studying him. The sleeves of his T-shirt were too long, covering his biceps completely. In fact, the whole shirt was too large, not revealing much except for the base of his neck and a bit of his shoulders. Judith was somewhat disappointed, she would have liked to see all of him.

His legs were completely hidden under khaki cotton trousers, the left leg supported in a horizontal position, the large bulge of his bandaged knee stretching the fabric. There was no way of knowing what his legs looked like, but Judith could safely assume the thighs were muscular and well-defined. Was the skin tanned or pale? Bare and smooth, or covered with hair? Would she ever get to find out?

In front of them the doors of the lift were an unpolished metal surface, reflecting only vague shadows. But the three walls of the lift were dark, tinted mirrors, and by turning her head slightly Judith could see the man's profile repeated endlessly, subsiding into oblivion.

The Major stared right in front of him, not caring much for the mirrors. The lift stopped with a faint jerk and the doors opened onto the main corridor of the basement. Judith was lost in her thoughts and her contemplation of him and took a few seconds to realise it was time to get out. The Major turned his head towards her slightly, as if wondering why she still hadn't moved.

'Don't you know where we're going?' he asked. 'I can navigate if you like.'

She bent down to release the break on the wheels. 'I'm not too sure,' she lied, pushing the chair forward. 'I've never been down here before.'

'Right behind that corner,' he pointed as they came out of the lift. She pushed him along slowly, this time standing as close to his back as possible, her knees rubbing through the leather back of the wheelchair, gently hitting his buttocks in turn, her breasts mere inches behind his head. She was playing some sort of childish game, as if she wanted to prompt some reaction out of him. But still he didn't seem to notice her proximity, or at least didn't mind.

They passed the frosted glass door of the doctor's lounge and Judith couldn't help the tremor that shook her body, remembering that night, not too long ago, when she had been invited to visit this lair.

'Doctors' Lounge,' the Major read aloud. 'Have you ever been in there? I heard that in every hospital it's the most interesting place.'

Judith laughed, trying to sound casual. 'I wouldn't know, I only started to work here last week.'

'Young, pretty, and inexperienced. What a lucky man I am.'

Judith didn't reply, although she was wondering what he meant by that. She expected him to say more but he kept quiet until they arrived at the physiotherapy department.

'In we go,' he said cheerfully as he pushed the door open using his good leg. The sound of rustling fabric welcomed them and a man wearing a white nylon track suit appeared, gesturing for them to come forward into the adjoining treatment room.

'Desmond, old chap!' Major Johnson said joyfully. 'It's such a pleasure to see you again. Look at the pretty lady who drove me here.' He turned his head and looked at Judith.

But Judith wasn't looking at the Major anymore. The sight of Desmond had frozen her brain in stupor. She pushed the wheelchair close to the massage table, but without entirely realising what she was doing. Her brain had ceased to function the moment Desmond had appeared.

She thought she recognised him, she had seen him before, in a dream or another life. His skin was dark as the night, his head completely bald, a shining ball so black it reflected a slightly blue veneer.

She had seen him a thousand times yet today she was looking at him for the first time. He was that pirate from the south seas, the genie from the lamp, the dark slave of Roman legends. He was every man in one.

The word "impressive" wasn't strong enough to describe him. Desmond was tall, very tall; and big, very big. His broad shoulders and narrow hips made him look more like a sculpture then a man. The fact that he wore white only enhanced the darkness of his skin. He looked at Judith as well, vaguely puzzled by her stare, and smiled.

Two rows of teeth shone like a thousand tiny lights, like white snow in the bright sunshine, accompanied by the faintly yellow gleam of a single gold tooth towards the back of his mouth.

Judith smiled in return, still hesitant. He looked almost unreal, a devilish figure, both threatening and beckoning at the same time. He took off his nylon jacket to reveal a white polo shirt, the stretched fabric clinging to every curve of his chest, mounds and valleys of dark, tight flesh, ripples of black velvet.

Bending forward, he helped the Major out of the wheelchair. The Major slipped his arms around the thick, dark neck and Desmond practically lifted him off his feet, almost carrying him in his arms onto the narrow table. There was nothing Judith could do but stand there and watch.

The Major was dwarfed by Desmond's impressive size, holding on to him like a small child. Judith watched as Desmond silently pulled down the Major's trousers, his big hands carefully slipping them over the bandaged knee.

Just as she had imagined, the Major's legs were quite a sight, muscular and tanned. But compared to Desmond he almost looked like a little boy. Even the way he smiled suddenly seemed demure, as if he were in admiration, yet afraid of the big, black man.

But despite his size Desmond was not frightening. His movements were slow and caressing, his big hands handling the patient's limbs as if they were made of delicate crystal. He undid the pins that held the bandage fastened and slowly unrolled the long piece of elastic fabric. Without a word he examined the injured knee, his thick finger gently tracing the path of the pink scar, slipping his other hand under the joint to support it.

The Major looked at him and smiled, and then shyly removed his T-shirt. Only then did Judith realise he was completely naked, and almost turned away in surprise and embarrassment.

In her mind a question rose: if the Major was here to exercise his knee, why was he completely naked? This didn't make any sense. She looked at him again. By now he lay on his back, eyes closed, whilst Desmond finished unwrapping the knee. The contrast of the black man's hands on the Major's paler flesh was mesmerising.

But even more impressive was the sight of the Major's phallus, slowly coming out of its slumber and gradually growing turgid, as if awakening under the touch of the therapist. The glistening head slowly appeared from under the foreskin; the shaft was getting thicker and faintly twitching.

It all became very clear to Judith: Major Johnson was the kind of man who liked to be touched by another man. Now she knew why he had been so eager to get to the physiotherapy room. No wonder he had remained unmoved by her touch!

Once again she looked at the black hands. Desmond was massaging the thigh thoroughly, his fingers digging deep in the muscle, kneading it in preparation for the exercises. He then moved down to the calf, repeating the treatment, warming the flesh that had been kept idle after the surgery.

And all the while the Major grew stiffer, clearly aroused by Desmond's touch, unconcerned – or glad? – that Judith was watching them. Desmond didn't pay any attention to her either, as if she had become invisible. But she was there with them, watching closely, her hands once again clenched on the handles of the wheelchair, her knuckles whitening under the tension, betraying her excitement.

For a moment she could almost feel Desmond's hands on her as well. She, too, would get aroused by his touch. The thought was so vivid in her mind she felt her vulva contract, screaming its desire to be touched by the large fingers.

Judith had to let go of the wheelchair as a cramp set in her wrist. She remembered how she had felt watching Edouard with Lady Austin, the previous week. Once again she was witness to a most arousing, if unusual, scene. And this time Desmond and the Major knew she was right there with them. But still they didn't seem to care.

She forced herself to look elsewhere, unable to stand the increasing pounding of her heart. The scene that was taking place just a few paces away from her was most impressive. She wanted to watch, yet she was afraid to. Her eyes travelled around the room, looking at the long row of jars and pots on the shelves but without really seeing them.

After a moment she closed her eyes, but couldn't remember what she had just looked at; she couldn't concentrate on anything. The only sight that rose in her mind was the man on the table being massaged, caressed even, by the black man, and how he was visibly enjoying every moment of it.

She tilted her head back and forced herself to look at the ceiling. To her amazement the flat, white surface she had expected to see – a ceiling just like any other – failed to materialise.

Instead there were rows upon rows of sturdy metal tracts, from which bundles of thick chains hung. At the end of each chain leather cuffs of different sizes were attached. For a fraction of a second her surprise was such that she almost forgot what was going on in front of her, but she heard the Major groaning and the sound brought her back to reality.

By the time she looked down Desmond had lifted the injured leg in his arms, and the Major's phallus had attained respectable proportions. The contact shared by the therapist and his patient seemed to be getting more and more intimate. The sight made Judith uneasy.

Suddenly she felt the room becoming hot, almost suffocating, the air squeezed out of her lungs with every crushing beat of her heart. Yet she quickly realised it could only be her imagination.

She couldn't stand to watch them, she had to get out of there; get out before she fainted with excitement. Reacting instinctively, she quickly opened the door to the next room and set out to explore it as a way of escaping Desmond and the Major.

She turned on the light as she entered, closed the door behind her and breathed a sigh of relief. Now she was alone. All she had to do was to find a way to spend her time until they were finished. The image of the Major's stiff cock was still imbedded in her mind. But there was no reason for him to be naked in there, no reason whatsoever. And Desmond hadn't seemed the least bit surprised. What exactly were they up to?

She was tempted to go back and continue watching them. Yet she couldn't bring herself to open the door again, not just yet. Her reaction angered her. Why was it that wherever she looked she seemed to be constantly surrounded by naked bodies? And why was it so disturbing, so frightening, so arousing? And why did it have to be her patients?

She forced the thought out of her mind and looked around her. This was another similar treatment room, slightly smaller, with a massage table in the middle and shelves loaded with lotions and ointments. Only in this room the chains that hung from the ceiling were not tied up in bundles but hung freely, bringing the leather cuffs just a few feet from the floor.

Judith walked amongst the chains as if in a forest, pushing them aside with the back of her hand as she crossed the room. The metal felt cold and unforgiving against her skin, the thick links bright and solid. Looking up to the ceiling once more, she realised the chains seemed to be fixed in a certain pattern, yet she failed to understand their purpose.

This wasn't the first physiotherapy room she had ever seen, but never before had she noticed such an elaborate system. As she turned around, the side of her face met one of the leather cuffs and she let out a small cry, slightly startled by the contact.

She laughed nervously, her nerves on edge, kicking herself for being so stupid. She seized the cuff between her fingers to examine it more closely. The leather was soft and pliable, the buckle slightly worn. As she pulled on it she realised the chain was in fact hanging from a pulley, so that its length was adjustable.

Toying with the buckle, she managed to secure the cuff around her wrist and tugged on the loose part of the chain, pulling her arm up. Although the chain was cold, the leather around her wrist felt warm and almost comfortable. She pulled back and forth a few times, forcing her arm to go up and down, playing with the chain like a child discovering a new toy.

The noises it made distracted her for a while, until she seemed to hear an echo to the metallic clinking. She stopped.

But the echo continued. As she turned her head towards the door, she realised the sounds were actually coming from the next room and she immediately understood the chains and pulleys were being used in there, most probably by Desmond.

Her heart began to pound again. What on earth could they be up to? She licked her dry lips. Would she dare peep? She freed her wrist and slowly walked to the door, pressing her ear against it.

The noises had stopped but only to be replaced by sighs and groans. And that only served to increase Judith's curiosity and rekindle her arousal. Once again, in her mind she saw Desmond's dark skin spreading itself over Major Johnson's paler flesh. The lovely dick appeared as well, throbbing in reply to the therapist's touch.

What had gone on after she had left the room was a mystery, but Judith was convinced the chains had been used, probably the cuffs as well. But could it all be a coincidence? There was only one way to find out, she would have to ask.

She turned around one more time and cast her eyes around the room. There were no windows, there was no other door and no way out. She suddenly got scared, she needed to get out, but she was also afraid of what she would now see on the other side of the door.

The best of two evils. Her curiosity won over her fear and she decided to go back to Desmond and the Major. Her heart still pounding, her eyes closed, she mentally prepared herself for the worst and forcefully opened the door. She took a deep breath and opened her eyes.

To her amazement, Desmond was gently helping the Major back into the wheelchair, fully clothed. Both men looked up at her and smiled.

'Enjoying your visit?' the Major asked cheerfully.

'Er . . . Yes,' she replied.

'Time to head back now,' he continued in the same tone. 'Can I hitch a ride home with you, Miss?'

Judith slowly walked forward, as if finally awaking from a dream, her steps still hesitant. She looked around again. Nothing had changed, except for a jar of cream that had been taken off the shelf and now lay open on a small side-table. Its contents exuded a faintly sweet fragrance that mixed with another scent which hung around the room, the latter one vaguely familiar, not unpleasant but rather acrid.

Her eyes were diverted towards the ceiling. All the chains were neatly tied up in bundles, there was no way of knowing whether any had been let loose recently.

The Major followed her gaze and smiled. 'What are you looking at?'

'The chains . . .' She cleared her throat. 'What are those chains for?' Her tone suddenly grew strong, she wanted to know and was no longer afraid to ask.

Desmond didn't reply but Judith noticed a slight twitch at the corner of his mouth.

'What are the chains for?' she insisted.

Still not a word from Desmond. In fact, Judith realised at that moment she had not heard him speak a single word since she had arrived.

Major Johnson laughed loudly. 'As they say in the Army,' he stated in a judicial tone, 'that's for us to know and for you to find out . . . Can we go now?'

Chapter Nine

*I*t took Judith a few minutes to remember where she was. Her body seemed to be floating, snugly wrapped in warm cotton. Yet gradually her mind began to come round out of the comfortable embrace of slumber and her thoughts began to focus on reality.

She finally opened her eyes and looked at the alarm clock. Her sleepy brain concluded she had been sleeping for almost fourteen hours. Raising her arms above her head she stretched with a yawn, then lasciviously twisted her hips this way and that a few times. A day off, at last, and nothing to do but sleep.

Noises from the street were finally reaching her ears. She could hear the lorries complaining at the street corner, the cries from the children coming out of school. It was the middle of the afternoon yet it was as dark as the early evening.

As her mind slowly emerged from its slumber she also recognised the noise of the rain hitting the roof above her head. A dark and wet day, a day to spend in bed.

She rolled onto her stomach and grabbed her pillow with both arms, parting her legs on either side of it, pressing her naked hips against its soft roundness. Her bare breasts rubbed against it sensually, digging into the warmth she had herself imparted.

She didn't often sleep naked, in fact she hadn't done that in years. But now it seemed her body couldn't stand any obstacle anymore, her skin needed to be free. Her nipples grew stiffer under the caress of the soft fabric, pushing at the down on the other side.

This wasn't like her she had changed. Her feet used to automatically hit the floor a second after her eyes opened, and she could have slept just as well if her bed had been a wooden bunk. But now she liked to lay under the duvet for hours, simply enjoying the feeling of her bare skin lightly brushing against the downy fabric, to cuddle her enormous pillow and wrap her legs around it, her hips gently thrusting against the soft cotton.

Every morning and every night, her naked body could now find the sweet, comforting caresses it seemed to constantly crave. When had it all begun? Always the same reply sprung to mind: when she had started to work at the clinic. Before that her body was almost a non-entity, something that simply asked to be fed, washed, and exercised.

Now her body, more than food or sleep, needed to be pleasured above all; to be pleasured time and time again. And the pleasure she could give herself wasn't sufficient anymore. She needed the touch of another body, of warm flesh against hers. She needed to feel it, to taste it even, like an overwhelming hunger she couldn't seem to appease. The change had been subtle yet sudden, she couldn't remember exactly when or how it had happened.

Outside the house the rain pipe was leaking again. Judith could hear fat drops escaping and hitting the windowsill just a couple of feet from her bed. Their rhythm was regular and hypnotising.

This curiously reminded her of the first morning at work, in the operating theatre, when Edouard's voice had cast such a strong effect on her. Had she been hypnotised as well?

That recollection jerked her thoughts and she abruptly sat up in her bed, throwing her pillow aside. She suddenly realised what had happened to her. Now she understood. The realisation sent her heart pounding and her mind working fast. Of course, it had to be, it made so much sense! Why hadn't she thought about it before?

The more she thought about it, the clearer it became. If, from the moment she had started to work at the clinic, her sensuality had so violently awoken, it could only be for one reason: she had been hypnotised. There was no other explanation.

She grabbed her head with both hands and forced herself to remember more, to put all the details together. It had all started that morning, in the operating theatre. As Lady Austin was being put under, she had been hypnotised as well. It was all very possible, a master could make her do anything he would want, even make her forget she was in a trance ... It was preposterous, yet so simple.

So that's how it had happened. Edouard had hypnotised her. He had suggested that her body would now always be in a state of arousal, couldn't be without physical contact, or something like that.

He must have devised a way to trigger her senses. He had probably told her about something specific that would make her react without even realising it. Then right afterwards everything would go back to the way it was before; only a few minutes spent recovering and then it was back to work, as if nothing had ever happened. That would also explain why she had never felt this desire to just linger at leisure after having climaxed. This way she would go back to her duties as quickly as possible!

Everything made sense now. She had been set up, programmed ... By Edouard ... But was anybody else aware of this? Robert Harvey? Of course ... He had been the first to 'test' her. The fact that she was unable to resist his advances was the proof She hadn't seen him much since then, only in passing really, but that could be because of their conflicting schedules. Besides, it was only a few weeks ago, he would surely try to seduce her, to 'test' her again.

Who else? Tania and Jo? Less likely. On the other hand, maybe they were hypnotised themselves? Maybe all the nursing staff was programmed this way, so that they were unable to resist the sight of a naked body.

Lady Austin? That was doubtful. Or maybe not, she could be in on this with Edouard. After all, they were lovers . . . Or was she hypnotised as well?

This was still confusing, yet the pieces of the puzzle were starting to neatly fit together. Judith threw her blankets aside, jumped to her feet and almost ran naked to the bathroom. The thoughts racing through her mind were making her frantic, she needed to think clearly.

She turned the taps but didn't wait for the water to get warm. She hopped in the shower right away, presenting her face to the cool stream, hoping to wash away all traces of sleepiness and restore some thinking power to her brain.

The water hit her face hard and she shuddered in surprise. But she needed that to help clear her head. The water trickled down her face, assaulting her puffy eyes and she forced herself to put some order to her thoughts.

So far she had established there was a strong possibility the people with whom she had been in contact with at work could have been either hypnotised, or they were aware that Judith was under a spell and had taken advantage of the situation.

She had managed to determine the status of Robert Harvey, Tania and Jo, and Lady Austin, not to mention Edouard himself. Of course, Edouard was at the root of all this . . . But what about the others?

Mrs Cox? Now, that was a little more tricky. Looking back, however, it was possible the supervisor knew that Judith was in a trance, and although she was aware of the situation, she didn't agree with it but might not have a say in the matter.

That would explain her behaviour: the supervisor knows the young nurse is always aroused despite herself, so she does her best to help her by providing release when Judith needs it most. After all, it's part of her job to look after the nursing staff. Hence the reason for what she did in the shower room, and why she had asked all those questions in her office!

Doctor Marshall? Surely he knew what was going on, possibly he was at the heart of it all as Director of the Clinic. He could be the one who decides which members of staff get hypnotised, and Mrs Cox is in charge of making sure things don't get out of hand.

Desmond? He knows something, but he could be some kind of puppet, like the others. That was only a supposition though, for Judith had no proof something had actually taken place between him and Major Johnson.

What about those guys at the gym? Coincidence? They could have been 'planted' there to test her ... There was always a chance the Directors of the Clinic might want to monitor her activities just to be sure she was still under their spell.

So there it was, it all fell into place! There was definitely something fishy going on at this clinic, and now she knew what it was. But what about the patients?

Were they also hypnotised and submitted to the whims of the doctors? If so, that was not only highly unethical, it was also illegal. She would have to get proof and go to the police.

But how could she? She would need to get out of the trance first. Yet the fact that she had been able to piece this all together was proof that her mind could fight their suggestions, and that she was strong enough to go against it.

She had no option at this point but to confront Edouard, tell him she knew what he was up to and that the game was over. If she could avoid his eyes, and pay no attention to his voice, she wouldn't fall prey again. She would have to be strong. She knew she could do it, and she still had forty-eight hours to prepare herself.

* * *

He laughed so loud Judith could almost feel the floor shaking under her feet. She sat in front of him in the leather chair, motionless, determined to fight him every step of the way, but she had never expected this reaction from him.

He stood up and walked to the cabinet just a few feet from his desk, took a tissue out of the box and wiped the tears hanging at the corner of his eyes. His face was red from laughing, drops of sweat pearled on his forehead.

'Hypnotise you?' he repeated for the seventh time, almost choking. '*Ma chère*, what an imagination you have!'

The laughter resumed, louder than before. At some point he had to brace himself on the corner of the bookcase, his knees slightly giving under him.

Judith was becoming quite impatient. She had been expecting him to deny her accusations, but not like this. She waited until he calmed down and continued the speech she had rehearsed in her mind so many times over the past couple of days.

'I told you I know everything. It's no use denying it. And I know Mrs Cox does not agree with this. So unless you take everybody out of their trance I will ask for her help and together we will go to the police.'

'Mrs Cox?' he burst out laughing again. 'The police? This is really too much...' And he continued to laugh, always louder.

Judith bit her lip and lowered her head. His reaction was throwing her off balance and she was worried he might actually be trying to turn the tables on her. But she knew she could beat him. All she had to do was to remain true to her convictions and keep fighting.

After a while his face gradually returned to its normal colour and his laughter slowly subsided. He looked at Judith again and she held his gaze despite the dangers she knew she faced by looking at him. But he didn't scare her, not anymore.

'You realise these are serious accusations?' he asked, coming back to sit behind his desk.

'I know. But I also know what you are doing is unethical and illegal, so I am asking you to stop now.'

'Did you talk to anybody about this? Any expert on hypnotism?'

'Yes, I did. That's how I was able to find out what you were up to.' She was only bluffing, of course, but at this point she didn't have any choice.

She had been expecting him to deny everything angrily, even to rant and rave. But he had the opposite reaction and that completely destroyed her plans, so now she had to improvise.

'You're lying,' he said, suddenly recovering his seriousness.

As he spoke Judith felt she was quickly losing ground. She had to think fast, to come up with strong arguments and show him she knew what she was talking about. Yet in her mind everything was getting confused again and she was starting to panic instead.

He got up and walked to the front of his desk, standing just a few inches from her. At this point she should have looked up at him – at least that's what she had planned to do – but she didn't have the nerve to.

'If you really had consulted an expert,' he continued, clearly enunciating each word, 'you would have learned that what you are accusing me of is absolutely impossible. Even the greatest masters of hypnotism cannot suggest to a person the things you mentioned. Even in a trance, you cannot make people do what they wouldn't do when they are wide awake. And you cannot put a suggestion in a person's mind that would remain long after he has been taken out of the trance.'

Judith sensed he was perhaps expecting her to look up at this point but she didn't dare. The other morning, when this idea had germinated in her head, everything had seemed so logical. Now she wasn't so sure anymore. And she realised how stupid it would all look if indeed she were wrong.

She closed her eyes, keeping her head down, feeling as if her life were drained out of her with each successive beat of her heart. Her determination was vanishing quickly, only to be replaced by an overwhelming feeling of embarrassment.

He was right, of course; his explanation made perfect sense. She had heard that before, and more than once. But she couldn't go back now.

However, the more she tried to think, the more extravagant her theory appeared; and she had this image of a house of cards on the verge of collapse as each of his words shook the fragile foundations.

On top of it all, there was no doubt she was making a fool of herself. In an ultimate attempt to turn things to her advantage she decided to play her last card.

'Then how can you explain what's been happening to me these past few weeks?' she asked defiantly. She looked up at him as she spoke, despite knowing that her eyes would probably betray her embarrassment. But she had nothing to lose at this point.

He looked down at her tenderly, his pale eyes still alight with an amused sparkle. 'There is only one word to explain this,' he said softly. 'It's called "life".' He bent down and took her hands in his. 'Just look at yourself, Judith. You are young and beautiful, how can people not be attracted to you?'

He bent down and delicately seized her hands. Surprised, she didn't protest and obeyed his silent invitation to stand up. Slowly, he led her to the back of his office, all the while still smiling.

She didn't know what he had in mind but didn't have the mental strength to fight him and risk making the situation worse than it already was for her.

He gently guided her towards the far wall where she came to face a large mirror. She didn't speak, still taken aback by the logic of his argument, surprised by his behaviour, and stared at her reflection.

'Do you see what I see?' he asked softly, standing behind her, his face above hers in the mirror. 'I see a sweet, healthy young lady, perhaps still a bit innocent. She has grown up in a small village and now she comes to work in a big city. Almost immediately she is surrounded by people who are attractive, but who also have much more experience in sexual matters. Naturally she is overwhelmed...'

He stood tall behind her, his hands resting on her shoulders, his touch ever so light. Looking at her in the mirror, his pale eyes travelled up and down her body, a tender smile resting at the corner of his lips.

'I see a young body that has just begun to experience pleasure and is eager to find out more. Believe me, Judith, there isn't anything anybody can force you to do without your consent. All that has happened to you is completely normal. Maybe it seems extreme because it is all happening so fast, but that is just a coincidence.'

His hands on her shoulders closed into a soft but firm grip. Still he kept looking at her in the mirror.

Judith didn't know what to think anymore. He was making sense, of course. Or was he simply trying to turn things around?

'You might think that I am trying to hypnotise you right now,' he said as if reading her mind, 'but I cannot put you in a trance unless you agree to it. I have no control over your mind unless you let me.'

Once again this was something she had heard before. At this moment she realised how foolish she had been. The thought almost made her laugh. There was no 'hypnotic' conspiracy, of course. It was just her imagination running wild. And there was nothing wrong with the desire she was feeling, nothing at all. Edouard was right.

'Look at yourself,' he continued. 'Not a man on this planet could resist you. Tell me honestly, Judith, is it really such a bad thing?'

His hands then slid off her shoulders, down the length of her arms. She could feel him close behind her, and still getting closer, almost pulling her body towards him. She could also smell him, a rich, clean aroma that was a bit reminiscent of a forest after the rain.

'I can prove it to you,' he said. 'Will you let me?'

She nodded. He let go of her arms and gently encircled her waist with his left arm. His right hand glided up the side of her ribcage and gently brushed her right breast. In the mirror she saw her nipple grow stiff and peak through the fabric of her uniform. She shuddered.

'You see? This is just your body responding. I have no control over your mind. Everything you do, it's because you want to.'

He was right. There was no-one to blame for what had happened to her, it was just a natural reaction. At that moment she felt an enormous weight lift from her shoulders. All she had to do was to accept that her impulses were nothing to be afraid of, and in fact something she had to deal with and gain pleasure from.

She leaned back and practically fell into his arms. Why fight it? If her body wanted to be pleasured, so be it. She felt his cheek brush hers and closed her eyes, immediately abandoning herself. It was futile to look for any sort of explanation. She was young and beautiful, and sweet pleasure was within her grasp.

His lips gently took hold of her earlobe and began to suck on it. The wet and smooth caress translated into a warm wave that extended all the way down her abdomen, once again triggering that familiar feeling at the junction of her legs.

'Take everything life has to offer, Judith. It is there for you, make the most of it.'

She tilted her head back on his shoulder, listening to the calm tone of his voice. Was he hypnotising her right now? She didn't care anymore. All she knew was that she wanted to find comfort in his words, and pleasure in his arms. That was real; she was not imagining it.

His hands made her turn around and face him, encircling her tiny waist with both arms. He smiled sweetly.

'Tell me to stop and I will,' he whispered, his face just a moment away from hers. 'You are in control, always.' He bent down further and caught hold of her ear again, this time gently pushing his tongue inside it, sending shivers down her spine.

'No,' she heard herself say. 'Don't stop, not now.' She wanted him. She hadn't been able to chase from her mind the image of his shadow on the curtain in Lady Austin's room. She remembered the sight of his erect cock and now she wanted to see more than a simple shadow.

He began undressing her as she stood motionless. His fingers worked fast, undoing all the buttons of her uniform before pushing it off her shoulders.

Judith didn't try to help him, content to just enjoy the smooth caress of the fabric as it slowly fell to the floor, brushing her skin on its way down. He used his hands only to shed her clothes, all the while caressing her solely with his tongue.

She felt it, soft and wet, licking the side of her neck, gliding down towards her breasts and quickly finding its way inside the cups of her bra as he dropped to his knees. It seemed to be animated with a life of its own, snaking around her stiff nipples in turn, bathing them in a warm moistness, increasing the excitement she was already feeling.

The hook of her bra gave without any resistance under his fingers and the cups immediately glided aside as his tongue pushed them away. Her breasts peaked up, finally freed, swelling with the heat of her arousal, causing Judith to moan loudly as they were assaulted by the cool air of the room.

As his tongue surveyed every contour of her breasts it left a wet trace behind, cooling the heat that throbbed on her skin, creating delicious shivers along its length. She could hear him breathe loudly as he tasted her skin, sighing occasionally as if he were getting just as much pleasure from this as she was.

Every contour of each milky globe was soon bathed in this wet warmth. He flicked her nipples with the precise tip of his tongue time and time again, and sucked on them between each long lick until they became engorged. Judith felt her vulva contract violently in reply, her pussy rapidly getting wet with her own dew.

He continued discovering her with his mouth, tasting

every inch of her abdomen, his head pushing her arms up to gain access to her armpits, then slowly licking down the underside of her arm, all the way to the palm of her hand, stopping only to briefly suck on her fingertips.

His tongue then foraged inside her belly button for a moment, his nosed pressed against her belly, before moving on to the other arm.

All the while he kept his hands off her. From the time his fingers had eased her panties down, they seemed to no longer serve any purpose. He needed only his tongue to caress her.

And soon she felt him on her hips. By then he was down on all fours, slowly crawling around her as she stood still, worshipping her with his mouth. Her eyes remained closed, her mind went numb. All she could feel was this hot wetness gradually covering her, slowly, deliciously, inch by inch.

His tongue bathed the whole swell of her behind before slowly sliding down between her buttocks. Judith moaned loudly as its tip briefly pushed at the puckered rose of her anus. The sensation was overwhelming and she suddenly felt her knees become weak under her.

But a second later she felt his hands push her feet apart as he came to kneel in front of her. His tongue licked at her ankles and traced a sinewy path up her calves, stopping briefly behind her knees to suck at her tender skin, before continuing until it came to taste the softness of her inner thighs.

By then her legs were parted wide, and Judith had to put her hands on his head for support. She heard him grunt as the pointy tip of his tongue brushed her stiff clitoris, but only for a split second, before moving back down her thighs.

Then his hands got to work, taking each foot and pushing it back one after the other, forcing her to step backwards in a silent tango until she came to rest against the wall. At the same time he crawled forward, his tongue never losing contact with her skin.

Only once her back rested against the wall did he cease to caress her so methodically. Instead, he reached up and grabbed her buttocks in his hands, pulling them apart forcefully. His tongue immediately darted at her vulva, assaulting it with all his might.

Judith moaned loudly, surprised by the change in him. In a fraction of a second he had turned into a ravenous madman, suddenly losing control, licking and sucking as if he wanted to swallow all of her, roughly penetrating her vagina with his tongue, occasionally grazing at her clitoris with his teeth.

His mouth opened wide and practically grabbed the whole of her pussy in a tight suction; it was most deliciously painful. Judith screamed with pleasure, her cries of joy echoed by the grunting noises he made as he relished her.

She looked down at him and was almost surprised to see he hadn't even shed his clothes. He was half-kneeling, half crawling on the floor, his hands clinging to her behind, his fingertips pushing at the entrance of her anus.

His mouth was still devouring her swollen vulva, and getting more and more impatient, his tongue sliding deep inside her and then back out again, his lips nibbling and sucking at her clitoris endlessly.

Judith felt her sweaty back sticking to the wall behind her, her skin glued to its cool surface. She slid down inch by inch, her arousal so intense that her legs no longer supported her. The whole of her weight practically rested on Edouard's mouth and she dug her fingers in his hair, pressing his face towards her vulva.

She felt him choke against her flesh, gasping for air as he continued his assault on her pussy. His nose dug deep into her curly mound and she could feel his warm breath brushing her skin as it managed to find a way out despite the close contact.

He grunted loudly and Judith realised he was actually talking, in French, but she couldn't make out his words. Then he turned to her clitoris once more, sucked it into his mouth and closed his lips around it in a tight grip.

Judith started to pant, feeling her climax finally approaching, yet not wanting to peak just yet. She wanted to feel his mouth on her still; she wanted his tongue to possess her, to fill her completely. But she couldn't fight the wave of pleasure that rose up her thighs, grasped her vulva and made her scream in a loud moan of pleasure.

Tears pearled at the corners of her eyes as her orgasm exploded within her. At the same time she felt Edouard slowly getting up, his tongue tracing a path up her belly, his face soaked with her warm juices, sliding wetly against her skin.

He pressed his clothed body against her, pinning her to the wall as he finally stood on his feet. She nestled her face against his chest and slid her arms around his waist, under his white coat.

She was a weak, naked puppet in his arms, her energies completely spent. But he was not finished with her, not just yet. Her mind was numb and she felt him move as in a dream, barely realising he had unzipped his trousers and eased out his erect phallus.

He bent his knees and used them to force her legs apart, presenting the purple tip of his cock to the entrance of her vagina. Slipping his hands under her armpits to support her, he impaled her forcefully, thrusting upwards, lifting her off the ground simultaneously.

Judith awoke from her torpor as his successive jabs rekindled her arousal. His hips jerked up violently and she felt herself lifted off the floor each time under the strength of his assault.

The rough fabric of his trousers grazed at the soft skin of her thigh, and the metal buckle of his belt dug into her tender skin, enhancing the heat that enveloped the whole of her pelvis.

She moaned as she held on to him, feeling his member thrusting into her repeatedly, her body crushed against the wall. He pushed her up laboriously, heavily panting under the effort, groaning with every jerk.

As she repeatedly slid up and down his thick shaft to the

hilt, Judith felt her vulva stretch and her bottom hit his engorged balls. Her pleasure returned, growing more intense with each of his jabs. They screamed in unison, both swept by a simultaneous orgasm. Her vulva clenched as it milked his seed and she felt him throb within her.

He dropped to his knees and she followed him, collapsing on the rough carpet. He lay her down and almost immediately zipped up his trousers.

Judith remained motionless, feeling her life draining from within her, the whole surface of her skin now so sensitive it throbbed slightly. She opened her eyes sleepily and looked at him.

Édouard was sitting on the floor next to her, once again fully clothed. Not a hair on his head had been displaced, his neck tie was perfectly done and there wasn't a single crease in his shirt.

In contrast, Judith lay completely naked, her skin red and hot, her hair undone and spilling all over the carpet, her limbs weak. A distinct, sweet smell hung in the room, a smell Judith was by now only too familiar with; the smell of pleasure.

Her vulva was still occasionally shaken by mild contractions; after-shocks of the earthquake that had just devastated her. She slowly brought her hands to her breasts and caressed them lightly.

Édouard smiled and bent down to deposit a gentle kiss on her lips, his tongue briefly toying with hers.

'You taste wonderful, *ma chérie*,' he said in a whisper.

Judith felt wonderful as well, now that she knew she didn't have to be afraid of her desires, but could enjoy them instead. She laughed out loud, suddenly realising the unusual sight they offered: she, lying naked, her body still shaking from pleasure; he, casually sitting on the floor, looking just like nothing had happened.

She turned onto her stomach, the rough carpet scratching her sensitive skin, and soon she felt his tongue on her again, this time slowly discovering her back, tracing the curve of her armpits and each of the rounded bumps of her spine.

Thinking back to her mood when she had first entered the office, she couldn't help laughing again, and she heard him laugh in reply. There were still questions left unanswered in her head – a lot of questions, in fact – but it didn't really matter right now.

There would always be time to find out more later.

Chapter Ten

The attendant took her aside and looked around before bending down to speak in her ear.

'You've got to save my life,' he whined. 'It's almost midnight and I'm supposed to be off now, I really can't stay a minute more. I was called to help on the third floor and it took longer than I had thought so I fell behind in my list of tasks. All that's left to do is to help the guy in room 627 with his bath. I know it's not part of your duties, but if you have a minute could you take care of that? He says he doesn't mind waiting. Everybody else is asleep in their bed, so you shouldn't be too busy. Please?'

Judith looked around as well. They were alone by the side of the nursing station, the other nurse who was assigned to work the night shift with Judith was nowhere to be seen.

She hesitated for a moment, knowing that when the attendants weren't finished with their tasks at the end of their shifts they were expected to stay and work overtime. The nurses had more important things to do.

She looked at him and was surprised by how young he looked and decided he was rather cute. Then she glanced down again to read his name on the tag pinned to his breast pocket.

'Listen, Ray,' she began, 'you know that nurses are not supposed to do the attendants' work...'

'I know,' he interrupted her impatiently, 'but my friends are waiting for me outside. We're off to this party and it's late already. I would have been finished by now if it hadn't been for that problem on the third floor... The guy in 627 is very cool, he won't say anything, I'm sure. Please?'

Judith hesitated, looking at him and trying to decide whether she should let him off. Yet he seemed sincere and there would be no harm in helping him out. She knew he was about the same age as her yet he looked much younger; his cheeks seemed as soft as a baby's. His eyes were a pale brown, almost amber, and she thought, curiously, that his hair was just about the same colour.

He looked sweet and his voice sounded slightly worried, with a tinge of desperation. She felt her heart melt. He was right, there was hardly anything to do before her first round at one o'clock, and room 627 was one of hers. Besides, if anybody found out about it the blame would be on Ray who left without finishing his tasks, not her.

'Where is the patient now?' she asked.

Ray smiled, knowing he was winning. 'I just put him in the tub, he's soaking now. All you need to do is to scrub his back and then help him out of there. He's got a bad leg but other than that he's fine. He's in an island tub and he's on some kind of muscle relaxant. Desquel, I think. He shouldn't give you a hard time.'

Already he was pulling away, smiling at Judith. He winked before turning around. 'Thanks!' he whispered. 'I'll make it up to you.'

Judith went back to her station and sifted through the order sheets. The team who had just finished on the evening shift had left nothing to be done. All the medication had been distributed, the observation charts filled, the patients tucked up, except, of course, for the patient in room 627.

PATIENT WAS PUT IN THE BATH TUB AT 23:50, the

last nurse had written and put her initials in the next column.

Judith checked her watch and took out her pen. PATIENT WAS TAKEN OUT OF THE BATH TUB AT 00:30. She put her initials. That would give her about 20 minutes to get him out of there.

The island tub Ray had mentioned was the kind installed in the middle of the bathroom, on a small pedestal, high enough and far away from the walls so that the nursing staff could go all around it to help the patient, making things much easier for everyone. This would only take a few minutes, yet Judith didn't want to rush the patient.

The other nurse assigned to the station was checking on her own patients, rooms 600 to 615. Room 627 was the last one at the other end of the corridor, so chances were nobody would come and check up on Judith for a little while.

She re-arranged the papers on the desk and looked around quickly before heading down the corridor in a fast, silent pace. She had been assigned to this floor just last week, during the day shift, but she couldn't remember who was in 627 anymore. Besides, it wasn't unusual for patients to request a change after a couple of days, if a better room became available. This particular room was at the very corner of the building and had windows on two sides, offering a better view than the other rooms, and therefore making it quite popular with many patients.

When Judith entered all the lights were out, even the tiny lamp above the head board. A pale triangle of light painted the wooden floor at the far end. It came from the bathroom door, which was only slightly ajar and let faint splashing sounds escape. The lights in there had not been turned on to their full power and she concluded that the patient probably wanted to relax in semi-darkness. After all, it was after midnight already.

She walked over to the bathroom and glanced in. Just as Ray had told her, the patient was in an island tub, his back to the door. A thin cloud of steam was rising from the water and all she could see of the patient was his broad shoulders and the back of his head. She didn't recognise him and concluded it must be a new patient. She knocked gently on the bathroom door, not wanting to startle him, and slowly entered.

'I'm coming to help you out of there...' she began. She swallowed the rest of her sentence when the patient turned his head up and smiled at her.

'Very nice of you,' he replied with a smile. It was Mike Randall, laying in the bath tub with water up to his waist, covered only with a small towel over his loins. His left leg was still in a cast, covered in a plastic film and held up a few inches above the bath tub by a thick rubber strap to prevent it from touching the water.

He looked comfortable, his arms dangling on either side of the tub, his upper back propped up by a rubber pillow. Judith slowly came forward, fascinated by the sight of his near-naked body, enthralled by the way his tanned skin contrasted against the whiteness of the enamel.

Mike was wide awake tonight and did not seem to remember her.

'I was just about done,' he said. 'Just relaxing now. Can you do my back?' He leaned forward and handed Judith a large blue sponge.

Without a word Judith grabbed the sponge and plunged it into the warm water, gently brushing the side of his ribcage with her wrist in the process. The moist heat of the steam rising from the water almost choked her for a minute, forcing her to breathe deeply.

As her hand hit the water she felt the heat rise up her arm and instantly radiate through her body. She didn't know whether it came from the water or his body. Slightly blushing, she looked at him. He looked at her, still smiling. He leant further to give her better access to his back, his chest now practically resting on his cast.

The fragrance of the soap assaulted her nostrils, a refined, distinct smell that hung in the room and which she would most probably associate with him from now on. She gently rubbed his back, working up and down along the length of his spine and then across the width of his shoulders. She let her hand disappear under the waterline, pressing the sponge all the way down until her fingers came to hit the bottom of the tub, where she could feel the cleft of his buttocks.

He laughed softly. 'You are very daring,' he said. 'We've only just met!'

'No, you're wrong,' she replied. 'I was with you when you came out of surgery.'

'That was you? I thought I had been dreaming about angels...'

He let out a sigh of satisfaction as she slowly squeezed the sponge over his shoulders, making the water trickle to rinse off the soap. His voice grew soft as he continued talking to her, in that flirtatious tone she had heard him use in one of his films.

However, she wasn't really paying attention to his words. Still holding the sponge in a light grip she traced the line of his muscles with her fingertips. She was fascinated by the way his wet skin felt, and somehow hoped she could drop the sponge and simply let her hands run over it.

A few days ago she had taken advantage of his sedated state to caress his chest. Now she was pretending to wash him to continue her discovery of his body. She brushed his shoulder, lost in her thoughts, desperately wishing that the sponge could miraculously vanish...

His hand came up suddenly and seized her wrist. She let out a small cry and dropped the sponge, which splashed soapy water around as it fell back in the tub.

Still holding her hand he leant back and brought her wet fingers to his lips. 'Now I remember you,' he said before kissing them gently. 'You're the nurse with the nice touch. I thought you only existed in my dreams...'

Judith started to tremble as she felt his lips nibbling at her fingers. Once again she marvelled at the sight of his naked chest, the taut muscles, the tight skin now glistening and bringing even more definition to the ripples of his flat stomach.

Her eyes wandered down and paused over the small towel which barely covered his genitals. His leg held high caused the towel to strain and run up his thigh. If he tried moving his other leg at all there would be a strong possibility that his maleness would be revealed in its entirety.

She couldn't stop looking at the slight bump in the middle of the towel, and wondering what lay underneath. He followed her gaze.

'Good old Desquel,' he laughed softly. 'Always available when it's not really needed.'

At first Judith couldn't understand what he was talking about but then she remembered the attendant had mentioned the patient was still on that medication. Desquel was popular in surgery, a powerful, non-addictive painkiller but with a slightly inconvenient side-effect: certain men were unable to achieve an erection whilst they were taking it. Obviously, Mike had also been told about this possibility.

So that's what Ray had meant when he said the patient wouldn't give her any problems. Somehow Judith felt relieved, knowing Mike wouldn't feel at all tempted to make a pass at her under these conditions. Therefore she could easily resist temptation. But suddenly she noticed a twitch in the fabric and the towel began to rise above the water line.

'But then again,' Mike continued, 'they stopped giving it to me a couple of days ago...'

Judith pretended not to notice anything and pulled her hand away from his to quickly reach down and pull the plug out. The water spiralled down the drain with a gurgling sound and she turned around to grab a large towel, throwing it across her shoulder.

Despite her efforts to keep calm, a storm was now raging within her. She had to help him out of the tub, dry him off and then help him to bed. That meant close contact with his naked body and his glistening skin. Just standing near him was enough to feel the heat of his body, compounded by the lingering warmth of the bath water.

How would she react to the moist touch of his arm around her shoulders? Perhaps she would also have to slip her own arm around his waist. She would most probably be tempted to touch more of him ... Would she be able to restrain herself? Now she wished she hadn't let Ray go. That was all his fault; she shouldn't have agreed to this. If only she had known, she could have avoided finding herself in such a compromising position.

On the other hand, she was probably nothing to a man like Mike Randall. He most probably saw her as a nurse just like any other; one of those horrible women who like nothing better than to stick needles in people's behinds and force them to swallow all sorts of foul-tasting medications.

Yet his behaviour was quite revealing; the way he had kissed her fingers, and then blatantly directed her attention to his aroused genitals. She might have to fight off his advances, and this would require enormous strength from her, both physically and mentally.

He waited for the water to drain completely then braced himself with his arms on either side of the tub. Bending his good leg underneath him, he raised himself up until he came to rest his buttocks on the edge of the bath tub. Judith helped him by unhooking his cast from its support, slowly lowering his leg until his foot touched the floor.

He now sat astride the side of the tub, the towel around his waist soaked and dripping, threatening to come loose as the bulge of his erection kept straining the fabric, continually sending trickles of water down his thighs.

Judith came to him and held him whilst he swung his right leg out of the tub. Her arms were too short to encircle him completely and she felt his wet skin slipping under her fingers. She let him lean against the tub and handed him the towel whilst she went searching for his bathrobe. So far, so good, she thought. The worst part was over, and on the whole it had gone quite well. She had felt a vague fluttering in her loins as she watched him get out of the tub, and saw his muscles playing under his skin. But at this moment she figured all she had to do was to cover his body. Then at least her attention wouldn't be diverted by the sight of his bare flesh.

She found his robe hanging on the inside of the bathroom door and took it to him. When she turned around, however, she saw him pulling at the wet towel impatiently, tossing it back in the tub in a wet bundle.

She froze in surprise for a second as she saw his turgid phallus pointing in her direction and looked up at him, rather puzzled.

'The towel was dripping,' he explained in a childish tone. 'I can't get my cast wet, can I? I can't bend down with that cast, could you please dry my leg?'

He handed her the towel with a smile. Judith licked her lips nervously and sensed her breath becoming shallow in excitement. Now he stood completely naked in front of her, except for the cast. He was asking her to touch him, to bend down in front of him and pat his leg dry.

She knew that by doing what he asked she would have to bring her face just a few inches from his erect member, which was still getting bigger. She felt her crotch grow wet at the thought of getting this close to his luscious body, and having to run her hands all over his muscular leg, albeit through the thickness of the bath towel. She had to think fast to find a way to avoid this contact or else she would not be able to resist this sweet temptation.

Stirred by a flash of inspiration she stepped forward and almost forced him to put the bathrobe on, even fastening it for him at the waist. He let her cover him without uttering a word, an amused smile on his lips, perfectly aware of her confusion.

The robe came down to mid-thigh and Judith was somewhat relieved. She could still see his phallus pointing through the cloth but the rest of his body was almost completely hidden, making it less compromising for her if she had to offer her shoulder as a support.

She bent down briefly to pat him dry, starting with his foot and working her way up his calf, stopping slightly above the knee. But although she tried to look casual and professional, all the while she sensed her breath quickening. She felt his muscles hard under her fingers, and almost wished she could touch him directly. But even more disturbing was the motion of his hips as she knelt in front of him.

She could feel his erection brush the side of her head repeatedly, as if he was doing it on purpose, and she desperately tried to retain her composure, not to move her head away too quickly, pretending she hadn't noticed anything. As his hips swayed next to her face she thought she heard him moan but quickly willed the impression away.

All her efforts seemed in vain. If he hadn't moved his hips so suggestively on purpose, then her imagination was once again getting the best of her. What if he really tried to make a pass at her? Would she be able to refuse him? There were hundreds of women out there who would probably want nothing better . . .

Once she stood up he threw his arm around her, supporting himself on her shoulders and they got out of the bathroom to laboriously make their way to his bed. He moved forward in short hops, his left leg trailing behind, pressing his body against hers to keep his balance. The knot of his bathrobe belt came loose and as the robe fell open his cock slowly appeared, gradually getting harder with each step he took.

The bathroom door slowly closed behind them, and soon Judith found herself trying to guide her patient in the dark. The only light came from the lamppost outside the window, which cast a pale blue light on the bed. They approached it inch by inch, his body now heavy on her shoulder.

She could feel the moist heat of his body through the

cloth of his robe. Because of the way he held on to her, she had no choice but to bend forward slightly, keeping her head down, thus watching his thick shaft bob up and down, the purplish head slowly emerging from beneath his foreskin, gradually coming alive.

Her own arousal began to mount as well, as she watched the glistening plum jump towards her lips time and time again, almost begging to be kissed. In the light of the lamppost she thought she could see a fine drop pearling from the tiny mouth. By the time they reached the bed his bathrobe was completely opened, and his member stood fully erect. Judith helped him climb into bed and lifted his cast up to lay it next to the other leg.

Although the trek from the bathroom had gone rather well, he seemed relieved to finally reach his bed and lay down quietly, his bathrobe spread underneath him, his taut body once again revealed. Judith took one last look at him. Outside the room the wind blew through the branches of a nearby tree and the light from the lamppost cast their moving shadows all over his smooth skin.

The effect was surreal and captivating. He just lay there, still smiling, his eyes half-shut. Judith knew she had to leave. Not only was she afraid she wouldn't be able to fight the temptation to run her hands all over this gorgeous body for much longer, but she had been away from the nursing station for quite a while now and her colleague might start looking for her at any minute.

She turned around to leave but at the very last moment she felt his fingers grabbing hold of her arm and she was gently pulled back towards the bed.

'Do you remember your promise?' he asked in a whisper, his eyes still half-shut and staring at the ceiling.

'What promise?'

'That morning, when I came out of surgery, I asked you if you would take good care of me, and you promised you would...'

Judith didn't reply. Obviously he remembered more about that day than she would have expected. But exactly how much?

'I remember your hand caressing my chest,' he said as if reading her mind. 'I felt your touch soft and warm . . .'

Judith remembered as well, of course, but was that his way of asking her to do it again? She looked down to his engorged phallus and saw it twitch slightly in the blue light.

'You promised,' he repeated, 'you can't leave me like this now . . .'

Of course she couldn't, but she had to. She was so confused, remembering how warm and soft his skin felt in the palm of her hand, how she had wanted him that day. Yet she knew perfectly well that he was a patient, and that she had to go back to her desk immediately.

He loosened his grip on her but his fingers continued to caress her arm. She felt a tingling sensation at the surface of her skin and let out a faint sob. Only then did she notice a large mirror on the wall by the foot of the bed. She looked up and stared at their reflections, a tiny white figure standing next to this gorgeous, naked flesh.

'You want me, I know you do,' Mike continued. 'Besides, aren't you supposed to do everything your patients ask you?'

'I . . . don't know,' she stammered. 'This wouldn't be right. You are my patient . . .'

'You must be new here, then. I heard it's a policy of this Clinic to offer special care to clients who ask for it. That means giving them everything they ask for . . .'

Judith was disappointed by this sad excuse, thinking it was indeed a strange way of trying to get to her. Yet at the same time she wished it was true, so she could let herself yield to the force of her desire. She began to tremble and immediately sensed his fingers growing insistent on her skin, travelling up and down along the length of her arm, the bone of his wrist brushing the peak of her erect nipple each time.

He must have felt the confusion within her, for his tone grew even softer and his invitation more open. 'I want you, Judith. I want you to undress for me, to show me that gorgeous body of yours. I am hot for you, wouldn't you want to feel my skin against yours?' He reached up and gently seized her neck in his fingers, slowly pulling her head down towards his.

She didn't offer any resistance as her lips came to meet his and she felt his tongue invade her mouth, its softness sending a shiver from her breasts to her loins. She had to put her hand on the bed to stop herself from falling on top of him, but he anticipated her move, grabbed her wrist and brought her hand to his chest instead. She slowly bent her elbow until she came to gently rest against him, pressing her chest against his, once again letting the heat of his body radiate through her.

He let go of her mouth after a brief moment and pulled his head back slightly. 'Undress for me, I want to see all of you.' His voice was still soft but his tone was more authoritative. In the darkness she saw his eyes sparkle, and read his desire. He wanted her.

She hesitated a moment, but suddenly realised how good it would be to feel her bare skin on his, if only for a moment. There was no doubt in her mind that it wasn't right, mainly because he was her patient. But if no-one ever found out about it, what harm would there be? Besides, when she had been hired to work at the Dorchester Clinic, there was absolutely no mention on her contract of what to do in such a situation . . .

Closing her eyes, she also realised she was now trying to find excuses, however futile they may be, to justify this desire that was still growing within her. She also knew it was useless; she was vanquished.

She stood back and undressed quickly, her fingers trembling but precise. Her dress fell to the floor and her bra and panties followed right after. She couldn't fight her desire any longer, it was pointless. Right now he wanted her, and she wanted him. All she had to worry about was that somebody might see them.

Standing completely naked, she quickly drew the curtain around the bed, making sure that if someone entered the room they would think the patient asleep. The bed was now contained in a small space formed by the window on one side, the curtain on the other, a blank wall at the head of the bed and the wall with the large mirror at the other end.

She took some sort of wicked pleasure out of walking around naked in the blue light, knowing his eyes were studying her every move. Coming over to the other side of the bed, by the window, she climbed and knelt on the bed.

She watched her own shadow rise on the curtain and felt her arousal bloom. All she needed to do was to turn her head slightly and she could also watch herself in the mirror, she could see her now-naked body bending down to worship his.

By now her excitement was such that she practically fell on top of him, covering his chest with hers, pressing her swollen breasts against his hot skin, straddling his right leg with hers.

She knew he couldn't move because of his cast, and the thought of being in control of the situation excited her even more. She grabbed his mouth within hers forcefully, now wanting to taste all of him, her hips thrusting up and down rhythmically, grinding her wet pussy onto his hard thigh.

He couldn't do anything but yield to this passionate embrace, and he gently caressed the side of her hips as they melted onto his thigh, letting his fingertips wander over the swell of her bottom, his nails grazing at her delicate skin, just stopping short of her swollen love-lips.

Judith groaned with every breath, now slightly pulling away from him, her hands sliding between her body and his, caressing both his chest and her own breasts simultaneously.

She kissed, licked and suck his mouth, his jaw, his neck, his chest. She heard herself gasping and moaning loudly, no longer in control of her own breathing, as she writhed on top of him.

From the moment she had climbed onto the bed she had been given a certain power over him; he was at her mercy. If she wanted to get off and go back to her station, leaving him alone and frustrated, she could do just that. Even if she chose to stay, because he couldn't move unassisted, she was in charge of both her own pleasure and his.

She sat up on his thigh and let her own weight crush her wet vulva against him, her hips never ceasing their thrusting motion. He reached up and grabbed her breasts, feeling their fluid weight in turn, letting his fingertips gently worry her erect nipples. She sighed.

This was better than she could ever have imagined. Of course he was at her mercy, but it was also up to her to satisfy him. 'Ask me anything,' she announced in a whisper.

'Sit on my face,' came the reply.

She smiled and looked at him. She hadn't expected that. Rather, she would have thought he would ask her to pleasure him first. Changing position, she slowly crawled along his chest and turned around to straddle his face. He reached up, grabbed her hips and eased them down gently until her moistness met his mouth.

His tongue on her flesh was a revelation. Judith felt herself melt onto him, his lips studying her methodically, his tongue reaching deep inside her. Her hips resumed their dance, using his mouth as a soft surface against which to grind.

His hands kept surveying her thighs, his fingernails gently scratching at her soft skin, sending tingling, hot waves all the way up to her pussy.

Judith looked up and was almost surprised to see herself in the mirror on the opposite wall. She saw his body, hard and tense, lying on the white sheet, brushed by the blue light, the shadows of the branches playing against the curves of his muscles. His stiff prick stood up against his belly, twitching sporadically.

But most impressive was the sight of her own body, straddling his face, writhing incessantly. She didn't recognise herself, not tonight. It was another woman she saw tilting her head sideways, her eyes half-shut, her face betraying the storm of pleasure that ravaged her.

She watched the woman bring her hands up to caress her own breasts, as her face began to contract in repeated spasms of pleasure, the eyes barely able to remain open, the mouth frozen in successive oh's and ah's.

Her gaze came back to the statuesque body that lay underneath hers, and to the stiff cock that still remained untouched but now craved its reward. She bent down and grasped it delicately, gently pulling the foreskin back to completely expose the swollen plum. At first she bathed it in long licks, from the base of the shaft all the way to the tip of the head, inserting the tip of her tongue at the entrance of the tiny mouth, feeling her man's hips jerk smoothly every time.

Her hair fell forward and covered his hips. At the same time she took him in her mouth, completely, to the hilt, and began sucking gently. She heard him moan under her and his mouth grew impatient on her vulva.

In reply she lowered her hips even more, almost choking him, now grinding her pussy forcefully against his face. Yet she didn't increase the intensity of her ministrations of him. He had to earn his reward. He had to make her come first.

She let go of him for a while, sitting up again in order to concentrate on the wave of pleasure that was being born deep inside her at this very moment. Once again she looked up in the mirror. She wanted to see herself come.

She smiled at her reflection. Yes, it was her. How beautiful she looked on the verge of her climax, her hips now swaying rhythmically, her hands clasped on her breasts, kneading them furiously, her fingers pinching her engorged nipples.

She opened her mouth to scream her joy but no sound came out. Instead, her whole body arched under the strength of her pleasure and she leapt forward in an ultimate spasm, falling against the hard rock of his flat stomach.

Her vulva lay half-way down his chest, her thighs now straddling his shoulders. He inserted his finger in the gaping entrance which lay just a few inches from his chin. The moist flesh sucked at it readily, in successive spasms, as Judith's body shook under the intensity of her climax.

At the same time she was highly aware of it all, her limbs numb but her mind still very much alive. With great effort she lifted her head and looked in the mirror again, somehow fascinated by its presence, unable to find a reason for this attraction.

She saw the woman sprawled over the man's body, her face almost hidden behind the curtain of her own hair, her smile still betraying her pleasure. At the same time she felt the thick prick stir between her breasts. Now it was time to reward the man.

First she rolled onto her side, sliding off him. Then she stood up next to the bed, the cold floor assaulting her naked feet. She stared at the body that lay on the white sheets, once again wanting to force it into submission.

She walked over to the other side and opened the door of the bed-side cupboard. Fumbling in the dark she managed to locate the leather restraints.

There was a chance he might object to what she had in mind but she remembered the procedure she had been taught at nursing school: first she had to grab the wrists quickly and secure the strap around them, then use her own weight if necessary to pull the other extremity and tie it to the head of the bed.

She acted swiftly and precisely, and by the time he realised what she was up to it was already too late. He whined in complaint but she ignored him, quickly picking her bra off the floor and gagging him with it. She thought of tying his feet as well but it was not really necessary, once she sat on him he wouldn't be in any position to go anywhere.

She climbed back on the bed and knelt next to him again, amused by the worried expression in his eyes. This time he was all hers. Once again she straddled him, this time setting her knees on either side of him, her inner thighs rubbing against his hips, and she bent down until she came to completely lie on top of him. She gently nibbled at his chin whilst her hands caressed the strong muscles of his biceps.

She could feel his heart heavily pounding in his chest. What was he feeling? Fear? Arousal? Anticipation? A strange mixture of all three? At least she knew he wasn't indifferent.

Her foot grazed the side of his cast and a series of weird associations sprung in her mind. When the cast would come off he would most certainly need extensive physiotherapy . . . With Desmond.

In a flash she imagined them together, the tanned athlete and the black therapist, their contrasting flesh melting together. Maybe she would get to see it for real, one of these days. But she got him first; right now he was hers, and hers alone.

She caressed his chest and his stomach lovingly, using only her fingertips, surveying every inch of his smooth skin. He was hot under her, and seemingly still getting hotter, his skin now exuding a moist, fresh aroma.

Against her belly his prick pressed harder and harder, trying to throb its way inside her. The engorged head seeped at the mouth. He was more than ready. But it was still too early for Judith, he would have to wait.

She could see his eyes sparkle in the dark, at times worried, at times lustful, and she took a wicked pleasure out of torturing him like this.

Her hands increased the intensity of their caresses on his skin, and little by little she began using her whole body to discover his, stroking the entire length of her arms against his, rubbing and pressing her erect nipples across his chest.

Her tongue also danced along his neck, travelling from one ear to the other, gently sucking on his earlobes for a moment before continuing its journey. She bathed him thus, remembering how she had felt when Edouard had done it to her, hoping it would have the same effect.

After a while her mouth worked its way down his chest, nibbling at his pectoral muscles in a succession of wet kisses until she came to suck on his nipples. They were already stiff and engorged, but grew even bigger in Judith's mouth. She sucked on them greedily, flicking the tip of her tongue over them at a maddening speed, teasing them incessantly whilst her hands massaged his hard muscles.

He began to writhe under her, moaning loudly despite his gag, as if surprised at his own reaction. He lifted his head briefly. Judith stopped her ministrations and looked up at him.

His eyes were begging her to untie him, his maleness now growing impatient on her belly. She smiled wickedly.

'You asked for it,' she whispered. 'Now let me have my way.'

She went back to concentrate on his nipples, satisfied that he was getting impatient, quite determined not to let him loose for a while still. Yet at the same time the engorged cock that throbbed against her chest was calling to her. It wanted her, and she decided she wanted it too.

Putting her hands flat on his stomach to support herself, she sat up and rocked her pelvis back and forth a few times, feeling his thickness brush her moist vulva, covering him with her dew. She heard him moan again. Now she was happy to have tied him up, she could take him on her own terms.

Soon her clitoris quivered against his hardness and she longed to feel him inside her. She grabbed hold of his shaft and presented the swollen head to her entrance.

She lowered herself upon him, slowly, feeling him stretch her gradually, but not letting him enter her completely, before lifting herself up again. Her entrance teased his rigid member, never giving it the satisfaction of total penetration.

His hips jerked up in a vain effort to impale her but she lifted herself up even more, pressing hard on his stomach to prevent him from moving again. This was an uneven fight however, his range of movements limited by the weight of the plaster cast around his leg. Yet Judith still wanted to show him she had the upper hand.

'Stop this,' she warned, 'it's no use.'

But as she glided up and down upon his length she gradually conceded. Soon she began to ride him, at first by simply rocking back and forth, then increasing the movement of her hips as she felt him growing bigger inside her, her arousal now mounting quickly. She was becoming a victim to her own game, having meant to hold out as long as possible to torture him, but realising she was the one who could no longer wait.

But by now she was acting solely with the intention of reaching her own climax. It didn't really matter if he came as well in the process, he had earned this reward. She heard herself panting, the muscles of her thighs soon tied in a burning knot as she rapidly moved up and down upon his shaft, her knees locking under the strain.

Her vulva was melting onto his member and quivering with delight, as Judith willed herself to continue her assault despite the pain in her exhausted legs. The swollen head stroked her inside, up and down the smooth walls of her tunnel, triggering that sensation which would soon take her to the point of no return. Her stiff clitoris rubbed itself on the hard shaft as well, only enhancing the pleasure she could already feel was about to explode.

She was breathless, highly aware of the pressure building up within her, yet her climax almost took her by surprise. Her head jerked back and forth a few times as successive sobs escaped from her mouth.

Her vulva contracted around his member and provoked his own climax. She hardly felt him quiver inside her, but she recognised the spasm that shook him, as if escaping from her own body to transport him right after.

She let herself collapse on top of him once more, this time recoiling on his chest and nestling her face in the groove of his neck. She listened to his heartbeat slowly returning to its normal rate, as was hers.

Although she would have liked to stay a little longer,

she knew she had to shake herself from the cloud that now surrounded her, and fight the temptation to stay with him any longer.

His regular breathing told her he was completely relaxed now, and probably falling asleep. She rose with difficulty and felt his limp phallus slide out of her, falling back with a fat flop on his stomach.

Her patient was now in bed, she had done her duty. She undid the restraints and stored them back in the bedside cupboard, then took her bra from his mouth and began to dress.

The back panel was soaked with his saliva and felt cold against her warm skin, right between her shoulder blades; a silent reminder of the daring way she had treated him. She laughed softly. She wasn't sorry for what she had done.

She finished dressing and pulled the blanket on top of him, looking at him one more time, still bathed by the blue light coming from the window, before making her way to the bathroom. Her hair needed to be tamed before she returned to her nursing station.

In the bath tub the wet towel still lay in a bundle, and its sight gave a smile to Judith's lips. This was something she wasn't going to forget for some time. She quickly gathered her hair up and checked her image in the mirror one more time: prim and proper, who would have thought? Glancing at her watch she suddenly realised she had been gone for over an hour.

She turned off the light and almost ran out of the room, desperately trying to think of a good excuse in case her colleague started asking questions. The best she could do was to tell the truth: she had to assist a patient out of the bath tub and help him settle for the night. The rest didn't matter.

Once she got to the station, however, the other nurse was busy preparing an injection. Judith quickly grabbed the order chart and pretended to absorb herself in it. For a second she felt this crazy urge to turn to her colleague and tell her all about what she had just been up to.

She could still smell him, feel him inside her, and her sore knees were still complaining about the way she had abused them.

It wasn't easy keeping a straight face.

Chapter Eleven

'Good evening, my sweet...'

Judith's neck stiffened and her heart quickened. Jo's voice in her ear was unmistakable. Its hissing sound sent a shiver through her limbs. It was reminiscent of a rattle-snake, but just as sickly sweet as the morning she and Tania had cornered Judith in the shower room. That morning was over five weeks ago already, but suddenly it seemed like it was only yesterday. She clutched her pen to prevent her hand from shaking, but released her grip when she felt the plastic crack under her fingers.

'So, we'll be spending the night together,' Jo continued. 'I'm sure we'll have a nice time.' Her voice shook slightly and it was clear she was fighting a giggle. Yet Judith wasn't in a laughing mood. What was Jo planning to do to her this time?

There were only two nurses at each station during the night shift. This was the second time Judith had been assigned to do a series of night shifts, but so far she had worked with a different nurse each night. Luckily, she hadn't been assigned to work with either Tania or Jo, who worked regular night shifts, but it was too good to last.

This was her last night before going back to day shifts, and her worse nightmare was about to come alive. Yet at the same time a strange sensation seized her, her body cruelly reminding her what the girls had done to her that morning, and despite her fears she felt a weird anticipation, some wicked desire to somehow fall into their clutches again.

Her mind racing, she stood up and walked toward the filing cabinet. She had to buy some time, calm her nerves and think of a way to stay outside of Jo's reach for the next eight hours. When she turned around again Jo was standing by the desk and still staring at her, smiling sweetly. For a moment she almost seemed friendly.

Judith looked straight into the blue eyes, trying to see in them what made her so afraid of the blond doll. But in fact, Jo didn't look threatening at all. She was shorter than Judith, and a bit plumper. The body was voluptuous, the breasts and the hips generous, the stomach nicely rounded.

Her blond hair was only loosely tied up, something that would perhaps make the directors frown, and her earrings were definitely too big. The make-up was overdone, too. Large patches of blue powder weighed on the eyelids, and a red blotch covered each cheek. The pouting lips were red as well, dark as blood and shimmering. The nails were painted a matching red, something else that wasn't in line with the regulations of the Clinic.

A doll, that's what she was. Something to cuddle softly, to play with, and then put aside in a corner when playtime was over.

In Judith's mind a wicked thought arose: the best way to fight her fears would be to tackle them head on, to turn the tables on the naughty nurse. All she had to do was to corner her colleague and frighten her the way she and Tania had frightened Judith, so the victim would become the attacker. But how? She was never keen on practical jokes, she never had the wicked imagination needed to be really successful. However, given enough time she would perhaps come up with something good.

The phone rang and interrupted her thoughts. Jo picked it up and Judith returned to the filing cabinet. She fished out the procedure sheet and rapidly glanced through it.

There were rounds to be made at 2 o'clock, and after that the nurses had to go to the stock room to do a brief inventory and order missing supplies for the next morning. The store room was right behind the station, and quite a distance from the patients' rooms. The two nurses would be alone in there, no-one could hear them.

Judith smiled and bit her lip. That would be the perfect moment. She had to attack first and surprise the girl, scare her as much as possible. But how? She had about three hours to think of something, something good. If she was alone with her she knew she was strong enough to have the upper hand.

She turned around to face Jo, determined to be just as sweet and show her she wasn't at all afraid of her. But instead she came face to face with Carol Martin, the night supervisor.

'I've been looking for you,' Carol said. 'We have a problem on the fourth floor. One of the nurses is ill and the other has just called in to say she would be late. Problems with her car, I think. I need you to go down there and mind the desk until she gets here, then help her with the rounds.'

Judith glanced at her watch, suddenly disappointed. It was already a few minutes past midnight, there was no way of knowing how long she would be away from her own desk, and away from Jo. But she had no option. Besides, being away would certainly buy her time and Jo would not become suspicious. It didn't really matter if she was away for the next couple of hours anyhow; she could set her plan in motion anytime after that.

She grabbed her handbag and made her way down to the fourth floor.

Judith paused in the stairwell and glanced at her watch. She had chosen to walk up the stairs to get back to her own station. This way, there wouldn't be any noises from the lift to betray her arrival. It was almost 3 o'clock; if Jo had worked fast and if there hadn't been any problems, she could very well be doing the inventory already.

Judith walked towards the desk quickly but silently, almost clinging to the wall, carefully passing each room. She briefly pressed her ear to each door, trying to figure out where Jo could be at this hour.

The nursing station was deserted and Judith slipped her handbag under the desk. She quickly glanced at the order chart and saw a long row of check marks, along with Jo's initials. The rounds had been done.

She tiptoed to the stock room and carefully pushed the door open, peering inside. Jo was standing near a stack of bed sheets, her back turned, holding her clipboard in one hand and using the other to toss the sheets whilst counting them aloud.

Judith slowly entered the room and silently shut the door behind her, her heart beating fast, desperately trying to pace her breath, lest it became so loud it would betray her presence.

She had decided to quickly pounce on the girl and take her by surprise, to simply grab her forcefully and perhaps even grope her a little. After that, she would have to improvise.

Of course Jo wouldn't know what hit her. Hopefully she would be scared out of her wits. Already Judith felt a warm flow collecting at her crotch, the excitement of the attack strangely fuelling some sort of arousal. This peculiar desire wasn't really directed at Jo, but rather at the concept of surprising and frightening the girl. Tonight Judith was in charge.

Her hands pushed at the door behind her to make sure it was completely shut. Rapidly she estimated the other nurse's position and distance. In her mind the plan was already in motion.

Reaching up along the wall she turned off the light and waited a second, wanting to make her attack even more startling. Then she stepped forward and almost immediately felt Jo's plump body stopping her advance.

Obviously the other girl hadn't realised what was

going on for she hadn't even turned around yet. In the dark, Judith pushed her forward, slipping one arm around the curvy waist and pressing her other hand against her victim's mouth.

'Not a word,' she muttered in the girl's ear, trying to change her voice and fighting a giggle. Already she felt elated and now she wished she could see Jo's face. But attacking like this in the complete darkness was even better than she would have expected.

She heard the clipboard falling to the floor and felt the tiny panic-stricken hands trying to pry hers off the painted mouth.

Judith pinned her victim face down against the stack of sheets, preventing her from going anywhere, not even giving her any room to move. She felt the thick lips protesting under her hand, and the heat of Jo's frightened body piercing through her uniform.

As she felt Jo writhing in her embrace, she suddenly became excited, now wanting to impress not only fear upon her victim, but arousal as well. Under her hand squealing sounds were trying to escape and she increased the strength of her grasp. At the same time she let her other hand roughly brush the rounded breasts, surprised to notice the nipples immediately growing hard under her fingertips.

Yet she could still feel Jo trembling against her and at this moment estimated victory was hers. She had succeeded in both frightening and arousing the girl.

Judith resisted the urge to laugh out loud, satisfied and almost surprised by the immediate success of her revenge. The joke was over, and she had vanquished her own fears. From now on she knew there was nothing Jo could ever do to frighten her.

And now all she had to do was to wait a little while without releasing the girl – just to make her worry a bit, wondering who this attacker was and what she wanted – and then she would let her go.

Yet at the same time Judith felt a strange desire to continue, to discover the rounded body that kept on writhing in a more and more sensual manner, the hips gyrating lasciviously, the buttocks pushing against Judith's thighs. For a minute she wondered what it would be like to caress the girl as she had herself been caressed.

She moved back slightly, hoping Jo would take this opportunity to escape. But instead she felt a tiny hand grab hers and bring it back to caress the engorged nipples. The soft buttocks continued pushing back against Judith's thighs and the body grew limp in surrender. Jo had stopped fighting. Judith's heart began beating faster.

Things were getting out of hand. She hadn't expected Jo to react like this ... Now she felt like she was falling into her own trap, being both aroused by the close contact with this plump body, and frightened by the way her own body now craved to caress the blond girl.

What was she to do? Her mind was telling her to stop right there, but her body was eager for her to go on, as if she would then miss out on something. If she kept going she would likely discover another source of pleasure and this notion quickly made her hesitation vanish.

She couldn't stop, not just yet. She decided to keep up the game just a little bit longer, just to see how Jo would react. Possibly the girl would soon begin to yearn for pleasure, and right at that point Judith would stop. That was the easiest option; some sort of compromise in reply to the dilemma between her reason and her senses. Just a little longer ...

She brought both her hands to the girl's breasts and gently cupped them, curious yet shy, no longer thinking but rather letting her body dictate her behaviour. Instinctively she knew Jo probably wore the same kind of underwear as she did, a lacy bra and matching panties, and the thought excited her even more.

Guided by Jo's hands, she fumbled to undo the buttons at the front of the girl's uniform, then slowly slipped her hands inside, her fingers instantly melting onto the warm skin.

Jo moaned gently and tilted her head back against Judith's shoulder, turning her face sideways to kiss her attacker's neck.

At that point Judith wondered if Jo knew who was caressing her like this, but immediately she realised that not knowing was probably even more exciting for a girl like Jo. The thrill of an unknown attacker, albeit female, probably added to the excitement she might have experienced through the attack itself.

Judith let her fingertips glide over the lacy cups of the bra, her nails gently scratching the erect nipples. Her own nipples grew stiff as well, her breasts swelling in arousal. She was holding a woman in her arms. How strange, how pleasant.

The need to possess the body she held in her grasp soon became overwhelming, yet Judith thought she could never bring herself to inflict on Jo the same treatment the two naughty nurses had submitted her to in the shower room.

The heat of the body pushing against hers was inviting; the rounded curves begged to be caressed. Judith suddenly wished she was a man, wanting to survey those curves with larger hands, and possess the girl with a strong, virile passion.

She heard Jo moan gently and felt tiny hands straying, fingers slowly pulling up her own dress to get at her thighs. Still holding the breasts in her cupped hands, she stopped thinking and abandoned herself to fully enjoy this new sensation. In her mind she saw the red fingernails slowly tracing the path of her thighs; she saw the breasts she held in her hands swelling under the soft caress. She moaned in reply and instinctively started to cover the girl's neck with gentle kisses.

Jo's aroma was sweetly perfumed with cinnamon undertones. A fine layer of sweat covered the offered cheek and Judith quickly brushed it with her chin. She was amazed by its softness; how different it was from a man's rough skin.

The hands once again grabbed hold of Judith's to guide

them under Jo's dress. At that moment Judith understood that although she had meant for Jo to be her victim, they were now equals.

Still standing behind the plump body that continued to press itself against hers, Judith began to caress it, marvelling at the softness of the skin her fingers had found.

Jo brought her hands up above and behind her head and gently encircled Judith's neck, abandoning herself. In the dark she put one foot up on a step stool in front of her, effectively parting her legs for the benefit of her attacker.

Judith saw her own image rising in her mind; how she had herself offered her body to her previous lovers, and what a sweet invitation it was indeed. Her hands glided up the girl's thighs, feeling their hot, fluid plumpness. She shuddered as her fingertips finally reached the lacy fabric of Jo's panties, hesitating a moment.

Once again she felt she shouldn't go on. But the warmth that had taken over and stunned her senses only urged her to keep going. In her arms the girl moaned again, as if inviting her to continue her search. This intoxicating feeling rendered Judith's mind numb. Only her senses were now guiding her on this unusual road to pleasure.

She placed the whole of her hand on the girl's crotch, letting its feminine wetness pierce through and bathe the palm of her hand. At the same time a familiar smell rose to her nostrils, the smell of lust, similar to the aroma of her own excitement.

The girl that writhed in her embrace was wanton, and her excitement was inevitably contagious. As Judith let herself be invaded by this voluptuous aroma she felt her own arousal bloom and at this instant decided that she wanted to feel Jo's naked skin. After all, Jo had herself boldly caressed Judith once, it was only natural to return the favour . . .

She undertook to undress her victim quickly. The uniforms they were wearing were similar, both fastening through a long row of buttons at the front. Strangely, Judith felt like she was undressing herself. Jo didn't display any resistance but didn't try to help her either, as if she had accepted she was a victim tonight.

Judith's excitement gave her fingers an unusual precision and even in the dark she was able to remove everything Jo wore without even seeing it. And again she wondered whether the blond girl knew the identity of her seducer.

Her hands worked fast and in a matter of seconds Jo stood completely naked. Being unable to see the naked body only made Judith more eager to discover it. She ran her hands all over it, delicately feeling the whole surface, endlessly marvelling at its warm softness.

Jo stood passively, moaning gently every time Judith's hands brushed her breasts or the inside of her legs. By now she had to brace herself by putting both hands on the pile of sheets in front of her, her legs parted wide in anticipation, in invitation.

Where Judith's hands went her mouth would soon follow, but not just yet. She pressed her clothed body against the naked back, cupping both breasts and worrying the puckered nipples whilst her lips lightly brushed Jo's neck and shoulders. She continued her discovery in this fashion for a while, her hands surveying the front of the plump body and her mouth caressing its back.

She worked her way down gradually, letting her tongue run down each bump of Jo's spine, sucking at them briefly. Her hands on the girl's breasts became a little rougher and grasped the rounded globes in a tighter grip, pinching and pulling at the nipples between her thumb and forefinger.

Soon Judith ended up on her knees, her hands now holding the girl's thighs and her face resting on the rounded buttocks. She had ceased to think a long time ago, yet she was still highly aware of what she was doing. Her caresses were not automatic but carefully planned, blindly obeying the orders dictated by her own desire.

She could also feel her own body alight, consumed by the desire to caress the girl in ways she wouldn't have dared only a few weeks ago. But now she was ready, she wanted to know a female body. She stood up and grabbed Jo by the shoulders, forcing her to turn around. Still pushing her against the stack of sheets she bent down and quickly took hold of a nipple in her mouth.

Jo let out a small cry of joy, tentatively putting her hands around Judith's neck and shyly pulling it even tighter to her generous bosom.

Judith took a demure lick at the puckered bud she now held in her mouth. It seemed to grow bigger, to swell as she teased it gently, its smokey taste pleasantly strange.

Her nose gently brushed Jo's cushiony breast, resting against the soft skin and caressing it with each breath. At the same time her hands wandered along the girl's thighs, stroking them endlessly in an up and down motion.

Jo's knees seemed to buckle under her, and Judith suddenly felt powerful, encouraged by the way she could get the girl to react to her caresses. She was still pinning the girl to the stack of sheets even though Jo wasn't showing any resistance. Yet Judith felt she was in charge, calling the shots, and Jo would have no option but to obey anyway.

Sensuously, wickedly, she let her fingers glide up the inside of her victim's thigh and only briefly brush the moist vulva. She heard Jo moan and felt her tremble, but Judith's own flesh reacted even more strongly.

She began to pant and engulfed Jo's breast deep in her mouth, locking her lips around the tender skin in a strong suction. She sucked at it as if it were the very air she breathed, the effect of her caresses somehow transferring onto her own body. She was feeling what she was doing, as if she were caressing herself. Her own vulva clenched violently as she touched Jo's again, ever so lightly, her fingers teasing the wet folds only in passing before continuing to caress the warm flesh of the rounded thighs.

Yet her fingers began spending more and more time brushing the wet bush, their eagerness continually increasing, discovering a treasure that was different, yet so similar, to her own.

She realised she probably knew what to do to make the girl climax, but she didn't want to make her reach her peak just yet. First Jo had to be deliciously tortured, perhaps even kept waiting forever without ever receiving the pleasure of release...

Tonight Judith was determined to be cruel. She remembered that fateful morning in the shower, and she also remembered the girls hadn't kept their promise to make her come. Now it would be her revenge.

Her mouth then turned to the other breast, bathing it with the warmth of her tongue, and began gently teasing the erect nipple with tiny butterfly licks, the tip of her tongue only darting at it lightly but rhythmically.

This role reversal wasn't only surprising for Judith but also terribly arousing. Once again, she curiously wished she were a man right now, to be able to possess the girl with all her might, to impale her and fill her passionately.

Her hands became frantic, kneading the soft skin of Jo's thighs with both hands whilst her mouth decidedly began its descent along the girl's belly. She felt Jo's warmth against her cheek as she glided down in a soft caress, and only stopped when she felt the downy mound tickle her chin.

By now she was kneeling in front of the girl. Jo still hadn't moved, content to be caressed. Judith could smell the musky dew, quite similar to her own. She remembered Edouard's words when he had cornered her in the corridor a few weeks ago: 'I can smell your desire...' Now she knew what he meant. The musky smell of a woman's arousal, its sweet and heady fragrance, could only serve to enhance a man's own desire.

And right now Judith's mouth was just a few inches away from this wet treasure, so compelling, so inviting. She buried her lips in the soft curls, her tongue shyly yet eagerly searching for the tiny shaft she now longed to taste.

It seemed to be waiting for her and throbbed with delight when she found it. She gently suckled its hardening bud, letting her tongue slide along its length, and brought her hand up to discover more of what lay amidst this soft bush.

Her fingers lost themselves along the wet folds, feeling their watery softness before being sucked in the silken cavern, the smooth walls of the vagina closing around them in a delightful grip.

Her mouth soon followed them, her tongue digging deep inside the girl whilst her other hand reached up and her thumb came flickering over the swollen clitoris. She tasted the girl's sweet dew, her taste buds awakening to this new nectar that now seemed to flow into her mouth.

Judith felt her own vulva react violently, demanding to be caressed as well. By now she was teasing the girl exactly the way she liked to be teased herself. And somehow she could feel it in her loins, her body alight with a fire on the verge of explosion.

She let go of the treasure she was holding in her mouth and stood up again. Without a word she took Jo's tiny hand and guided it to her own flesh, under her dress and inside her soaked panties.

Jo followed the silent instructions obediently, and her hand mimicked Judith's, both women caressing each other's silken flesh in a smooth, back and forth motion.

Only Judith bent forward slightly, eager to grab hold of the girl's pulpous breasts and again taste their smokiness. Jo's fingers on her vulva followed the tempo set by Judith's hand, and soon both women began moaning in pleasure as they kindled each other's arousal.

Judith forwent her previous intention not to let the girl reach her peak. By now it seemed they had entered some sort of silent pact, whereby giving and receiving pleasure could not be dissociated.

Judith's hips began swaying violently, as if desperately

trying to extract pleasure out of Jo's hand. Judith's hand on Jo's vulva also became frantic, torturing the stiff clitoris hard and fast. Judith was still pressing her clothed body against Jo's naked skin, moans of pleasure escaping from her throat with each breath. Both women reached their climax almost simultaneously, Jo sighing loudly, Judith almost grunting, her mouth still gripping the girl's breasts.

They had to lean against each other for a while, Judith's pleasure subsiding quickly, but Jo weakly holding on to her.

A second later Judith's brain began functioning again, suddenly realising she couldn't afford to abandon herself completely, she had to get out of there. With her foot she quickly scattered Jo's clothing around the room. She had to buy time and make sure the girl wouldn't get out of the stock room too soon lest she discovered who her attacker was, if she didn't know already.

Next she took some of the sheets from the stack and tossed them aside, reducing the height to make the limp body lean against it instead. She forced Jo to turn around, making her bend over the diminished stack, face down, and then covered her entirely with a couple of sheets. By the time Jo regained her senses, got out from under the sheets, retrieved her clothes and finally exited the room, Judith would have disappeared from the station, only to come back some time later.

For a second she was tempted to lock the door on her way out, but decided against it. Instead she left the room without turning on the lights, grabbed her handbag, and once again made her way to another floor using the stairs.

The door of the lift closed in front of her and Judith checked her watch: 5 o'clock. She had waited in the nurses' lounge for almost thirty minutes, just as if she had been on her break. Her timing was perfect and she smiled to herself, rather content that Jo would probably never find out who her attacker was.

The lift stopped with a squeaky hiss, sounding louder than usual in the silence of the early morning. With any chance Jo would hear her arriving this time.

She walked to the station decidedly, almost giggling, yet still trying to keep a straight face. Jo was sitting behind the desk, filling forms in for the morning shift.

'I hope you don't mind,' Judith said, 'but I decided to take my break before coming back up. Did you have time to do the inventory or do you need me to help you with it?' She tried to sound casual, a bit uncertain, trying to recapture the impression she must have given Jo when they first started their shift.

Jo didn't even look up, seemingly fascinated by the forms she had to complete for the laboratory tests.

'It's all done, I'll be going on my break now.'

Judith let out a small sigh, trying to sound relieved at the thought of not having to spend much time alone with her colleague. After all, Judith was supposed to be Jo's prey, wasn't she?

Chapter Twelve

The paper seemed to burn in her hands. Judith sat down in an armchair in the nurses' lounge adjacent to the locker room and read the letter over again, trying to make some sense out of the words that were now dancing in front of her and losing their shape as tears filled her eyes. All around her nurses were coming in and out of the room, laughing loudly, not paying attention to her. Many were on their way home and often slammed the metal doors of the lockers, only adding to the noisy confusion.

But Judith couldn't hear any of this anymore. Her mind was completely absorbed by the letter she had just received.

The envelope was included with her pay packet, marked 'personal and confidential'. At first she had thought it was probably something insignificant to do with her salary or taxes, but the first line of text had sent a bolt of sorrow through her heart and tears to her eyes.

NOTICE OF CONVOCATION TO A DISCIPLINARY HEARING
FOR: Miss Judith Stanton
REGARDING THE EVENT THAT TOOK PLACE:
the 17th of this month

ON FLOOR: 6
DURING: the night shift

She was required to attend the meeting which would take place the next morning in the Board Room. The 17th was two weeks ago already, but Judith had not forgotten that night: it was the night she had been with Mike Randall.

Obviously somebody had seen them and reported her. Probably the other nurse who was on duty that night, or maybe even Mike himself! But why had the directors waited so long before taking action? After that night each passing day had given Judith a sense of security, she was sure no-one would ever find out. Until now . . .

A disciplinary hearing for a nurse who had not completed her probation could only mean instant dismissal.

The offence was serious. Back in nursing school she had been told several times that physical relations with patients were regarded as highly unethical. Some hospitals even considered it as some kind of abuse since it was often implied the patient was under medication and therefore not really aware of what was happening.

It was her fault, there was no doubt about it, and the blame would be on her. She should have walked away that night, she should have been strong and resisted temptation. Now it was too late.

She tilted her head back against the wall and took a deep breath. She remembered every second of the time she had spent in Mike Randall's room; how his skin looked under the blue rays of the floodlight; how hot his flesh had felt under her touch . . .

Her sorrow quickly turned to anger. She folded the letter and put it back in the envelope, wishing she knew who had squealed on her. Somehow she doubted it could be Mike himself, what would he have to gain? Her colleague? That was a strong possibility; she could have been motivated by jealousy.

At that moment Judith realised she hadn't seen her

since that night. Now what was her name? ... Mary ... Mary Jenkins.

She stood up and went back into the locker room, reading the name tags on each of the narrow doors until she found the name: C. Jackson ... J. James ... M. Jenkins. The door was locked, of course, but the nurse who occupied the next locker was sitting on the long bench, tying up her shoelaces.

'Excuse me,' Judith inquired, 'have you seen Mary recently?'

'Mary Jenkins? No, not for a while. She hasn't been in for over a week now. Nobody knows why, maybe she's been ill or something. Why? Does she owe you money as well?'

Judith gave a faint smile. 'No, nothing like that. I was just wondering, that's all. Thank you.'

She turned around and went back to her own locker, in the next row. Time to go home. Thankfully she hadn't received the letter earlier during the day; she wouldn't have been able to carry on. She opened the narrow door and stared at the three uniforms quietly hanging in the locker. She had bought them only two days ago and still hadn't worn them. Her trembling fingers caressed the smooth fabric, wondering whether her short career could already be coming to an end. If she were dismissed it would make it even more difficult to find a job elsewhere.

She grabbed her coat and her bag and quickly closed the door with a bang, then made her way out of the locker room, desperately trying to hold back her tears, at least until she was out of the building.

Why had she bothered to wear her uniform this morning? After the hearing there was no doubt in Judith's mind she would be out of a job. She sat still, her limbs strangely steady, waiting to be called into the Board Room.

When she had arrived she had seen Mary Jenkins go in. At this very moment her colleague was probably still describing what she had witnessed that night, giving them all the details of how Judith had pulled the curtain around the bed, how she had undressed and wilfully hopped into bed with her patient. They would then quickly build up a case against Judith and just present her with the fact once she was called in.

Judith shuddered. She wanted to scream her pain, protesting she hadn't done anything wrong. But, of course, she had known all along that it wasn't really right either.

The clock ticked slowly, each second increasing the feeling of impending doom that hung about her. Last night she had thought about it for what seemed hours. There was always a slight chance she might just be reprimanded, in which case she would gladly accept any kind of punishment if in turn they would let her keep her job.

At that moment she had promised herself she would never again let her lustful desires get the best of her. She would restrain herself. She would pick up guys in bars to satisfy her needs if she had to. But not at work, never again.

She was startled when the door opened and Mr Armstrong, the personnel manager, came out.

'We're ready for you, Miss Stanton.'

She stood up quietly, feeling strangely calm, and followed him into the large room where she was invited to take a seat at the large oval, mahogany table. On the other side sat Doctor Marshall and Mrs Cox. Judith couldn't stand to look at them. This wasn't fair, she thought. They had been so blunt with her that day in Mrs Cox's office, making her take her clothes off and masturbate in front of them. And now they were about to fire her for giving free reign to her passion.

Mr Armstrong sat next to her. Judith furtively glanced around the table to see who else was there. She felt a cold chill as she noticed Robert Harvey sitting at the far end. What was he doing here? Then she remembered he was chief surgeon, and as such would be involved in administrative matters.

So there was only the four of them. However, three of

these people knew something about her, something very personal. The three of them had seen her naked body writhing with pleasure, they had all heard her cries as she had climaxed.

Again today she felt as if she was naked before them. Only this time it wasn't nice at all. Turning her head slightly, she saw Mary Jenkins sitting in a far corner, like a witness. Judith instantly felt betrayed and couldn't stand to look at her either. What was about to happen was not only very embarrassing, it was also very personal. How could they let Mary stay and watch?

'Miss Stanton,' Mr Armstrong began, 'I need to ask you a few questions about the night of the 17th. Now, it is very important that you answer in all honesty, do you understand?'

'Yes.'

'That night, you were working the night shift on the sixth floor, right? Which rooms were you responsible for?'

'616 to 630.'

'And Miss Jenkins here, which rooms was she looking after?'

'601 to 615.'

He paused and glanced at the table. Only then did Judith notice the small tape recorder and a feeling of panic seized her. They were recording her every word! How could they?!

She felt her face flush in outrage but before she could say anything Mr Armstrong had turned to her again. 'During your shift that night, did you at any time go into room 612?'

Judith felt surprised and her anger vanished for a moment. Room 612? What did this have to do with her?

'No ... No ...'

'Did you see Miss Jenkins go into that room during the shift?'

Judith's hands began to tremble. Why was he asking her this? His question took her aback, she had to make an effort to remember. That night her mind had worked on automatic pilot, completely dazed after what had happened in Mike Randall's room. Room 612? Wasn't that Mrs Gibson's room, the one who was in for a facelift? Yes, now she remembered Mary having to tend to her quite often; the patient had spent an agitated night.

'Yes. She went in there quite a few times...'

'Now,' he said slowly, 'this is very important. When she came out of the room after checking on the patient, did you ever notice Miss Jenkins taking something out of the room?'

Judith began breathing fast, getting suddenly excited. Obviously there was something else going on today, maybe this hearing wasn't about her ... She forced herself to concentrate, to recapture the images that were now so vague in her mind.

'Yes, I saw her taking something.'

'What?'

'I don't know...'

'Try to remember. Was it sheets? Clothes? A tray?'

'I'm ... I'm not sure. It was something small ... In her hand ... Black ..'

'Miss Stanton, this is very important. Please make an effort.'

'It was like a purse, a black leather purse ...'

'Are you sure?'

Judith breathed a smile. So this is what it was all about. Did her colleague take something from the patient's room? Then she remembered the words of the nurse in the locker room: 'does she owe you money as well?' Mary had been off work for a couple of weeks and nobody knew why. Could she have been suspended pending the hearing because she had stolen money from a patient?

'Quite sure,' Judith announced, suddenly relieved. And indeed she was sure. Now she distinctly remembered Mary going to check on Mrs Gibson towards the end of their shift, even though the patient had finally fallen asleep some time earlier. She had something with her when she had come out of the room, and she had put it in her handbag.

And now Mary's job was in Judith's hands.

'Did you see what she did with it? Did she ever bring it back to the patient's room?'

'I don't know.' Now she felt sorry for her colleague, and quite ashamed to have thought Mary had squealed on her. However the administration seemed to have pretty strong evidence against Mary already, and nothing Judith could say at this point would make a difference.

'Do you know whether it could have been her own purse? Is it possible she could have taken it to the patient's room for some reason, without you seeing her, and brought it back again later?'

'I don't know.'

'But you are sure she did take something that looked like a purse out of the patient's room?'

'Yes, I'm absolutely sure about that. But I wouldn't know whose purse it was.'

Mr Armstrong turned to Doctor Marshall. The men stared at each other for a few seconds until Doctor Marshall silently nodded. Mr Armstrong turned to Judith agam.

'Thank you,' he said with a smile. 'You may go back to your station now.'

Judith smiled in turn and stood up, her eyes quickly looking for some sign of acknowledgement from those seated on the other side of the table. But no-one was looking at her, they seemed to be busy exchanging glances between themselves.

At that moment Judith really felt that her own job was secure, for now. Before leaving the room she also looked at Mary, still sitting in the corner. The tear-stained face looked up at her with a faint smile.

Judith felt sorry for her colleague, but there was nothing she could do. She had to tell the truth otherwise she would have risked her own job. And after this she knew she would never do anything to risk that again.

Chapter Thirteen

The bell rang on the station board and Nurse Hardcastle sighed in exasperation.

'Lisa Baxter! Again!' She turned to Judith. 'Would you be an angel and go see what she wants this time? She's such a pest this morning! I've been to her room four times already. I'm just about to kill her. I have better things to do than help her put nail varnish on her toes!'

Judith laughed and made her way to room 218. One of the drawbacks of caring for rich people was that the nurses were often mistaken for servants, and the patients failed to realise the staff had more important things to do than cater to their every whim.

At the Dorchester Clinic, it seemed to be even worse on the second floor, where the patients were younger and the atmosphere was not unlike a wild party at times. From starlets who thought spending thousands of pounds just to get rid of a few tiny lines around their eyes would open the doors to fame, to affluent young men whose egos needed a little boost in the form of well-placed pectoral implants, the whole second floor looked more like a university college than a private clinic. And the patients all had one thing in common: they had a tendency to believe the staff had nothing to do but to wait on them.

Nevertheless, Judith felt more comfortable around this younger crowd and since she had started to work at the Clinic she had often wished she could be assigned to this floor more often.

The first thing she did as she entered the room was to turn down the radio, blasting so loud she could hear it all the way down the corridor. There hadn't been any complaints, but there were rules to be observed otherwise things would rapidly get out of control.

Lisa's room, like most rooms on the second floor, was decorated differently from the rooms on the upper floors: still luxurious and comfortable, but with a more youthful look. The small leather sofa in the corner was a deep red instead of pale orange. The bedcover also looked younger, featuring a rather psychedelic pattern in red and green instead of the usual, more subdued mint and peach print. In a corner sat an enormous panda bear, adding a black and white note.

Lisa was sitting on her bed, knees apart, brushing her long hair with one hand, the other still paused on the call button. She turned to the nurse.

'It's about time,' she whined in a comical voice, her nose still covered in bandages and forcing her to breathe through her mouth. Her blonde hair fell in straight strands, untamed, over her shoulders. The thick fringe on her forehead made her look even younger than she was.

She was wearing white satin pyjamas through which the twin peaks of her nipples were plainly visible. Judith remembered the sight of her naked body, the nipples the same colour as coffee, the way they had puckered when she had touched them . . .

That was already more than two weeks ago but Lisa was still here. Something had gone wrong in the operating theatre that morning and the procedure had to be rescheduled. As a result, Lisa had been sent home and had to come back a couple of weeks later.

Needless to say, from the moment she had set foot in the Clinic the second time around she had been very demanding, constantly throwing tantrums to members of the staff who had been advised to humour her. There were fears that if Lisa Baxter wasn't entirely happy with her stay, she might in turn complain to her friends who would otherwise someday become patients of the Clinic themselves. Since word of mouth was the only form of publicity for the Dorchester Clinic, it was important to avoid ending up with dissatisfied patients .

'What can I do for you, Lisa?' Judith asked as she turned towards the bed. She stopped about three feet away, somewhat intimidated by the girl's impatient tone, unwilling to irritate her any further.

'I want you to open the window; it's too hot in here!'

'We've told you before, we can't open the windows just now. It's too cold outside, you can't afford to catch a cold as long as your nose is still covered in bandages.'

'Then take the bloody bandages off!'

Judith bit her lips in an effort to kill the smile that rose to her lips. Lisa was fuming with anger, almost screaming, but the snuffling voice coming out of her mouth was incredibly out of place and made her sound like a cartoon character.

'Two more days, dear,' Judith replied, coming closer to the bed. 'And you'll be allowed to go home right after. Just be patient and bear with us.' She tried to remain calm and talk in a reassuring tone, having been warned by her colleagues to always remain polite and kind even if this particular patient became difficult. If Lisa started to complain to the directors, at least she wouldn't have anything to say against Judith.

In an effort to pacify the girl she approached the bed and gently took the hairbrush from her. Standing behind Lisa, she quietly ran her fingers through the girl's hair, draping the light mane over the back of her hands.

'You're becoming quite impatient,' she stated, trying to sound friendly. 'I bet you can't wait to get out of here. Has your boyfriend been to visit?'

'No,' Lisa replied, gradually calming down. 'He's such a wimp, he's afraid of hospitals!'

'Somehow I can't imagine you going out with a wimp!' Judith laughed.

'We're not really together. He's hardly my type, but he's such a good fuck.'

Judith gasped and almost dropped the hairbrush, although she knew she shouldn't be surprised to hear such a sophisticated girl using that kind of language. Nowadays, even rich, spoilt girls weren't immune to dirty words.

She tried to think of something to say, to change the subject, sensing that if Lisa wasn't entirely happy with her boyfriend she might start getting angry again. But before she could come up with another topic, Lisa spoke again.

'Do you have a boyfriend?' she asked.

'No, not really,' Judith replied

'I bet you're having it with the doctors here then, right? They're all so luscious! What do you think my chances would be? I have a friend who was in here a couple of months ago and she told me she had it with this doctor called Harvey. She said he was really something else! Do you know him?'

Judith pretended not to hear her and gave her back the hairbrush with trembling fingers. Lisa continued talking, as if she didn't really care whether the nurse was listening, but by now Judith couldn't hear her anymore.

Slowly she walked away from the bed, like an automaton, her mind completely absorbed by what Lisa had just said.

Robert Harvey had been to bed with one of his patients? That couldn't possibly be. How could he? A doctor with one of his patients . . . Of course, that wasn't really surprising. He was good-looking, therefore probably popular with his patients. And Judith had no right to point the finger at anyone, considering what she had done with Mike Randall . . .

And then there was also Edouard, with Lady Austin . . . That wasn't surprising either, but now this was becoming a little too much for Judith to take. 'I have to go back to the nursing station,' she breathed before opening the door and walking out.

In the corridor she had to lean against the wall. The mention of Robert Harvey was once again having a powerful effect on her, bringing back memories so powerful she could feel her skin react, and she shivered despite the comfortable temperature. She also remembered Edouard, the moment they had spent in his office, the way he had caressed her with his tongue . . .

The images were still vivid, bringing back this longing she had tried to quieten after the disciplinary hearing. On the whole she had been rather successful, having avoided being alone with her colleagues as well as the patients. She had also managed to keep her lust under control, concentrating on her duties and remembering the dread she had felt at the disciplinary hearing whenever she saw an attractive body. She had vowed to fight her lust, but her body was now seized with desire, her arousal stronger than ever, all those suppressed feelings surfacing again, coming back with a vengeance.

She slowly walked back to the station, her knees buckling under her, her steps uncertain. Hopefully, once she got back to work, there would be things to do, something to keep her mind occupied. As she turned the corner she bumped into Ray, the attendant who was responsible for her ending up in bed with Mike Randall.

'Hi there!' he chirped, grabbing her by the shoulders to stop her from falling. 'You don't look so hot. Are you all right?'

Judith felt her face flush. She was unable to think any longer. A sensation that was only too familiar had seized her, her flesh suddenly set alight and throbbing. She put her hand flat on his chest to retrieve her balance and raised the other on her forehead.

Ray took her arm and opened the door to a nearby utility room, ushering her in. 'What's the matter? Seen something you weren't supposed to?'

'No, I'll be fine,' Judith replied with a faint smile. 'I just felt faint for a moment, but I'm better now.'

'Your face is all red,' he said, making her lean against a sink and caressing her cheek with his finger. 'You're all warm. Do you want to go outside for a moment?'

'No, I'll be fine,' she repeated.

He took a towel from the stack next to the sink and wet it with cold water. Then he neatly folded the towel and delicately wiped her face, tenderly patting her red cheeks. 'Listen,' he said, 'I'm really grateful for your help the other night. I've been looking for you to say thanks. Did everything go OK? I hope you didn't get into any trouble because of me . . .'

Judith looked up at him. Why did he have to mention that night? If he had done his job she never would have ended up in Mike Randall's bed. The best way to fight temptation was to avoid it altogether. But now it was too late. Yet deep within herself she had to admit it wasn't really Ray's fault; she was the one who couldn't resist the sweet temptation.

And even now the mention of that evening only served to trigger her arousal, and that was the last thing Judith needed right now. She looked up at Ray, feeling her vulva clench, wondering if he knew the storm that was raging through her at that very moment.

He took her chin with his fingers and gently brushed her lips with his. 'Thanks again,' he whispered. 'You've been really sweet.'

His kiss took away the last remnant of the wall of defence she had tried to build up around her. Instinctively she pressed her body against his, oblivious to the look of surprise she read on his face. She demurely slid her arms around his neck, returning his kiss, sighing as she felt his arms encircling her waist.

Their lips barely touched but sensually brushed again and again. She closed her eyes and dissolved in his embrace, slightly opening her mouth in an invitation for him to discover its smoothness. She heard him laugh a few times, as if he was both amused and happy by her behaviour. Still he kept on kissing her, his lips growing insistent on hers.

Soon she felt his tongue searching hers, its caress rapidly increasing her arousal. Involuntarily her legs parted and her hips pressed against his thigh. He seemed to immediately guess what she wanted, for his hand wandered down the side of her leg to slide back up under her skirt. His hand felt hot and dry, soft yet scratchy like wool. His fingers travelled up her thigh in large, tantalising circles.

Judith rapidly grew impatient, enjoying his caresses but not wanting to be merely teased much longer. She seized his hand and brought it to her crotch, quickly guiding his fingers inside her panties, moving back slightly to allow him better access, her mouth never letting go of his.

As he softly caressed her silken mound she tossed her head forward and grabbed hold of his arm, forcing his hand to rub back and forth along her wet slit. She held on tight, clutching his biceps with both hands and resting her cheek against his shoulder, her mouth now gasping for air.

He let her move on his hand, standing motionless as she began to frantically ride his wrist, using his arm as a rigid pole against which she pressed her clothed body, his fingers sucked into her wet tunnel. As she opened her eyes she was almost surprised to him standing there. For a moment she had thought that once again she was with her imaginary lover, and all that mattered was her own pleasure.

In this respect, Ray was perfect. He anticipated her needs, clenching his hand into a fist and using his edge of his wrist to tease her tiny, swollen shaft in an up and down motion. He seemed amused by this little wanton that writhed in the palm of his hand, abusing his arm to attain her pleasure, almost bouncing up and down on his fist. Yet he didn't move, did absolutely nothing to stop her.

'Are you always like this?' he whispered in her ear. 'Maybe I should ask to work day shifts more often . . .'

Judith moaned in reply. If he was making fun of her,

so be it. Right now she needed him to fulfil the needs of her body, no matter what he might think of her.

There were voices coming from the other side of the door. Judith knew only too well that anybody could walk in on them at any second. Yet the danger of being discovered was only more exciting for her.

Her nipples pushed hard against the lacy fabric that held them prisoner, but Judith had no time for them. Right now the centre of her universe was between her legs; her slick and tender flesh was begging to be tortured, to submit in pleasure.

The whole of her body was also ablaze. She pressed herself against his arm, brushing the swollen breasts against the bulge of his biceps. Her hips continued to swing up and down, faster, harder.

She sealed her lips on his shoulder, gagging herself to smother the cry of joy that rose in her throat. She didn't care where she was, who she was. Her body was asking and she had to give.

Her climax came and went like an arrow through her loins, piercing her violently and suddenly. She whined loudly, collapsing against Ray's arms. Her heart seemed about to leap out of her chest, pounding furiously. Each beat sent a pulse throbbing through her vulva, like aftershocks of the quake still rumbling through her.

She gasped for air a few times and gave a long, final moan.

Ray just had time to catch her before she fell, guiding her limp body to a broken swivelling armchair near the large sink. The chair had a broken wheel and had been left there to be taken away and repaired. Despite its wobbly balance it did the job, giving Judith a chance to rest until her senses came back.

'You're really something else,' Ray laughed softly, crouching next to her.

Still panting, Judith looked at him and smiled. 'I'm sorry, I don't know what got into me.' He smiled in reply and let his eyes travel over her body. Judith looked at him as well.

Although he no longer seemed surprised by what she had done, she sensed he didn't want to touch her; his eyes rested on her in a way that was merely curious and not lustful.

Judith laughed in turn. 'I really needed that,' she said. 'My life has been hell since I started working here.' His smile changed to a confused expression but he didn't say anything. And she kept on talking, the words came out of her mouth naturally, as if he had been a dear friend and confidante. 'It seems everywhere I look people are trying to seduce me,' she explained. 'Their looks, their touch, even their words excite me. I don't know how to handle this anymore. It's got to the point where I'm afraid of losing my job.' A sob rose in her throat and she stopped talking.

For once it felt good to be able to express her feelings, to tell of the effort she had to make to keep her passion under control. Instinctively she knew she could trust Ray even though she didn't know him very well. She could still get him into trouble for having left her to help Mike Randall out of the bath tub the other night. He had asked her to do his job and so Judith had readily assumed he wouldn't betray her secret. In fact Ray wasn't surprised at all, and once again she saw an amused sparkle in his eyes.

'You just started working here then,' he said. 'You haven't been told, have you?'

'Told what?'

'This is all happening on purpose. It's supposed to be that way.'

Judith still couldn't make sense of what he was saying, and it occurred to her that he was trying to make fun of her.

'What are you talking about?'

'The Special Care Programme, have you heard about it?'

She vaguely shook her head. Indeed she had heard it mentioned a few times, but she hadn't figured out what it was all about, and had never even thought of asking.

'This clinic offers more than medical care, Judith,' Ray slowly said, emphasising each word. 'We are here to care for the patients, to do everything they want us to, *everything*.'

This still didn't make sense to Judith. What exactly did he mean? Before she could ask him he stood up and started to walk towards the door, looking at her one more time before stepping out.

'Don't fight it,' he said. 'Just let it happen. Enjoy it.' The door closed behind him.

His words prompted her memory, and were reminiscent of what Edouard had told her in his office. If her body craved to be pleasured she should just give in. Ray had just told her something similar. Yet somehow Judith doubted they were talking about the same thing.

She slowly stood up and flattened the front of her uniform with the palm of her hand. Once again she had to get back to the station before they came looking for her. This feeling was becoming only too familiar.

Her head sunk into her pillow. Judith opened her eyes and blinked several times, examining the ceiling to see if the images would appear again.

And still they danced in front of her; places, faces. If she closed her eyes the images would disappear, only to be replaced by words in her ears. She turned around and pulled the duvet over her head, trying to escape. But they wouldn't leave her alone, wouldn't let her sleep peacefully.

First it was Edouard's shadow on the curtain around Lady Austin's bed. The way he had kissed and touched the patient whilst Judith silently stood on the other side of the curtain, watching them. She should have known right then and there that something was up.

Later on, Lady Austin's words had also added to the puzzle by mentioning Robert Harvey: 'He can't keep his hands off me when I come here now.' And she had asked Judith to touch her, even to the point of complaining when Judith had refused!

And now the nurse's mind was in a daze. Just like that other morning, when she had come to the stupid conclusion that she had been hypnotised, to serve as some sort of sex slave to the directors of the Clinic. It was actually the other way around, if she could believe Ray. No wonder Edouard had found her accusations so hilarious!

She had been seeing those around her as sources of pleasure, most probably because they were probably feeding on her sensuality, as if she was an involuntary bird of prey.

Now she also understood what Mrs Cox meant: 'After you've been here a few weeks, you will have a different perspective on such situations.' Of course. She was blossoming, the force of her desire only barely awake back then.

But what exactly was going on at the clinic? Ray had mentioned the Special Care Programme, something she had first heard Doctor Marshall talk about at the monthly staff meeting ... 'Because Miss Stanton has not finished her probationary period with us I shall not discuss in detail the issue of our Special Care Programme which she doesn't know about yet ...' She hadn't paid any attention to it back then, but now she realised she should have asked about it.

There was also the cryptic message Mike Randall had given her, although at the time she had thought he was only joking: 'Aren't you supposed to do everything your patients ask you?'

Finally, she now understood the meaning of Jo's words in the shower, speaking about Tania: 'Not a man on this planet can tease a woman the way she does. That's why she got her job here, by the way ...' That morning, Judith had vaguely understood this as meaning that Tania had slept with someone as a favour in order to get her job. But in fact it was the other way around! She had been hired precisely *because* of her skills ...

But where did Judith fit in? Nobody had told her that contact between patients and staff was allowed. Or was it just her imagination running wild again? The more she thought about it, the more improbable it seemed. Yet at the same time it would make things much simpler if it were true. Or was that only wishful thinking on her part?

She sat up in her bed. Of course, it wasn't just her imagination. Now she had something tangible on which to base her assumptions. She had to find out. And this time she wouldn't be stupid enough to confront anybody armed with foolish accusations. She would find out for herself.

Without asking any questions, all she had to do was to keep her ears and eyes open, even snoop around if she had to, but she would keep her mouth shut at all costs.

Strangely, this time she didn't feel any fear at having figured out the truth, if indeed she had. The thought of having been hypnotised and acting against her will had confused and scared her. Now her excitement was fuelled by a feeling of sudden reassurance.

She turned onto her back once again, now hoping to see something on the ceiling, the solution to this enigma. She needed more clues, more information. Everything had to come to her; she couldn't find out the details by coincidence.

Surely there was a way of finding out where the truth lay. There had to be.

Chapter Fourteen

As the doors of the lift opened onto the corridor of the basement, Judith thought she could see a book opening instead; a book in which everything was written, all the answers to her questions.

She slowly walked the length of the corridor, the soles of her shoes making a funny, squeaky sound on the bare tile floor. She didn't know what had prompted her to come downstairs and see Desmond, but somehow she knew he could help her in her quest.

The man was mysterious, in his own way, and this made him strangely attractive. Would he talk to her? He hadn't uttered a word last time . . .

Judith knew she would find a way to get him to talk. If she put together all the information she had so far, she could only come to one conclusion: what Ray had said was true, and as a member of staff Desmond would also be expected to provide physical pleasure to the patients, which is probably what had happened when she had left him alone with the Major.

But how could she be sure? She would have to bluff, to pretend she already knew, and that she was coming to the physiotherapy room to learn more. That was a bit weak, but quite believable.

She turned the corner and immediately stopped in her

steps. Next to the door of the physiotherapy room, on the floor, lay a large spool of chains. Thick, coldly shining links, wound around a metal cylinder that was about waist high. Her heart began to beat fast. What could the clinic possibly need those chains for? Were they just meant as replacements for the chains already hanging in the treatment room? Or were there plans to extend the facilities and build another treatment room? In either case, Judith still didn't know the purpose of using chains in physiotherapy in the first place, but she knew she would find out soon enough.

They seemed to glare back at her, defiantly, reflecting the crude light of the ceiling fixtures, gleaming cruelly, yet invitingly. There was something both threatening and beckoning about them, as if they were instruments for both torture and pleasure. She walked past quickly, seeing her tiny reflection mirrored thousands of times and almost ran until she entered the lobby of the physiotherapy department.

Desmond didn't see her come in. He was in the adjoining treatment room, helping a patient back in her wheelchair, his large back to the door. Just like the other day he was wearing a white polo shirt and track suit trousers. And just like before his movements were gentle and caressing as he delicately deposited the body that seemed ever so frail compared to him.

Judith waited silently, not really knowing how to make her presence known. She glanced around furtively, trying to see whether anybody else was around. This late in the afternoon most of the patients had usually been given their treatment and returned to their room.

'Hello, Judith. Can I help you?'

Judith turned around and recognised Vicky, a short, dark physiotherapist who often had her lunch at the canteen at the same time as her. Vicky was fumbling with her coat, trying to put it on whilst still holding her handbag in one hand.

'I'm waiting for Desmond, I need a word with him . . .'

Vicky smiled. 'Don't keep him here too long, it's after

four. We're supposed to be closed by now.' She walked past Judith and left.

As the door closed Judith ventured another look in the treatment room. Desmond now was kneeling next to the wheelchair, trying to adjust the leg support but obviously experiencing some difficulties.

The mechanism was jammed for some reason, and he had to pry it forcefully. From where she was standing Judith could see the muscles of his shoulder and upper arm playing under his skin, his fingers clutched around a large knob which stubbornly refused to budge.

The patient was a middle-aged woman who winced every minute or so. Both her legs were neatly covered in bandages but still she seemed rather uncomfortable and was probably growing impatient, needing the leg support to be fixed as soon as possible to relieve her pain.

Judith was about to enter the treatment room and ask Desmond if he needed help when the main door opened behind her and another nurse walked in, pushing a wheelchair. She walked past as if Judith wasn't there and headed straight for the treatment room.

'Here,' she told Desmond and the patient. 'I think we'd better use this one. The other should be sent to be repaired instead.' She pushed the wheelchair next to the other one and gestured to Desmond to transfer the patient.

He stood up, unrolling his heavy body, and bent down to pick the patient up in his big arms. The lady demurely slipped her arms around his neck and he lifted her as if she had been a mere twig. The nurse pushed away the defective wheelchair and pulled the other one closer. Desmond bent down, gently deposited the patient once again and watched silently as the nurse rolled the chair and the patient out of the room.

Judith held the door open and both the nurse and the patient thanked her with a smile. As the door closed behind them, she now knew she was alone with Desmond. She made her way into the treatment room.

Desmond was busy tidying up the place, putting the

jars back on the shelf, discarding the dirty towels into the large laundry basket. If he saw Judith come in, he didn't acknowledge her presence.

Once again she realised she hadn't heard him speak a single word and started to wonder if he was mute. She came near the treatment table and hoisted herself onto its smooth leather surface. Legs dangling over the side, she began staring at Desmond, trying to figure out what she would say to him once he decided to stop ignoring her.

As he turned to face her a large smile appeared on his face, his white teeth making his skin look even darker.

'How can I help?' he asked.

She was so surprised by his baritone voice that it took her a few seconds to react. Yes, Desmond could talk, and each of his words was a velvet caress, as if flowing from a cavern, deep and warm.

He came closer and stood right in front of her, tilting his head slightly, like a intrigued child. Obviously he had no idea what she had come for; how could he? Judith tried to think of what to say, of asking the question that abounded in her mind but without actually saying it. She decided to bluff it.

'I've been told,' she began, 'about the Special Care Programme, about the staff and the patients. I know everything . . .'

His smile shifted to the corner of his mouth and Judith thought perhaps he could tell she was lying. Or maybe she was completely off the track . . . No, if he didn't know about the Special Care Programme he would look puzzled, not amused.

'But there are still things that intrigue me,' she continued, 'and I want to know more.'

His eyes looked down, glancing towards her legs, and the smile disappeared from his face, but he didn't reply. Judith knew she was on to something, otherwise it would show in his face. He knew, he could confirm her doubts. But instead he turned away and went back to the shelves, placing the pots and jars in order, his indifference telling Judith he had nothing to say to her.

'I want to know,' she insisted.

'What does it matter what you know,' he finally replied. 'What is important is what you feel . . .'

She wished he had stayed and stared at her some more. Perhaps she could have smiled and tried to charm him somehow. But now her mind was working on finding words instead, something to say that would make him a little more talkative.

She looked up in exasperation; this was tougher than she would have thought. Above her head the chains were still attached to the ceiling, quietly hanging in bundles, the leather cuffs relaxed and yawning. The chains . . . What were the chains for? Treatment or pleasure? She had to find out.

Desmond still had his back turned. Judith reached up above her head and grabbed one of the cuffs, pulling hard. The thin piece of string that held the bundle together gave easily and the chain unrolled, coming down in a loud, rattling cascade.

He turned around suddenly and looked at Judith. In his eyes she read both surprise and admiration, and immediately knew she had done the right thing. But now that she had his attention, what else was she to do?

The leather piece was lightly resting on her lap, the chain released to its complete length. Delicately seizing the cuff between her fingers, Judith held out her hand and presented it to Desmond.

'I want to know,' she repeated. The tone of her own voice surprised her, halfway between a plea and an order. It must have had some sort of effect on Desmond for he silently walked back towards her. This time he wasn't smiling but had a rather severe expression.

He came so close that she instinctively parted her legs. Their bodies touched and she felt his hard stomach press against her breasts, thinking – and hoping – he was going to touch her with his hands as well. Instead he slowly reached up and pulled on a chain next to the one she had unwound.

It came down with the same clinking noise and the

cuff brushed her shoulder before landing on the treatment table. Desmond then pulled on another chain, and so on, until six chains came hanging around Judith, two at the head of the table, two at the foot, and two in the middle. For a few seconds the noise was deafening, then there was utter silence.

He looked down and peered into her eyes, silently asking her if she wanted him to continue. She tried to read his eyes but failed. What could he be thinking? A minute ago he seemed totally disinterested, and now he was doing exactly what she was wishing him to do ...

His hands fell on her thighs and she felt the warmth of his large hands through her dress. Despite his impressive size his hips were incredibly narrow and Judith could let him come close enough for their bodies to touch without having to part her legs very wide.

He just stared at her, as if waiting for her to tell him to continue. In reply she squeezed her thighs against his hips and almost immediately felt the snake uncoil at his crotch.

At that moment she realised what Desmond did in addition to giving massages to injured patients: he was also a slave to their desires. She didn't have to utter a word, and he would understand what she wanted him to do, in fact he probably took his own pleasure out of silent obedience.

His big hands rose to her chest and his thick fingers started to unbutton the front of her uniform. Another man undressing her, this was something she was beginning to get used to ... Only this time the man wasn't trying to seduce her. He was undressing her simply because he could feel that was what she wanted.

The buttons looked incredibly small in his big fingers, yet he never fumbled, slowly undoing them one after the other. His dark fingers contrasted with the whiteness of her uniform, his skin leathery against the crisp cotton.

As he worked his way down, the cool air of the room flowed inside her dress and strangely mixed with the heat of her body. He undid the last button and slid the dress off her shoulders, using only his fingers to gently grip the fabric, never touching her skin.

He brought his hands to her chest once more, taking hold of the clasp that held her bra fastened at the front. Judith looked down at his hands, fascinated to see his blackness so close to her own white skin, but still not touching it. He undid her bra and took it off her, gently folding it and placing on the small table nearby.

His hands then glided under her armpits and he gently lifted her off the table and onto her feet. Judith felt like a small child being undressed by an adult. His touch was just as gentle as if she were a baby, his movements just as loving.

Once she stood up her dress fell to the floor and he bent down to pick it up, folding it neatly and placing it next to her bra. Then he knelt next to her and lifted her feet one after the other, taking her shoes off. Her panties quickly followed, his thumbs grasping the elastic waistband to pull it down.

As she stood completely naked and barefoot on the cold floor he stood up and lifted her by the armpits once again to make her lie on the table, her calves and feet sticking out at one end. Moving to the end of the table and standing between her parted knees he then got to work, placing both hands on her right thigh.

Judith shivered as she finally felt his hands on her. Propping herself up on her elbows, she lifted her head and looked at his hands, now gently massaging her legs, black velvet on white silk. A heat wave travelled from his hands to her skin, and then all the way up her body to her breasts.

Her nipples contracted readily, her arousal coming to life. His hands were capable of holding the whole of her thigh in their grasp, enveloping it like a thick, soft stocking. She felt them move up and down both legs, massaging her tired muscles, kneading and awakening them.

Although strong and expert, his touch was also sensuous, his fingertips at times barely touching the tender skin on the inside of Judith's legs, slowly snaking up, stopping a mere moment from her soft vulva before changing direction and sliding back down again towards her naked feet.

After a while he concentrated on her feet alone, pinching her toes and pulling on them one after the other, inserting his large finger between them and prying them apart.

Judith now felt relaxed and let her head fall back, enjoying his treatment. The last things she saw before closing her eyes were the chains. She remembered that was what she had really come for, but right now she didn't care much for them. It could wait.

Desmond seized her ankles, one in each hand, and lifted her feet up, pulling them towards his face. Before Judith could realise what he was doing, she felt his lips close around her big toe and his tongue twirl around it.

A bolt of excitement flashed up her leg and through her loins, and she moaned loudly. His mouth then slowly travelled from one foot to the other, licking and sucking each toe in turn.

The feeling was incredibly powerful, his tongue silken and moist, bathing her feet in soft warmth. She felt a rush of dew collect at the junction of her legs, and her arousal mounted. So far he had only touched her legs and her feet, but she felt more excited than ever before in her life.

She wanted him to come closer, to work on the whole of her body, but she decided to wait before asking him. She knew he would get to it eventually. And her guess was soon proven right.

Putting her feet down, his hands slowly caressed her thighs in an upward move, his thumbs brushing the inside of her legs, his other fingers the outside. When he got to the soft junction his hands parted either way and his thumbs completely forwent her downy mound, his fingers merely tracing the sides of her buttocks.

His thumbs came together again over her belly-button and his fingers continued gliding upwards, covering the whole of her abdomen, his fingertips slightly brushing the underside of her breasts. She moaned again. Under his touch her skin kept growing hotter until it was almost burning.

By now he was bending over her, just a few inches above her limp body. For Judith was now so relaxed she could no longer move. She opened her eyes and looked at him, but he wasn't looking at her.

At the end of the table, between her parted feet, she could see the bulge of his erection pushing at the nylon of his white track suit. Did he want her? Most probably. And, of course, Judith wanted him as well. But not just yet.

His hands then moved to her arms and gently settled on her wrists. She liked the way he towered above her, she liked to think that once he held her hands she couldn't escape from his grasp, that she wouldn't want to anyway.

Slowly, his hands glided up, fingertips first, along the length of her arms. His thumbs lightly brushed the sides of her breasts and she shuddered. She liked the way he proceeded, slowly, inch by inch, covering areas of her body which weren't usually so sensitive whilst completely forgoing her breasts and her vulva. But by now Judith was also growing impatient. How long would he keep on teasing her like this? She parted her legs slightly, hoping he would get her message.

But he didn't seem to. His hands briefly paused on her shoulders and cupped them, closing around them in a snug fit, his thumbs pointing down on the edge of her breasts. His wrists were just an inch above her erect nipples, all he had to do was to bend his elbows and he would touch them.

Instead, his hands continued their discovery, his fingertips following the slow curve of her shoulders and gently closing around her throat. Judith's heart began pounding fast when she realised he could very well strangle her at this moment. Putting his thumbs together at the front and his fingertips touching at the back, he could encircle her neck completely. She stopped breathing for a moment, suddenly worried.

But he soon let go, his fingers running up along her scalp, burying themselves into the soft mass of her hair. He now held her head in both hands, the thickness of his large fingers pulling at the clip that held her hair up and quickly forcing it to slip off.

Then he let go to put his hands flat on either side of her head, and she finally felt his face descending towards hers. Soon his lips were on hers, thick, soft and cushiony, gently capturing her mouth. Still, only his lips touched her. The rest of his body was hovering above her, large and domineering, ever so close but not touching her, his elbows locked to stop him from crushing her.

But by then she wanted to feel his body on hers, even if it meant being smothered by this mass of muscles. Her hands refused to move when she tried lifting them off the table to touch him, as if she had been paralysed. Her mind and her body were no longer connected, her limbs refused to do what her brain asked. However, she knew there was no need to move. Soon, Desmond would take care of everything.

And even though his body had no contact with hers, Judith could feel his heat radiating through his clothes and enveloping her. She was ever so small underneath him, a frail and pale figure at the mercy of a dark giant.

His lips soon grew moist as his kisses became more and more passionate, gripping hers in a tight embrace, toying with them with his tongue.

Judith felt hot against the thin leather covering of the treatment table, sandwiched between two black entities, both soft and caressing, only one of them alive.

His lips let go of her mouth and gently slid down along her jaw to nestle in her neck. As she opened her eyes Judith could see nothing but the muscles of his shoulder playing under his skin, his big arms still locked to keep his body from touching hers.

Yet down there, at the junction of her legs, every now and again, she could feel his erect phallus brush her thigh through the nylon fabric of his trousers, the throbbing shaft quickly growing impatient. Obviously, Desmond had to make a tremendous effort, both physically and mentally, not to fall on her and possess her. But Judith instinctively sensed that, for this man, his own pleasure didn't matter. He was there to serve her.

She felt his ear brush against her cheek and was surprised by its leathery hotness. The whole of Desmond seemed to be made of fabric, at times velvet, at times leather. Always smooth, always dark, always warm.

She was tempted to stick out a timid tongue and caress his earlobe but, just before she could move, Desmond's head had already resumed its journey, now slowly following the sinewy path of her shoulder, covering her warm skin with even warmer kisses, his chin at times brushing against her swollen breasts.

Judith began panting. His lips seemed to trigger something every time they touched her skin, like a series of live wires directly connected to her loins. Never before had she been so aroused, his teasing seemingly not progressing beyond smooth kisses on parts of her body that weren't usually so sensitive. She could only guess what would happen if he eventually dared touch her breasts . . .

A second later she found out. He took his time, of course, his lips merely touching her skin, progressing at a snail's pace towards her erect nipple, pausing, coming back up towards her shoulder, then resuming their descent.

Judith shuddered and moaned at the same time, feeling an incredible, overwhelming desire to simply wrap herself around this taut body. She also wanted to grab his head with both hands and direct his mouth onto her swollen breasts. Yet despite this powerful storm raging within her, she was enjoying his deliberately slow method, each of his kisses, no matter where he lay them.

She writhed on the table, her body now coming out of its slumber, alight with a fire that seemed to extend all the way down to her toes. At the same time her hands recovered their strength and she took hold of Desmond's narrow hips, pulling them towards her crotch, wanting to feel his throbbing maleness against her own flesh.

But he immediately pulled away before she could feel no more than a mere brush of his erect phallus. Judith was somewhat disappointed, and rather puzzled. She was more than ready for him, and his desire was also obvious, so why wouldn't he want her to touch him?

He walked around the table and stood behind her head. In a couple of swift moves he caught each of her wrists and neatly wrapped them with the leather cuffs that were attached to the chains. He then pulled on the free end of each chain, adjusting its length so that Judith's arms were pulled up and she could no longer move them.

He then walked back down to the foot of the table and captured her ankles the same way. By then only Judith's back barely touched the table; her arms and legs were now prisoner's of the chains. Her head hung back, her blond tresses now set free brushed the table.

Her heart began to beat fast, both in apprehension and excitement. In her mind her doubts were now in the process of being confirmed. Soon she would know exactly what the chains were for. Although she had planned on receiving a verbal explanation, a demonstration would now be deliciously appropriate.

However her position soon grew uncomfortable. The joints of her shoulders and her hips were stretched to their limit and already felt slightly painful. Yet being restrained like this was a novelty, and the way her parted legs displayed her moist flesh in a sexy, wicked way aroused her even more.

Slowly progressing around the table, Desmond continued adjusting the chains, constantly forcing her legs to open wider. The air stream of the ventilation system descended straight unto Judith's exposed vulva, a soothing caress, yet not sufficiently cool to ease the fire that bathed her moist flesh.

Finally Desmond bent down and opened a drawer in

the large cabinet by the door, taking out a large piece of leather and bringing it to the table. He unfolded it slowly, and Judith was able to figure out it was some kind of corset, with about half a dozen straps and buckles making clinking sounds as he laid it flat on the table.

Supporting her back with one hand, he slid the corset underneath her, then brought the sides up and proceeded to fasten it around her waist. The piece of leather snugly covered her abdomen from the underswell of her breasts to the edge of her downy mound. On either side a thick metal hook was also fastened to the corset.

Desmond slid one arm under her back and lifted her clear off the table, seizing the hooks with his free hand, one after the other, and hooking her up to the last two chains that still hung at her midriff.

By now Judith hung in a horizontal position high up above the table, her arms and legs restrained and held apart, her waist harnessed to support the rest of her body.

Desmond came to stand behind her and took her head up in his hands to bring it to his level. He would no longer have to bend down to touch her, she had been brought up to his level.

A wicked smile played on his face as his lips came to touch hers, upside down. This time his kisses were nothing like what they had been before. His tongue went searching for hers immediately, caressing the inside of her mouth, at times also venturing outside and gently licking her chin.

Soon he held her head with only one hand and the other went where it had not dared before. Judith could see nothing but the blackness of his neck, but she could feel his hand now drawing closer to her swollen breasts. She moaned against his mouth. At last.

His fingers cupped them each in turn, the large hand able to cover the whole of the milky skin, the nipple growing harder in his palm. Soon he let go of her head completely and let it dangle backwards, then moved to the side of the table again.

Judith's body hung level with his chest. He quickly let

his hands run all over her, grabbing and releasing both her breasts, caressing her waist through the thin leather of the harness, then moving down to follow the curve of her hips.

She couldn't see anything but the shelf on the wall behind her, and upside down at that. Yet the touch of his hands on her naked skin felt even warmer than before and the image of his black fingers on her pale skin once again appeared in her mind.

One of his hands was on her legs, caressing the sensitive part behind her knees, then moving to the inside where the skin became baby-soft. Suddenly she felt the tip of his thick finger lightly rubbing the swollen bud of her clitoris.

Judith let out a faint scream, the muscles of her stomach contracting violently as she felt a bolt of lightning pierce her from deep within her loins to the very tip of her nipples, as if his finger was electrified.

Then it glided down her slippery folds, following the deep valley until it disappeared inside her slick vagina. She could feel it within her, searching her very core, triggering her pleasure from the inside. She moaned again.

He withdrew and slowly drew his hand up over her mound, his wet finger hovering above her curly bush and slicking the hairs. For a while his hand remained there and worked back and forth, spreading her love-juices from her wet folds to her bush, combing it with soaked fingers.

Each time he glided over her stiff clitoris Judith gasped, each passage seemingly briefer than the previous one, her bud now aching to feel his hand rubbing it instead of merely teasing it.

After a while she lifted her head up, laboriously, and looked at Desmond. He turned and looked at her in turn, as if sensing her eyes on him. For a while they held each other's stare, Judith trying to read intentions in his eyes, Desmond not letting anything show.

But she let her head fall back. Then she immediately

felt him raise one knee onto the table for support and his face swiftly dropped onto her chest. His hit was direct, his lips landing directly on her nipple and gently grabbing it.

The centre of her arousal shifted, her breasts quivering under the assault of his mouth, sending delicious waves down her abdomen. He laid one hand on her chest whilst the other supported her back, tilting her body this way and that, to provide better access for his mouth.

Judith's breasts were wickedly tossed from one side to the other, the tender skin on the underswell brushing against the edge of the leather corset time and time again. He devastated them with his mouth, his dark lips pinching her skin into tiny folds, his tongue circling around the erect nipple and flickering over it at a dizzying speed.

Judith rapidly grew even more excited and began writhing uncontrollably, adding to the motion Desmond had imparted to her body, tugging at the chains that supported her ankles.

This was more than she had ever thought she would be able to take; her arousal was extremely intense but her mind was unable to foresee the moment when her pleasure would finally release her. She could sense Desmond getting excited as well, but his behaviour never let anything show, his mouth and his hands still delicately caressing her.

At one point his hand strayed again, quickly hovering over the leather corset and once again seeking her wet vulva. His index finger slid over her slippery folds, back and forth, gently teasing her stiff clitoris and gradually increasing the pressure of his touch. His tongue continued to worry her nipple, and the line of contact between her breasts and her loins soon became overloaded.

Her pleasure pierced her and she bucked violently, tensing every muscle of her limbs and sending the chains rattling loudly a couple of times. Through her half-shut eyes she saw Desmond grin, amused by the results of his ministrations.

Judith's head fell back and her mind went numb. As usual, she felt as if she was floating on air, as she often did when she was swept by pleasure. Only this time she really was hanging in mid-air, yet her wrists and ankles no longer felt the restraint of the leather cuffs. She sighed and smiled, still reeling from her climax.

She felt Desmond getting busy around the table, going to each chain in turn and gradually lowering her until her back almost touched the table. Yet he never touched the cuffs, obviously not planning on releasing her just yet. Once all the chains were adjusted and Judith hung level with his hips, he slipped an arm under her back, lifting her in his arms to unhook the harness.

Judith was puzzled by his procedure. Why wasn't he undoing the buckles on her ankles and wrists? How long did he plan to keep her hanging like this?

He went to the foot of the table and reached up to the ceiling, unfastening some sort of mechanism that prevented the chains from sliding along the rails, and then did the same thing with the chains that held Judith's arms.

The noise overwhelmed her dozy mind, and she ceased trying to figure out what he was planning to do. All she knew was that the strain on her hips and shoulders eased up when he pushed her ankles and her wrists together and she felt relieved.

His hands took hold of her tiny waist, one on each side, almost encircling it completely with his large fingers, and he rolled her onto her stomach. He rapidly crossed her legs and uncrossed them the other way, the chains swapping places, and did the same with her arms.

Judith now lay flat on her stomach, her legs and arms spread out once again. And the strain returned to her shoulders and hips, at least until Desmond lifted her off the table and hooked the harness onto the chains.

And Judith finally understood what he was up to. Desmond wasn't planning on releasing her at all. All he had done was to turn her over and re-arrange the chains so that she now hung face down, her arms and legs still wide apart.

Her hair fell all around her face like a curtain, and if she peered down she could see her breasts dangling with the pull of gravity, her nipples slightly rubbing on the surface of the table. Although initially they puckered further from the leathery caress, this soon grew somewhat uncomfortable, the skin not really gliding but dragging along painfully as her body swayed in mid-air.

She was just about to protest when she felt Desmond's hands lifting both her breasts up with his hand. In his other hand he held a bottle of talcum powder, which he sprinkled on the table and then spread evenly in a large circle. Putting the bottle aside, he then ran his powdered hand across Judith's breasts.

Her body swayed slightly and she immediately felt the soft caress of the powdered leather on her nipples. This unexpected change sent a sigh of appreciation to her lips. Then she felt Desmond's hands give a slight push on her hips, and her body began swinging from side to side.

She watched her nipples brushing on the table, left to right and back again, the twin peaks seemingly growing stiffer and longer in an attempt to increase the intensity of the caress. The minty scent of the powder rose to her flaring nostrils and warmed her mind.

Despite the restraints of her wrists her hands were warm, and now itching to move, to caress, to tease. But she knew it was impossible. The black giant's mission was to take Judith to the height of pleasure, he would probably never let her touch him.

Yet she longed to feel him, to caress every inch of this mass of flesh, to lose herself in the embrace of his big arms, to discover the black rod that palpitated under the thin fabric of his trousers. But right now it was out of the question. She had wanted to know, and she had to remain a docile pupil until his explanation was complete.

As her body continued swaying, thoughts began racing through her mind and she gradually understood the real nature of this unusual situation. Although at first it seemed he was a slave to her desires, that he would want nothing but to give her pleasure, at this point it appeared there was a role reversal in progress. Judith was no longer in control, she hadn't asked for what Desmond was doing. She had, in turn, become his submitted slave.

The tables had been turned, once again. Just like when she had pounced on Jo in the stock room, the victim had become the attacker. It had been the same pattern with Mike Randall: he had asked her to pleasure him but in the end she had been in control of both her desire and his.

All this had happened, not by accident, but through the force of her own will. Even now, with Desmond, she had silently agreed to be hung like this, she could have backed out. Yet her instincts had told her that obedience was the key to sweet pleasure.

And indeed it was. Her nipples were on fire, the dry caress of the powdered leather now generating a strange heat that radiated throughout her body. Then she felt Desmond's hand on the side of her buttocks stopping the swaying movement. What else lay ahead?

Her body stopped moving, and Judith didn't have the strength to generate any sort of movement either. Once again her vulva was screaming to be pleased and she wondered how long it would take for pleasure to sweep her again.

She heard Desmond move, the rustling sound of the nylon trousers louder than before. Gathering some strength, she lifted her head and managed to turn it slightly in his direction.

Her neck quickly grew sore and she had to drop her head again, but not without having had time to notice that he was now naked. She sighed. He was there, just a few inches from her, yet she couldn't touch him. She lifted her head again, desperately trying to catch his eyes. But then she remembered he was there for her own pleasure as well, all she had to do was ask...

'Come here!' she said in a loud voice.

She sensed him obediently walking to the head of the

table. Through the tangled mass of her hair she could see his phallus, long and thick and dark as coal, the tiny opening in the black head silently gaping at the ceiling. She licked her lips, now wanting to taste him.

As if reading her mind he gently lifted her chin in one hand and brushed the hair from her face with the other, then slowly thrust his throbbing member into her waiting mouth.

Judith was elated. He knew what she wanted, he had obeyed her command. And now he pulsed on her tongue, slowly sliding back and forth, in and out of the wet embrace of her lips. She moaned loudly. Despite her precarious position, she was still in charge, her submission wasn't complete.

He supported her head in both hands now, standing immobile, letting Judith thrust with her head. However, she soon grew tired and slackened her rhythm. She thought he would take over by moving his hips, but instead, he gave a gentle push on her shoulder and Judith's body began swaying again, this time from head to foot instead of sideways.

Her nipples rediscovered the soft caress of the powdered table and her arousal mounted again, resurrected with a fury. Her mouth grew impatient, sucking and licking the hard rod that stiffened with delight, the tip of her tongue pushing at the tiny mouth that seeped in anticipation. She could feel him hardening still under this assault, yet the rest of his body never even twitched.

Obviously his erection was for her own benefit, as if she could continue her caresses forever and never feel the jutting of his pleasure. He was there for her to enjoy, he was completely hers.

She relished him as if he were the first and last man, tasting him with all her senses, at times letting go of him completely and feeling him brush back and forth along her cheek, nudging him with her nose. Her whole face toyed with him, like a kitten with a rubber mouse, moving on him back and forth and sideways, caressing him with her mouth, her tongue, her lips, her chin, her cheeks, even her nose.

All the while his fingertips on her jaw helped her keep her head up, supporting it but without guiding it. After a while however she was tempted to try his obedience again.

'Enough,' she said. 'Now go on with what you were doing before.'

He went away silently, and Judith's heart started to pound in anticipation. What would he do next? Obviously he couldn't guess what she wanted, for she didn't even know herself. But he must have some idea in his mind...

She soon found out when she felt him kneel on the table, between her parted legs. His hips caressed the inside of her legs and she felt his thick shaft nudge at her entrance. Immediately she wanted him inside.

'Fuck me!' she heard herself whine. 'What are you waiting for?'

He entered her and she screamed with joy. And again the swinging motion resumed, back and forth, his hands on her buttocks pushing her away and letting her swing back, her wet tunnel thrusting on him.

She felt him fill her and then escape repeatedly, the dark shaft possessing her through her own motion, its swollen head inserting itself and stretching the slick walls of her vagina in a delicious assault.

His hips brushed against the side of her legs, his smooth skin caressing hers. By then he was holding her by the knees, pushing her away and letting her slide back onto him. He didn't move this time either, letting only the swinging motion of her body do the work.

Her nipples were happy again, running back and forth on the table, connecting with her loins in a long, tickled line inside her abdomen. She moaned again, twisting her wrists in an effort to grab hold of the chain.

The metal felt cold in her palm but she grasped it with all her strength, bending her elbows and pulling herself even further up. Her level of energy amazed her. The swinging motion imparted by Desmond's hands on her wasn't enough anymore, she needed to increase the speed, the range, the intensity. She pulled hard, her biceps burning under her own weight, trying to increase the momentum of her body. She swung up and she let herself fall back down again, impaling herself onto Desmond's thick rod, feeling him penetrate her even further.

He laughed loudly, his deep voice reverberating around the room. His hand then landed on her behind in a sharp slap and sent needles through her loins, followed by a hot wave of pleasure. The dark giant seemed amused by this little wanton that now desperately pulled on her chains, sending them rattling frantically, using them to wriggle her hips onto his shaft.

She needed to move on him, no longer content to just swing back and forth passively. But the harness around her waist and the complicated position of her ankles were playing against her. All she could control was her arms, all she could do was to laboriously lift herself up and fall back down freely.

Her vulva impaled itself again and again, the thick rod filling her more and more each time, to the limit, in a somewhat painful but pleasant fit. The strain on her breasts was also considerable. They hung freely and bobbed slightly as she let herself fall back down, hitting the table with a sharp flap, sending bolts of pleasure-pain through the whole of her body.

Desmond didn't need to move, she could take care of her own pleasure. Already she could feel it mounting, burning inside her, along the line that connected her breasts with her tiny, swollen shaft.

Her climax was like dropping a large stone in a pond, sending one major impulse through her loins, followed by ripples upon ripples of smaller waves, all starting from the same point, all radiating through her body in circles of decreasing intensity.

She let go with an ultimate sob, her head dropping forward one last time. The sweat of her effort trickled down her back and underneath the leather harness, collecting in a wet line between her buttocks. She panted, exhausted but happy.

Yet it wasn't over. Desmond was still inside her, throbbing under the clenching seizures of her slick vagina. Just as she stopped feeling the reeling waves of pleasure subsiding into oblivion, he began to move.

His hand grabbed one of the straps of the harness to stop her from swaying, and his hips began thrusting. Judith screamed with joy, her tiny bud still sensitive yet ready to be awakened again. His free hand landed on her behind repeatedly, smarting the sensitive skin, making her moan each time. His momentum soon grew frantic, his hips thrusting forcefully inside her and out again, his thick shaft hardening still.

By now he moved so fast that she could feel his balls hitting her mound, his hips forcing hers apart even wider, each jab sending a wave through her body that once again made her breasts wobble.

She heard him grunt behind her, his voice echoing hers as she felt her pleasure mounting for the third time, insidious, slowly bubbling to the surface and growing thick at the same time. She was too exhausted even to moan, her limp body barely feeling anything but the pleasure that swept her.

At the same time she felt Desmond pull her against his hips and keep her there, the shaft inside her jerking violently and a strangled sob coming out of his mouth. A second later she felt him fall on top of her, his hands landing flat on the table on either side of her breasts, his face descending upon her back.

His member was still inside her, its size diminishing quickly, his honey oozing out slowly, its acrid smell filling the room. She recognised the scent, the same aroma she had noted after she had left him alone with Major Johnson: the scent of male pleasure. Now she knew.

But what Desmond had told her was also still present in her mind. It wasn't important what she knew, what really mattered was what she felt. And she felt good.

His arm slid across her chest and lifted her up, his other hand fumbling at the hook to release the harness. The man was obviously weaker by now, as was Judith, drunk with pleasure, still reeling from its effect.

The chains were released one after the other, her hands first and then her feet. Now she lay flat on the table, her ankles and wrists still prisoners of the cuffs, but the strain of the chains now neutralised.

Desmond hovered on top of her for a while, licking the sweat off her back with the tip of his tongue. After a moment he undid the buckles that held the cuffs around her wrists and gently massaged her tender skin.

Judith looked up and was almost surprised by the sight of his thick, black fingers on her thin, pale wrist. The soft leather hadn't left any marks, which was rather amazing considering the weight her arms had to support.

Desmond's large hand slowly brushed her hair off her face and his lips deposited a faint kiss on her cheek. She closed her eyes and smiled. He lay on top of her for a while, supporting himself on his elbows, his cheek softly settling on hers, the heat of his body a comforting embrace in which Judith forgot herself.

Chapter Fifteen

Elizabeth Mason's perfume was nice, but after a while could become somewhat nauseating. She was sitting next to the patient on the leather, looking as comfortable as if she were having tea instead of removing Lisa's bandages.

Judith was standing by her side, bending down towards her and holding a metal tray. This proximity, although necessary, was quickly growing tiresome for the nurse, her back now sorely complaining.

On top of that, Judith hated the way the doctor kept talking all the time, seemingly not needing to stop and breathe every now and then. Everything Doctor Mason said sounded childish, especially the way in which she described to Lisa every step of the bandage removal.

'Now all I need is to take these tiny scissors here,' she said, like a mother talking to a small child, 'and make just a little bit of a cut on the fabric. You be a good girl and don't move. All right, sweetheart?'

Lisa didn't reply, but then again she didn't need to. She looked at Judith and then rolled her eyes up in exasperation.

Yet the doctor's hands were quick and expert, removing each layer of bandage and discarding it into a small container that Judith was holding for her.

Judith couldn't understand why they hadn't brought a rolling table or some other kind of mobile tray. It would surely look out of place in the bedroom but would be much more useful. Or else it might have been more convenient to bring the patient to a treatment room.

Instead, doctor and patient both sat on the dark red leather couch, like two friends having a chat. Meanwhile Judith's back was slowly dying in pain, although all she had to hold was a small tray with a few pairs of scissors and a small bowl to receive the soiled gauze.

To her right the sun shone through the window at such an angle that it only hit Judith's arm. She felt it burning her, yet because of this unconventional set-up it was impossible for Judith to change places.

Layer after layer came off and the procedure was soon over. Lisa immediately reached to the side table to pick up a hand mirror and hold it up to her face. Her nose was a bit swollen and showed a few, tiny red marks, and two large purple blotches hung under her eyes. However, this was entirely normal and nothing would show after a few days. The nose itself didn't look very different, albeit slightly shorter.

Doctor Mason smiled contentedly, obviously pleased at having done a good job, but Lisa's mouth twitched a few times and a sob escaped from her lips.

'It's ... It's horrible!' she whined nervously.

Doctor Mason continued smiling sweetly. 'Not to worry,' she said. 'Once the swelling's gone it will be just perfect.'

'No!' Lisa cried. 'It's horrible! I hate it!'

Her smile quickly disappearing, Doctor Mason sighed and stood up. 'Just give it a few days. Once it's all healed, once you're back home, everybody will tell you how nice it looks ...'

'I can't face anybody with a nose like this!' Lisa screamed. 'How can I ever go home? I could never dare show my face!'

'You'll have to,' Doctor Mason added with a sigh of impatience. 'Mrs Cox will be here in just a few minutes to make you sign the release papers. You'll be going home tomorrow.'

'Tomorrow? But I don't want to! Not looking like this!'

Doctor Mason sighed again and stood up, looking at Judith. 'You deal with her,' she ordered. 'I have better things to do.' She walked out of the room and slammed the door behind her.

Judith bit her lower lip. She felt resentful, knowing that it wasn't ethical to leave a patient in such a distressed state. Now it was up to her to calm Lisa down, something that Doctor Mason should have done herself. This was especially tricky considering how difficult Lisa had been over the last few days. She deposited the tray and the bowl on the side table and sat next to Lisa.

'She's right, you know,' she told the girl. 'In a couple of days the marks will be all gone and you'll have the prettiest nose.'

'Really?' Lisa sobbed. 'I hate it, it's too short.'

'I think it's very nice. You just need a bit of time to get accustomed to it, that's all.'

In reply the girl tilted her head onto Judith's shoulders, letting her tears roll down the nurse's uniform. Judith didn't know what else to say. All she could think about is that she had to be very careful around Lisa, and that because her probation period wasn't over, any complaint from her patient would look bad and perhaps even compromise her future. She couldn't risk that, not now that she had come so close to finding out the truth about the Special Care Programme.

In addition, she knew that Mrs Cox was supposed to be coming to Lisa's room to make her sign the release papers, and she felt it was important that the girl calmed down beforehand.

She looked at her from the corner of her eye. Lisa's head was still gently resting on the nurse's shoulder, and she did seem to have calmed down already. Quite relieved, Judith encircled the girl's waist with one arm and gently caressed the silken hair with the other hand.

Lisa was sweet after all, a grown woman still not ready

to let go of her spoilt childhood. After a few seconds she snuggled up to the nurse, writhing against the white cotton of the uniform, and Judith felt the warmth of her young skin seeping through the silk pyjamas.

The small hand landed on Judith's thigh, hot and slightly moist. Lisa looked up at her.

'Do you think I'm pretty?' she asked, a tear still pearling in the corner of her right eye.

'Of course,' Judith replied. 'I think you're very pretty.'

'I think you're pretty too . . .'

The pale lips touched Judith's cheek and took some time before pulling away. Judith looked at her patient and smiled in turn. She was happy to have succeeded in changing the girl's frame of mind and pleased by Lisa's friendliness

'You're very sweet,' Judith said.

But just as she spoke, Lisa's eyes turned dry and lit up in a weird sparkle 'Am I really?' she asked in a rather sarcastic tone.

Judith was surprised by this sudden change and didn't reply.

'I like to think that I'm a bitch,' Lisa continued. 'People often tell me that I am. I don't know if it's true, but I'd like to be a bitch. That way I can get everything I want, and I can also get everybody to do whatever I want . . .' Her hand slid up Judith's thigh, snake-like under her dress, and her index finger came poking at the nurse's crotch.

Judith shuddered, both in amazement and, curiously, in fear. At that moment she understood there was a difference between the girl she had met in the operating room a couple of days ago and had again seen sitting next to her just a few minutes ago, and the other Lisa who was demanding and spoilt. This was like a double personality, and Judith didn't quite know how to deal with it. But above all she could only think of how she had to do her best to avoid making Lisa angry.

'I was told the staff here are supposed to do everything the patients ask them,' the girl continued. 'Is that true?'

Judith breathed deeply. What was Lisa up to? What did she know? Obviously, this idea that the staff was supposed to yield to the desires of the patients had to come from someone ... But who had told her? And why was she bringing it up now?

Did she only want confirmation from her nurse, or would she have the nerve to ask her to engage in some sort of sexy role-playing game?

Looking down, Judith saw Lisa's nipples growing stiff under the white pyjamas, and she felt her own nipples replying in turn. The girl noticed them as well and burst out laughing.

'You're just as horny as I am, aren't you? I should have known ... Come on then, be a good nurse and do as I please. If I can't get the nose I wanted at least I'll have something to remember.'

She smiled wickedly and covered the whole of Judith's crotch with her hand, making the nurse shiver despite herself. Lisa laughed again, obviously amused by the way she could get the young nurse to react, as if it was just a game to her.

Yet in Judith's mind there was nothing to laugh about. Once again she was about to become a victim to her own lust, even though this time she was highly aware of it and she was still able to fight it. But she could sense she had to obey, being somewhat afraid of Lisa, knowing she couldn't refuse to do what the girl would ask without running the risk of making her angry.

And just as before she hesitated, also knowing that she couldn't comply to the girl's demands because Lisa was her patient. She had promised herself she would never again be weak ...

And on top of it all, she also knew Mrs Cox could walk into the room at any moment. Curiously, this last thought only served to fuel her desires. If she were to be an obedient slave to her patient, and be caught in the act by her supervisor, maybe Mrs Cox would come to her rescue once again, release the nurse from the girl's hold and take care of Judith herself.

This was only a remote possibility, but it was worth trying. This would be a decisive moment. If what Ray had told her was true, if indeed she was expected to comply to special requests from her patients, then she didn't have anything to fear from having Mrs Cox walk in on them. This was perhaps the greatest gamble of her life, and suddenly made the situation much more exciting.

She tightened her embrace around the girl and let her fingers glide under the pyjama top, touching the soft skin of the waist, remembering the sight of the tanned flesh she had marvelled at just a few weeks ago in the operating theatre.

Lisa cooed and pressed herself against the nurse. 'Undress me,' she said. 'Now.'

From this moment Judith knew there would be no going back. The last flicker of hesitation disappeared from her mind but her free hand trembled as it undid the four buttons of the pyjama, the silk now feeling strangely cold under her fingertips. She wanted to abandon herself, to wantonly rediscover the naked body she knew was hiding under this thin layer of silk. How good it would feel to press her mouth against all this gorgeous skin. She had thought of Lisa often, but never actually thought this moment would ever come. And now it was all happening...

Against her neck the girl's mouth was already searching a sensitive point, the lips hovering and lightly brushing the underside of the earlobe. Judith closed her eyes for a moment, letting the heat of their bodies merge and awaken her senses.

Lisa smelled nice, a rich, probably expensive perfume that also emanated from her hair. Once Judith finished undoing the buttons she looked at Lisa again, as if trying to guess what would be asked of her next. In reply Lisa wriggled out of her top, the silk sliding off her shoulders and exposing her breasts.

The nipples seemed darker and smaller than before, but the skin was just as Judith had remembered, a tanned, light brown, the tiny hairs on her abdomen sun-bleached to a soft gold.

Lisa let go of Judith's leg and brought her hand up to her own breasts, caressing them with the palm of her hand. At the same time she looked at Judith wickedly. 'Touch me.' Her voice was harsh now, an unmistakable order.

Just like the other morning Judith pressed the underswell of the girl's left breast and pushed it up slightly, then let it fall back again, but without taking her fingers away. And just as before she saw the nipple contract and shrink slightly, becoming even darker. Her fingers followed the contour of the smooth globe, gliding around the nipple but without really touching it.

'Suck it. Now.'

Judith didn't mind Lisa's tone. In fact, she felt her desire increase at the thought of becoming her slave, of having no option but to obey. She silently bowed her head and let her mouth slide down from the girl's shoulder all the way to the pointed nipple, gently sticking out her tongue to flick over its stiffness.

Almost immediately Lisa's body went limp against her, and she felt the pounding of the girl's heart against her cheek. Letting go of the tiny waist, she pushed her back on the sofa, in a half-reclining position.

Lisa grabbed Judith's hands and brought them both to her naked breasts, guiding them and pressing them into kneading her warm skin. Judith silently followed the instructions and after a while Lisa let go of the nurse's hands to take hold of her head instead, immediately pulling it towards her cleavage. And again Judith obeyed the silent command. Whatever Lisa would want, Judith would do.

She sucked at the nipples greedily, surprised by her own eagerness, finding pleasure in licking the stiff buttons that seemed to grow bigger in her mouth. Soon she heard Lisa moan, and that aroused her even more.

Her own breasts seemed to throb in tempo with her heartbeat and the folds of her vulva, her dew now quickly gathering at the junction of her legs. Her clitoris also ached with stiffness, yet curiously Judith didn't want to be touched. All she wanted was to caress the lovely body she had desired from the very first time she had seen it, but not been able to touch until now.

By now Lisa held Judith's head against her chest with both arms, guiding the nurse's face from one nipple to the other, writhing under the soft assault of Judith's mouth.

Judith felt elated, wanting to swallow the whole of the girl's breasts, her tongue animated with a life of its own, darting at the erect nipples and worrying them incessantly. Her hands also kept busy, gliding all over the smooth flesh, gently at first but also getting rough at times, kneading the smooth globes in a tight caress, pinching the nipples and the sensitive skin around them.

After a while however Lisa pushed her away, grabbing the nurse's shoulders.

'Get down,' she said. 'On your knees. Now.'

Lisa parted her legs and Judith obeyed without protesting, now a willing slave, her heart pounding in anticipation of what would be asked of her next.

The wooden floor was hard under her bare knees but the sensation soon turned to some kind of numbness, her whole body alight with a passion that made her forget everything else. Once again she pressed her face against Lisa's breasts, her arms now encircling the girl's waist, her hands quickly surveying the softness of her back, using her lower arms to caress all of this warm, smooth skin offered so invitingly.

Lisa threw her arms up and stopped trying to guide Judith's caresses, satisfied that the young nurse no longer needed instructions. She continued moaning loudly, her body writhing slightly under the heat of their combined passion.

Judith was pleased that her caresses had such an effect on Lisa, but she suddenly wondered if somebody passing in the corridor would hear them. She had this vision of several people gathered in the corridor, their ears glued to the door, getting intrigued and excited by what they were hearing. The thought of being heard and attracting attention to what was going on in the room was exciting; the thought of somebody actually walking in on them even more so.

Through the window the rays of the sun now burnt her back and the top of her head, but that was also soon forgotten. Right now she cared about nothing but the desire to please her patient, to arouse the luscious body and be an obedient slave.

She held Lisa tight, burying her face in the soft cleavage, feeling the fluid heat of the young woman's breasts against her cheeks. Her own arousal grew and translated into a strong impulse to discover more velvet skin, more smooth curves. But she couldn't do anything about it. She had to wait for Lisa to ask.

By now Lisa was holding on to Judith's head, her fingers lost in the nurse's golden hair, her lips at times gently caressing the top of Judith's head. Soon her hips began to jerk slightly, and after a while Lisa let go of Judith's head to wriggle out of her pyjama trousers.

Judith didn't need to be told what to do then. She gripped the elastic band of the silk trousers with her fingers and pulled it down, helping Lisa lift her hips from the sofa to get rid of the garment.

The fabric glided down along the girl's tanned legs and Judith tossed it aside before going back to settle between the girl's parted legs. She could smell her desire, not unlike her own, sweet and heady. Judith continued kissing Lisa's breasts for a while and then slowly traced a long path of kisses down her abdomen, on her way to the soft treasure.

Finally her buttocks came resting on her heels and her lips began to gently hover above the curly bush. The fleece was also golden, sun-bleached, and neatly trimmed. It was quite thick but soft as baby hair, shining in the sunlight and fragrant with Lisa's dew.

Judith let her bare arms hang over the naked thighs for a moment, caressing the inside with her cheeks, turning her head this way and that to let her lips caress the soft skin as well. Just moments away from her mouth the wet vulva gaped and glistened, the tiny clitoris barely visible amidst the parted lips, but nevertheless throbbing with excitement, in sequence with the wet vagina that clenched sporadically.

She felt Lisa push her legs together, almost forcing her mouth towards the waiting flesh. 'Suck me!' she girl moaned loudly. 'Suck me now!'

Judith stuck out a timid tongue and tasted the soft folds, at first lightly, barely touching them, but soon covering the whole area with longer, deliberately slow licks.

Lisa moaned loudly and her hips jerked up towards Judith's face. It seemed she was already on the verge of climaxing, her legs shaking as her muscles tensed and relaxed in turn. Judith slid her hands under the girl's thighs and hoisted them unto her shoulders, bringing the writhing pelvis even closer to her face.

Her mouth took hold of the tiny clitoris and sucked it gently, her tongue flickering over it at the same time. Lisa screamed and Judith felt the legs on her shoulders grow heavy, the knees straightening and the toes pointing towards the opposite wall. At the same time Lisa ceased to breathe for a few seconds, only to expel a loud scream as Judith felt the vulva contract violently against her mouth.

The whole body then went limp again, and Judith sensed the wave that swept through the patient's loins, almost echoing against her own mouth. She turned her head slightly and continued to caress the soft thighs with her face.

Opening her eyes for a moment, she recognised a figure standing by the half-opened door. Mrs Cox.

The woman stared at them with a blank expression, but Judith immediately noticed the fingers clenched around the sheets of papers she was holding, the knuckles white and the grip so strong the paper seemed ready to rip.

Silently the supervisor walked to the bed, her gate somewhat unsteady, and simply dropped the papers on the bedside table. All the while she kept staring at Judith, the expression on her face never betraying her feelings; no anger, no surprise.

Still kneeling, fully clothed, between Lisa's parted legs, Judith continued caressing the soft skin, suddenly happy that her improvised plan had worked. She stared back at the woman through half-shut eyes and smiled smugly. There was nothing Mrs Cox could say or do, or else she would have intervened already.

At that moment Judith had the confirmation that what Ray had told her was true. There could no longer be any doubt about it. And Mrs Cox knew that Judith knew. What would happen next? It didn't really matter. All that mattered was that Judith was no longer afraid of losing her job. In her mind she knew they wouldn't let go of her now.

Mrs Cox turned around and left. Judith looked up at Lisa. The girl was looking at her with a wicked smile, her eyes half-shut as well, seemingly drunk with pleasure. Both women had managed to get what they had sought. Lisa to have someone to pleasure her, Judith to be caught in the act by her supervisor.

Yet she was still disappointed because she hadn't counted on Mrs Cox leaving the room like this. She wanted the woman to come to her rescue, in a funny sort of way, to be taken in by the scene Judith and Lisa offered. But instead she had walked out, completely disinterested, and now Judith would have to find another way to get Mrs Cox to come to her, to totally seduce her.

As she knelt between Lisa's parted legs, Judith wished for a moment that the roles could be reversed, that she would be the one sitting there, and have Mrs Cox torturing her tender flesh like an obedient slave.

At the same time her thoughts scared her. This was the second time she had had intimate contact with a woman, and her own desire was somewhat new to her. All her life she had only ever fantasised about men, but now her lust knew no bounds. And her behaviour had changed, too. Whereas up until quite recently she had been rather inexperienced and somewhat passive, now she craved contact in an almost aggressive way; these were uncontrollable impulses.

She wanted to pleasure and be pleasured, again and again, to be both slave and master, in turn, to others as well as to her own lust. And again today the way Mrs Cox had reacted wasn't what Judith had expected. Perhaps something didn't ring true, as Judith had not really been forced into anything she didn't want to do and the supervisor had instinctively felt it.

Against her face she felt Lisa's legs stir a few times. She sighed and looked up at her. Lisa winked, obviously happy to have received satisfaction. Judith was happy, too, but in her mind nothing was settled.

She was so close to her goal she felt she could almost touch it. She wanted Mrs Cox to come back and pleasure her, and she knew that eventually she would get her. But when?

Chapter Sixteen

All that was missing this morning was the red carpet, Judith thought. She stood quietly by the nurses' desk, filling out her reports, immune to the feverish excitement around her.

The other nurses were running all over the place, chuckling loudly. Marina Stone was expected any minute, and her imminent arrival sent a tension through the air that was like a storm about to break, electrical and stimulating.

The great Marina, the actress who could hold audiences on the edge of their seats, make them cry just by snapping her fingers, stir in them emotions that would linger long after they had left the cinema or turned off the television set. She would be here any minute.

Judith couldn't help feeling that everybody was overreacting. After all, this was probably a woman just like any other once the cameras stopped rolling. And from the moment she would set foot in the Dorchester Clinic, she would be a patient, just like all the others.

Apparently, she had been here as a patient a couple of years ago, and on that occasion she had practically never set foot outside her room and those who hadn't actually seen her doubted she had been here at all.

Yet around the nurses' station and in the corridor,

nobody but Judith could keep calm. As of yet no-one knew the real reason why Marina had decided to check into the Clinic. The odds were in favour of another face-lift, although liposuction on her chin was a strong second. But did it really matter?

One of the attendants had his head out of a window overlooking the street, although it was always strictly forbidden to open the windows on that side of the building because of the traffic noises and the fumes.

'Here they come!' he screamed before shutting the window. Silence fell for a second, yet the tension continued to mount. The staff members all looked at each other, their faces stretched by large grins, and a minute later the noises resumed.

'How long do you think it will take her to get up here?'

'Is the room ready?'

'What about the flowers? Where did you put the flowers?'

'Has the phone been installed in her temporary office?'

Judging from all this commotion, Judith figured that even a member of the royal family could never generate such excitement. And there was more to come, of course. The Great One hadn't even made it up to the floor yet.

Right now she was probably being greeted by Doctor Marshall, and maybe another doctor, the one who would be operating on her, and perhaps even Mrs Cox as well. Of course this would all be done discretely, with taste; there would be no bouquets changing hands, no flashes from cameras.

If she was satisfied with her stay at the Clinic then Marina would perhaps tell some of her prestigious friends and this could only be good publicity. Therefore everything had to be perfect.

'They're on their way up,' Nurse Parsons announced, hanging up the phone. 'Look busy.'

Suddenly, life went back to normal, or at least something that looked like normal. Everyone was still very excited but no-one could let anything show. The instructions had been very detailed. There would be no requests for autographs, no going into the actress's room without a good reason, and, naturally, no leaks to the Press. Marina would be given the best room, the one that had a small adjoining office, for her personal assistant and other members of her entourage. Everything would be controlled from there, for Marina would not do something so mundane as to press the call button if she needed anything; she had people who were paid to do that for her.

But of course Marina Stone would be treated just like all the other patients, with class and professionalism, but still keeping in mind she was indeed somebody special.

The doors of the lift opened and she stepped out, flanked by Doctor Marshall and Mrs Cox, looking glamorous, as always. Although she was shorter than she seemed to be on screen, Marina Stone had a certain panache that commanded admiration. Her dark green coat looked simple yet expensive, the style and colour perfectly suited to her brown hair which was held up in a complicated chignon. The position of her gloved hand on her handbag seemed calculated and her make-up was discreet but impeccable. She exuded class, and just stepping out of the lift looked like a grandiose entrance, a well-rehearsed scene straight from one of her films.

Doctor Rogers followed, one step behind like a faithful puppy. Judith thought it was quite unusual to see him without Doctor Mason for a change. He looked pale and even more frail behind Marina, his boyish looks giving him the allure of a bell boy and not a doctor. But if he was with them it could only mean he would be the one to operate on her, therefore the great Marina was coming in for liposuction, as that was Doctor Rogers's speciality.

Three people also came out of the lift; Marina's staff. The first one behind Doctor Rogers was a tall woman, probably her secretary, carrying a briefcase in one hand and a wad of papers in the other. She immediately looked around with sharp, inquisitive eyes, casting a brief but thorough glance all around, inspecting even the ceiling.

The other woman was shorter and her opened coat

revealed a pink uniform. She was carrying a large, shiny plastic bag and a vanity case. Although Marina was coming in for surgery there was no reason why she shouldn't look her best; taking along her hairdresser wasn't such a farfetched notion to people like her.

The last one out of the lift was a tall and burly man, with very short hair and broad shoulders. Judith couldn't decide whether he was Marina's chauffeur or bodyguard or possibly a combination of both. Nevertheless he looked very impressive and almost frightening. He was also carrying a bag: an enormous, black leather satchel that was obviously filled to capacity, bulging from all sides. In his big hand, however, it seemed almost weightless.

Such was the star's retinue, the few people she couldn't manage without, even whilst in hospital. At first the staff had been told she would bring along her own nurse as well, but Marina had changed her mind at the last minute and it was announced that a few chosen nurses would take turns caring for her exclusively. The names of those nurses had not yet been announced and wild rumours were fuelled by the anticipation.

At first it was supposed that Miss Stone would choose for herself, then it was said it would be exclusively male nurses. But in the end the decision was up to Doctor Marshall, upon recommendations from Mrs Cox and the attending surgeon.

Judith doubted she would be chosen, mainly because she had only recently joined the staff. However, when the star stopped at the nurses' station en route to her bedroom, Mrs Cox took her apart and put her hand on Judith's shoulder.

Judith kept looking at Marina, now standing by the station desk and chatting with the nurse in charge, but all her attention was focused on Mrs Cox, and how warm the woman's breath felt on her neck. At the same time her heart began to pound furiously. The last time she had seen Mrs Cox was in Lisa Baxter's room, the previous morning. She hadn't heard anything since, hadn't been called to the office, and still didn't know if being caught in such a compromising position would mean instant dismissal.

She dreaded what she was about to hear, yet at the same time felt a weird excitement at being touched by this woman who impressed her so much. The object of her recent fantasies was just a few inches from her, a hand on the nurse's shoulder and her mouth sensually close to her ear.

'Doctor Rogers has asked that you be assigned to his team for the operation,' Mrs Cox whispered confidentially. 'It would be in your best interest to accept ...' She didn't give Judith the opportunity to reply and turned around to join Marina as the star continued her tour on her way to her room.

Judith felt a sob rise in her throat and tears to her eyes. That could only mean one thing: despite what had happened with Lisa Baxter yesterday she wasn't about to get fired. At least not just yet. She was elated, once again seized with a feeling of victory. Things were working out just fine, but she still didn't have the final confirmation of what Ray had told her. How long would she have to wait for that?

Marina finally entered her room, the last one at the end of the corridor, followed by her staff, and the door closed behind them. Simultaneously several sighs were heard, a combination of admiration, relief, and envy. From then on it seemed to be business as usual, but it was all a pretence, and would likely remain so at least whilst the star was in residence.

Judith's mind was working frantically. For the past three days she had been going through her plan time and time again. Normally she would have been happy to get three consecutive days off work – her reward for having assisted Doctor Rogers in surgery – but since she had felt Mrs Cox's breath on her neck she had been unable to quell the hunger she was feeling deep within her, the warm desire to be near the woman again.

The lift opened onto the top floor of the building, where all the directors and doctors' offices were located, and Judith stepped out decidedly. She walked along the silent corridor and looked at her watch: 10 o'clock. Everyone was gone at this hour, but Mrs Cox's car was still in the car park so she was probably working late.

This time Judith would not let her supervisor have the upper hand. In the same way she had managed to get what she had wanted out of Desmond, she was planning to make Mrs Cox reveal what she knew, to confirm what Ray had said. After that, all she would have to do was to find a weak point in the armour the woman seemed to wear. She would make Mrs Cox yield, make her pleasure her tender flesh once again. This time Judith wouldn't step out of that office until she had got what she had come for.

The harsh light coming from the ceiling gave the corridor a strange aspect, too bright, surreal. It was just like being enveloped in that light, like a bright cloud, hot and blinding, almost lifting her off the ground and making her walk straight into the light.

She passed a series of doors, each adorned by a shining brass sign with a name on it. All the doctors and directors had their offices on this floor. All of them were identical, except for the name on the door. And to Judith each name had come to mean something very specific.

Elizabeth Mason's office was, naturally, right next to Tom Rogers's. There was surely some kind of link between them, other than being colleagues. It was more than friendship but Judith still hadn't been able to figure out their relationship. It didn't really matter, it had nothing to do with her. However this unusual couple were also strange because they hadn't shown any interest in Judith, other than as a capable nurse. They had stared at her in a strange way the very first day in the operating theatre, but after that they had never given that bewildering look of barely disguised interest she had noticed from so many of her colleagues. As if they had sensed just by looking at her that she was too different from them, that the new nurse would fit into this special world of theirs.

Suddenly Judith remembered that she had seen Doctor Mason's red Mazda in the car park, so there was a chance she was still in her office, probably working late as well. Judith hastened her step, not wanting to see her and eager to get to the other wing, the older part of the Clinic where Mrs Cox had her office.

She trembled, shaken by a delicious shiver, as she read Edouard Laurin's name before turning the corner, remembering the time she had come up to confront him with what she thought was a conspiracy to hypnotise the staff and turn them into sex slaves. The time she had spent in there was unforgettable.

As it turned out, if indeed Mrs Cox could confirm it, it wasn't so far from the truth. Yes, there were slaves at the Dorchester Clinic, but they were willing servants, slaves to their own desires.

She turned the corner and pushed open the fire door separating the old part of the building from the new one. The only people who had their offices in this wing, next to each other's, were Mrs Cox and Doctor Marshall. Judith remembered one of her colleagues telling somebody that Doctor Marshall had left early today. That would mean only Mrs Cox remained in this part of the building, isolated from everyone else. No-one was to know Judith was here, especially at this hour; no-one was to hear them.

She had planned to enter Mrs Cox's office without knocking and lock the door behind her. The surprise was on her, however, when she discovered the door was locked. She tried the doorknob a few times, gripping it tightly, her hands moist with anticipation, desperately trying to make it turn and wondering if it was just that she had no strength left in her hands.

But the door was locked, there was no doubt about it. And Judith couldn't bring herself to knock. In her mind, she felt so sure everything would go according to her plan that this setback looked more like a failure. Right now everything was working against her. She pressed her ear to the door, hoping in vain to hear even the slightest noise that would tell her if indeed there was somebody in there. But there was no sound to be heard. Either the door was too thick or there was nobody in the office. So where could Mrs Cox be?

With a sigh of resignation she let go of the doorknob and turned around, frustrated and angry. Perhaps the supervisor had gone home already. She could have been making her way down one of the lifts whilst Judith was coming up in the other. The timing was all wrong and Judith realised she wouldn't find anything out today.

As she slowly made her way back towards the lift her hand strayed and she mechanically, almost by reflex, grabbed hold of the doorknob to Doctor Marshall's office. She froze in her steps when she realised this door wasn't locked, and that only a slight twist of her wrist would make it turn with a faint click. She let it go suddenly, as if it had been burning, and waited, her heart pounding.

She was expecting to hear a voice inside asking who was there, or at least some sign that there was someone in there. Surprisingly there was nothing but silence. She pushed the door with her fingertips, her lips going dry and her cheeks heating up in excitement.

The door opened silently onto a dark room, the brightness of the corridor offsetting the faint light coming from a small lamp that was lit on the desk. Still not a sound. Judith breathed deeply and ventured into the room hesitantly. As her eyes became accustomed to the semi-darkness she cast a look around.

Doctor Marshall's office was not unlike that of Mrs Cox, albeit a bit larger. The desk took pride of place and was almost identical to Mrs Cox's, as was the large wall unit behind it, and this one was loaded with books. Judith got bolder and walked across to take a look at the series of photos on a shelf alongside the far wall; Doctor Marshall and Mrs Cox, looking much younger, a photo probably taken quite a few years ago; the opening of the Clinic, a beaming doctor cutting a red ribbon; a collage of Doctor Marshall with a number of famous personalities, possibly all former patients of the Clinic; framed press cuttings, all relating to the Clinic.

Obviously, this man was proud of what he had built, and for very good reasons. But how could he leave his office without locking the door? This was quite worrisome for Judith; she would have to come up with a very good explanation if he were to show up behind her and demand to know what she was doing in his office . . .

As she continued to look around she suddenly noticed something familiar on the floor between the desk and side-door. The satchel she had seen Marina Stone's escort bring in just a few days ago blatantly lay wide open. Only this time it was no longer bulging and on the brink of bursting open. Yet it wasn't empty either.

She crouched down and peered in. Her heart began to pound again and she reached in with a trembling hand. Wads of bank notes, from 5 to 20, crisp and new, freshly minted and neatly stacked. Her fingers shuffled them about quickly and she realised there was a small fortune in there. However, this wasn't anywhere near the amount the satchel had contained when Marina had checked in if in fact it had contained nothing but money.

Judith vaguely knew the costs of surgery and a four-day stay at the Clinic. At least she knew there was more than enough in the bag as it stood. Marina had brought in way too much money, but why? And where did the rest of it go? And how could Doctor Marshall leave his office with so much money quietly sitting on the floor?

Anybody could walk in and whisk it away, and no-one would ever find out about it. This was more than carelessness on Doctor Marshall's part, it was downright stupid.

A wicked thought crossed Judith's mind. There was more in there than she could earn in a year. How tempting it was to just grab the bag and leave . . . but at the same time she was somewhat indifferent to the idea of sudden riches. She had come here for another purpose, and she wasn't ready to leave without having found out what she had been waiting to learn.

As she slowly stood up a faint voice rose to her ears, noises coming from the other side of a door near to the desk, a door she noticed was slightly ajar. She tilted her head slightly to peek in and realised this was actually a way into Mrs Cox's office. Her fingers now numb, she opened the door slightly and tried to figure out where the noises and voices were coming from.

Mrs Cox's office was completely dark, and there was nobody in there either, but what Judith had heard was without a doubt coming from inside. She glided into the room and closed the door behind her. At first, all she could see was the light coming through the window, directly above a lamppost, casting an upward orange glow.

Then she noticed a tiny yellow light, a slim line at the bottom of the far wall which rose at a right angle before thinning out and disappearing. It took her a few seconds to figure out it was coming from under another door, a door she hadn't noticed on her previous visits to the office.

She walked through the darkness towards this source of light, unsure of what she would find on the other side. Yet she knew it was too late to go back, and at this point she was so intrigued she could only go on and try to find out more.

When she got to the wall she encountered a major hurdle: there didn't seem to be any kind of doorknob, how could she open the door? Her fingers frantically followed the crack in the wall, feeling it getting thinner and disappearing, and she soon felt like giving up. A wave of despair seized her. She knew she was close, how could this happen to her now?

Then, on the other side, she heard a loud moan. At first she felt her blood freeze in her veins. The cry was deep, the voice female. But an instant later Judith was swept with a strange heat, her loins realising that this wasn't a moan of pain but one of pleasure. Simultaneously, her nipples grew stiff and her breath shallow. Her brain ceased to think and her instincts took over.

Whatever was going on behind that wall, it was exciting, in more ways than one. Her hands then started to work frantically, feeling up and down the wall, desperately looking for some kind of handle, some way of opening the door.

When she got to the top she inadvertently pushed the corner in. It gave a click and sprung out unexpectedly. Immediately the yellow line grew thicker and the door opened slightly. Judith managed to venture a look inside and nervously licked her dry lips.

The first time Judith had been in this part of the Clinic she had wondered what else could be on this floor, for it had seemed quite unusual that there would only be two offices occupying such a large amount of floor space. But now she knew.

This room was bigger than both offices put together, only it seemed to be accessible solely through this secret door. At first Judith had the impression it was some kind of museum. The set-up was most obviously antique.

From what she could see it seemed the room was rather narrow but quite long, with a row of brass beds neatly lined up along the wall, flanked on either side by ancient, metal utility cabinets. Peering in, Judith could only see six beds but that was enough to make out that there was nothing posh about this room, unlike the rest of the Clinic. In fact, it looked rather gloomy.

The beds were old, the paint on several of the metal cabinets was chipped. On the ceiling old lead pipes were clearly visible, as were the bars in the windows. On the whole it looked much like a Victorian hospital ward, probably what the Clinic might have looked like at the turn of the century.

The yellow light was coming from several candles. Sorry curtains hung at the windows, tattered and turned grey with age. For a minute Judith wondered if she could come in, for there didn't seem to be anybody in there either. But at that very moment she heard yet another moan, stronger, betraying sensations she could almost feel herself, and that exerted such a pull on her loins that she just had to open the door and face whatever she would find on the other side.

She proceeded slowly, gradually stepping into another age, another world. There were about 15 beds in all lined up along the wall, and beyond them the rest of the room was set up to look like an operating theatre.

The smell of starch assaulted her nostrils as she walked past the first bed. The mattress was about waist high, the sheets crisp and neatly tucked. Looking down to the far end of the room she realised there were in fact several people there, two couples she couldn't recognise from where she was standing. She was obviously walking in on some secret get-together, now boldly inviting herself in. Nevertheless she kept on walking, as if in a dream, towards the unreal scene that was starting to reveal itself to her.

The first couple was a patient and a surgeon. The patient was lying on an old, narrow operating table, in a set-up very different from anything Judith had ever seen.

The patient was lying on his back, covered in bandages from head to toe, and the surgeon was standing next to him, with his back turned to Judith. Instead of the modern, green cotton garment, this doctor was completely naked under a large, dark rubber apron. All that was visible was a pair of rounded, smooth buttocks, topped by the apron strings neatly fastened around the waist.

The surgeon was quite obviously a shapely female, but there was no way of knowing who could be hiding under the worn, dark cotton hood; a gloomy head garment doctors used to wear a few hundred years ago, during the first years of modern medicine before surgical masks were invented.

As she walked closer, however, Judith noticed a few unmistakeable brown locks sticking out from under the hood. Her guess was proven correct when she got close enough to take a look at this doctor's hands: hands that belonged to Elizabeth Mason.

Doctor Mason turned around and looked at Judith, only her emerald eyes could be seen in this unusual head gear. She stopped for a second, one hand still clasped around her patient's ankle, the other holding a length of cotton gauze. Nothing in her eyes betrayed her emotions. If she was surprised to see Judith there, it never showed.

Her apron was fastened so tight it revealed the rounded contours of her breasts, the peaks of her large, erect nipples. Further down the small hole of her belly button was also emphasised by the tight rubber layer, which then fell straight down, almost touching the floor. Judith then ventured a look towards the patient who lay on the table, his arms and legs wide apart.

This silhouette was unmistakably male, but the identity of the patient would likely remain a mystery, for his head was completely covered in bandages. All that was uncovered was the underside of his nose, which showed the nostrils flaring sporadically.

His hands were thickly bandaged, looking like oversized bundles, and were both tied to a set of handles at the head of the table. The whole body was neatly wrapped in several layers of cotton gauze from head to toe, like a mummy, except for the most important part: his erect phallus, which reared, purplish and stiff, looking dark and mysterious in the midst of all these layers of white gauze.

The patient's thin frame made it easy for Judith to guess his identity. She also noticed that a lock of his pale hair had managed to escape through the bandages around his head. Such was the revelation of the real nature of that special relationship between Elizabeth Mason and Tom Rogers...

And right at this moment, Doctor Mason was busy tying up his legs at the foot of the table. The patient was now ready for the operation... What would she do with him? It was easy to imagine, at least for Judith. Yet to see these two prestigious doctors, surgeons she had assisted in the operating theatre, in such a set-up was unbelievable, almost fantastic, and the scene was even more surreal in the yellow glow from the candles dripping on the windowsill.

She could hear them both breathing loudly, Doctor Mason through the strange mask she was wearing, Doctor Rogers with great difficulty because of the bandages around his face. It seemed Doctor Mason didn't mind having a spectator, and although Judith was more than willing to stay and watch, she was too intrigued by what the rest of this strange room contained to stop exploring it so soon. She continued walking around, like a visitor to some live exhibit, her brain quickly processing every detail of the dim room her eyes could survey.

A little further away was another couple in another kind of set up Judith was eager to investigate. She immediately recognised Doctor Marshall, although the sight of his naked body wasn't anything like she could ever have imagined. She was startled and stopped in her steps, wondering how daring she could be, if she could make her presence known and move closer. For a while she watched from afar, not knowing how he would react if he saw her there.

His arms and torso were pale but muscular and covered in a lush carpet of silver hairs, tiny drops of sweat pearling on his chest and glistening in the candlelight. At this moment Judith realised that his hair was probably not a good indication of his age, for his body was that of a much younger man, chiselled and taut. She saw he was holding something in his hand, some kind of slim, metallic instrument that faintly reflected the yellow flames of the candles.

He looked up and saw her, but remained silent. For a moment Judith boldly held his gaze, expecting him to tell her to get out, almost surprised that he didn't. As he diverted his eyes Judith understood he didn't mind her presence and she approached him, fascinated by the way his cock pointed up and twitched sporadically, and how the delicate metal ring piercing his foreskin shook as the purplish head of his phallus bobbed up and down.

Gazing towards his partner, she concluded that the woman who was bending backwards over the wooden trestle, her wrists and ankles bound by leather restraints, her back supported by a black leather saddle, could only be Mrs Cox.

Hesitantly, Judith continued coming closer, unable to control her own feet anymore. She had to get close, to see more. As she approached them Doctor Marshall looked up at her again and this time a wicked smile appeared at the corner of his mouth.

His erect phallus stood up, pointing towards Mrs Cox's parted legs, but was nowhere near to entering the gaping vulva just yet. There again Judith was astonished to see him in such an unusual situation, but she knew this was only the beginning of her discoveries. There was more to come.

She stopped looking at him to quickly glance at Mrs Cox. The woman's breasts also pointed towards the ceiling, the nipples stiff and long. And Judith finally saw how foolish she had been that morning in the supervisor's office, when she had wondered why the nipples pointing through the woman's uniform had such a distorted shape. Of course, there was nothing unusual about the nipples themselves, other than the fact that they were both pierced by large metal rings. These also dangled and shone in the candlelight, and the slight pull they seemed to effect on the erect nipples was sufficient to trigger Judith's arousal.

There she lay, right in front of her, exposed and defenceless, the woman Judith had been waiting for. Yet this wasn't like any of the many scenarios she had been fantasising about!

On a small table next to the trestle were a series of instruments Judith couldn't identify, ancient surgical tools, also museum pieces. Next to them was an old, worn leather case, spread open and holding even more tools.

What Doctor Marshall held in his hand was also mysterious, a slightly curved metal rod about eight inches long, with a brown wooden handle and a stumpy, rounded tip the size of a large grape. There was no way of knowing the original purpose of this instrument, but it was easy to guess what he was about to do with it.

Judith walked around the trestle slowly, oblivious to the sighs that rose from the opposite corner of the room where Doctor Mason and her 'patient' were. Rather, she was mesmerised by the sight of Mrs Cox's precarious position, and even more so when she realised the woman was also gagged, her mouth held open by a leather strap with a knot in it.

This was something Judith had heard of before, the way loud or violent patients were kept from screaming, back in the days, many years ago, when such practices were considered the norm.

The look she saw in Mrs Cox's half-shut eyes had nothing to do with pain or distress, however. It was one of sheer pleasure.

To see her like this rekindled Judith's arousal and her heart began to pound in anticipation once again. She looked up to Doctor Marshall and couldn't contain a triumphant smile, somehow wickedly happy to see Mrs Cox displayed like this. Of course, this meant the woman wouldn't be able to walk out on Judith, and although the nurse wasn't responsible for this awkward situation, she couldn't help being pleased with it. She didn't know what else Doctor Marshall intended to do to the supervisor, but she already knew she now had a powerful weapon in knowledge.

By now the man was also holding something in his other hand, some kind of leather strap, worn and slightly fraying. Judith closed her eyes for a second, desperately trying to capture this scene in her memory, almost afraid of opening her eyes again lest it be just a dream, yet compelled to look on as the rush of dew between her legs grew insistent and she demanded more of the bizarre, exciting vision.

This vision was enhanced by the flickering light of the candles, each flame differing in intensity, in height, in projection, and casting hundreds of different shadows on the naked body that was arched over the trestle. In effect, the skin looked like it had been painted on, brightly lit patches contrasting with the other parts of the body where little or no light fell.

Doctor Marshall took one step closer towards his victim, and raised his hand to gently rub the protruding clitoris with the tip of the metal rod. The woman moaned loudly.

Judith couldn't imagine what had taken place earlier, but the sounds she had heard from the other room had indeed come from Mrs Cox's gagged mouth. There could be no doubt about that, judging from the glistening patches of dew that had trickled down on the inside of her thighs and glistened in the yellow light.

Loud moans were also coming from the other corner of the room. Judith turned her head only briefly, yet long enough to see that Elizabeth Mason was now up on the table, straddling her man, and just about to impale herself upon his thick member. In a sudden flash Judith understood the reason for such an elaborate set up: Tom Rogers, all covered in bandages, was totally isolated in his own world and his skin was unable to sense anything; only his erect prick was susceptible to sensation from contact with the outside.

Turning her eyes back towards Mrs Cox and Doctor Marshall, she could see that what was going on here was quite different. It was some kind of multi-faceted torture, where everything lay in the fact that the treatment had to be slow to be efficient. She had known that herself, when she had been tied up by Desmond. Soon Mrs Cox's arousal would reach such a point that her whole body would seem about to explode, yet she would still be denied the final release, the ultimate point where everything began, where everything ended.

Judith looked around once again, unable to see all of the room but subjugated by what her eyes could make out. One of the beds had restraints already secured to the brass bars at either end. Some beds had thick mattresses with starched sheets, others bare, rough straw mattresses.

All the windows were blacked out. Obviously it was not really necessary as this was the seventh floor and it would be difficult to peep in from the outside, but it did add something frightening to the already gloomy atmosphere that reigned in the room.

Judith was walking as if in a dream, both couples unconcerned by her presence in this secret chamber. They didn't even seem at all curious about how she found the room either. Both Doctor Marshall and Elizabeth Mason looked at her with an amused smile, and then at each other. No-one had uttered a word since she had walked in. Doctor Marshall was the first one to speak.

'Take your clothes off, nurse,' he ordered. 'Your uniform is not in line with the regulations of this room.'

Judith was about to retort that she didn't know any of these rules, but managed to hold back her words just before they crossed her lips. She was in no position to protest, all she could do was obey.

On the operating table, Tom Rogers's bandaged body began to writhe, his arms tugging at the thick lengths of gauze that held him down, his slim hips pushing up to enter the woman who was straddling him. Elizabeth didn't move much, content to let him exert himself for her own benefit. Her behind swayed gently, slowly, back and forth and sideways, seemingly trying to direct his thrusting prick within her tunnel.

She began tossing her head back and forth as well, at first in a slow, gyrating motion, but her movements became swifter and soon turned into a series of jerks so violent that her black hood slipped off her head and her dark, curly mane bounced all around her face, strands sweeping over her eyes and into her mouth.

Judith could almost feel the woman's pleasure, and her loins were seized in a strong, hot grip. Despite its nightmarish set-up, this room was made for pleasure, different, old-fashioned, forbidden.

Her eyes constantly travelled from one couple to the other as she took her clothes off, her burning feet finding relief on the cold tiles, her bare skin taking on a smooth, evenly velvety look in the candlelight. Once she stood naked Doctor Marshall beckoned for her to join him. She approached hesitantly.

Instinctively she knew very few words were ever spoken in this place. This was the realm of sighs and moans. Yet she would have liked to be told, she needed to know in no uncertain terms. But again Desmond's words echoed in her mind. It did not matter what she knew, all that was important was how she felt.

And right now she felt good, walking around naked, her body bathed in the yellow light, the scent of the burning wax invading her brain. In front of her was a woman, a woman she had wanted to submit to. This wasn't at all what she had planned. In fact, it was the other way around. But this was better than nothing, more than she could ever have hoped for. It was up to her to make it what she wanted. At last, here was her chance.

Doctor Marshall handed her the metal instrument and stood back, a silent invitation for her to proceed. In her hand the wooden handle was smooth and warm, obviously old and often used. She took a closer look at it, wondering what it could be. Perhaps it wasn't even a surgical tool at all, but somehow she doubted that. Everything in this room was genuine, it couldn't be otherwise.

As she approached the parted legs she saw the woman's knees tremble. At that moment Judith's loins went ablaze, her own vulva yearning to feel the exquisite torture of this unknown tool. She reached out.

At first she let the rounded tip slide up on the inside of the woman's right leg, feeling it glide smoothly over a few inches, its progression somewhat impaired once it began to tread over the wetter area. Amidst dark, wet pubic hairs, she saw the tiny bud of the clitoris gleam faintly, the rest of the vulva barely visible as the parted legs shielded it from the light. She directed the instrument towards it, wickedly letting it slide up ever so slowly, feeling the metal dig a slight furrow against the tensed muscle.

At last the metal tip came to touch the stiff bud. Judith held back, letting it brush only lightly at first, then redirecting it towards the dark, secret entrance that hid in the shadows. She felt elated and her own arousal grew as she heard the first moan coming from the woman's throat. Victory was hers.

How long would she wait before granting the woman the pleasure she would silently beg for? She didn't know just yet, but she definitely was in no hurry. She would savour her triumph, watch the woman writhe endlessly under the cold metal caress, bring her just moments away from her climax but deny it to her at the very last minute.

Judith felt naughty, finally allowed to release all her frustrations and tease the woman for as long as she would please. She inserted the tip of the rod into the slick vagina once again, then took the handle with both hands to make the rod rotate quickly.

The hips jerked in a spasm as the bulbous tip spun within it. Judith tried to imagine what this could feel like, to have this cold metal ball spinning inside of her, rotating on itself and caressing the smooth walls of her tunnel. She shuddered at the thought, her imagination so powerful she could almost feel the metal ball inside her as well. Would it be painful or pleasant? Probably a strange mix of both sensations in more or less equal proportions.

She slowly pushed the rod as far as she could inside the woman's tunnel and pulled it back out before re-inserting it again, repeating this motion time and time again, gradually increasing in speed.

Each time the rounded tip nudged at her entrance the woman moaned, and soon the insertions changed to rapid pokings. Judith slowly directed it towards the gaping vulva, then jerked her arm to thrust in forcefully, each insertion brief but forceful.

By now her victim was panting loudly, her breath escaping in tempo with each jab of the rod. Judith threw her head back and laughed loudly, wickedly happy with the woman's reaction. This was more than she had hoped for, and she knew there was still more to come.

She took the rod out and returned to caressing the thighs again, making the tip switch from one leg to the other with sharp twists of her wrist. As Judith gently hit the smooth flesh it responded with a faint wet slapping sound. She let the metal instrument slowly glide along the parted thighs and lightly brush the swollen clitoris now and again. Over the trestle, Mrs Cox seemed to relax and Judith thought the torture she would put her through would be like a roller coaster ride with intensely pleasurable episodes interspersed by more quiet, gentle teasing.

After a while, however, she was almost disappointed when she saw Doctor Marshall stepping forward to join her. He walked around slowly, looking at Mrs Cox's body but never at her face, his mouth now tightly shut in a severe, cruel expression. His gleeful eyes betrayed his lust, and Judith noticed several small drops pearling from the nether mouth of his erect phallus which was still pointing at the ceiling. He had been watching them silently, and was obviously excited by the spectacle of his woman being teased by a young, inexperienced nurse.

Judith pulled away for a minute, not really sure of his intentions. He looked at her and smiled complacently.

'Look at her,' he said cynically. 'When I met her a few years back she was just like you, sweet and innocent. Now, see what she's become ... A wanton creature, tortured yet beautiful in her quest for pleasure. I must admit she never ceases to amaze me.'

He stopped between the woman's parted legs and slowly ran the tip of the leather strap over the white flesh, its frayed edge making a slightly scratchy sound. He caressed her thus for a little while, then began to flick the strap from one thigh to the other. At first he just let it swing under the pull of its own weight, but gradually imparted some force to it, until it began to slap the smooth flesh which slowly grew red and raised.

The woman's hips jerked up a few times and her legs bucked. The slender muscles played under the skin, contracting forcefully against the restraints and as her vulva appeared in the pale light, Judith could see the entrance of her vagina clench violently. She was finding pleasure in pain, and at that moment Judith understood the woman's reaction when the nurse had confessed to being hit with a set of keys and having found it pleasurable.

So, in this respect Doctor Marshall was right. Judith had a lot in common with the woman who lay with her back arched and her extremities tied up. Their paths had crossed in their respective quests for pleasure and were now merging in an unexpected way. Judith was merely a novice compared to Mrs Cox, however. She still had a lot to learn, but the prospect of being guided through this realm of pleasure-pain was appealing.

The man moved back for a few seconds and the woman ceased moaning. Suddenly, Judith realised all was now silent in the large room. A powerful, eerie sensation seized her and, as she looked around, she was surprised to see that Doctor Mason and Doctor Rogers were gone. The only witness to their unusual encounter was a thick pile of gauze strips, scattered on the floor around the operating table. They had kept to themselves, enclosed in their own private world of pleasure, respectful yet oblivious of the others around them.

For such was this room, as far as Judith could make out. This was a place where people came to live out their fantasies, but without imposing on others. Everything had been carefully planned to offer a wide array of set-ups, all in respect to the old tradition of medical care, all imaginative and intriguing, all wickedly exciting and sexy.

Judith had found out more in one evening than she ever could have imagined. And she hadn't had to ask a single question. Now, more than ever, she understood the meaning of Desmond's words, for knowing the truth was one thing, but discovering it with her body was much better.

She began to relax her mind and let her senses take over. This room, with its appearance, the faint yellow flickering lights, and smell of burning wax, all merged into a powerful, arousing mental caress which she could feel through her loins. This was more intense than anything she had ever experienced in her life. Now, she became impatient to see what else there was to this unusual encounter.

However, she was puzzled to see Doctor Marshall go down on his knees behind Mrs Cox's arched back and take away the piece of leather that gagged her. He looked up at Judith and smiled cruelly.

'Since you managed to find us,' he said, 'would you please be the one to give Mrs Cox the *coup de grâce*? You may use your hand, or your tongue, as you please.'

At first Judith couldn't quite figure out what he meant but she understood immediately once she saw him insert the tip of his erect phallus into the woman's mouth.

Judith wasn't ready for this. Things were not turning out as she had hoped. It was too soon to bring the woman to pleasure, at least from her point of view. There was more to come, that's how she wanted it. She needed to torture her victim endlessly, and then get the woman to return the favour. She had only just begun teasing her. This was way too soon!

Yet she also remembered that this session had probably started quite a while before she had joined in, and, of course, there was a limit to the amount of time anybody could remain in such an awkward position. Doctor Marshall was right, everything had to come to an end sooner or later, and there probably wasn't anything Judith could say or do to change the situation.

Her heart pounding, she came to stand next to the arched body. She saw Doctor Marshall grab Mrs Cox's full breasts with both hands and hold them tightly, inserting his thumbs inside the metal rings and gently tugging on them. At the same time, Mrs Cox's mouth, albeit upside down, also closed tightly around his erect member.

The scene was surreal and exciting. Judith reached down and timidly lay her hand on the tortured vulva. She felt it melt under her touch, soft and fluid, the sinewy folds throbbing slightly. Even before she moved her hand she felt the clitoris grow stiff under her fingertips and begin to pulsate. Judith rubbed it slightly, almost lovingly, feeling the woman's dew soak her hand almost immediately. Its sweet, heady scent rose in the room and numbed Judith's will. The momentum of her hand grew in tempo with Doctor Marshall's thrusting hips. She heard the woman moan and saw her red lips contracting around the thick rod that now entered and withdrew from her mouth at a frantic speed.

Yet Judith stood immobile, her hand moving from the elbow only. She closed her eyes and listened to this symphony of moans, sighs and grunts. The unusual music rocked her, soft and lascivious, and she barely felt the hand snaking up her naked thigh.

At first she thought it was only her imagination, but as she opened her eyes she saw that one of Mrs Cox's hands had been released and it was she who had reached out to touch the nurse's vulva.

By now Judith's arousal was so intense that the mere contact of the woman's slim fingers on her stiff bud was enough to trigger her climax. She moaned gently, her voice joining the others, as she felt pleasure sweep her. How ironic that she should be the one to climax first, since she had barely been touched. However, as sweet as her climax was, it was rather swift and faint. She didn't feel the series of recessing waves transport her again and again, like she usually did. And although she had felt pleasure, she also felt cheated.

It seemed there was a hierarchy even in sensual delight, for by now Doctor Marshall and Mrs Cox were both panting loudly, seized by the first pangs of their climax, which would no doubt be powerful.

He came first and let out a loud scream that travelled around the room and startled Judith. She saw his face contract in a pained expression, yet there was no doubt that he was being swept by pleasure. His hips jerked and he pushed his phallus deep inside the woman's mouth, to the hilt, his muscular thighs seemingly trying to thrust in further still. Mesmerised, Judith witnessed the contraction of his scrotum as his seed was released between the woman's tightened lips. He withdrew almost immediately and fell back onto his heels, almost collapsing on the cold tile floor.

Then she noticed a faint tremor shake the body she had been caressing. Against her own thigh she then sensed the muscles of the parted leg contract in turn, gradually, from the foot up to the upper part of the thigh. Then the wave transferred onto the woman's abdomen, the smooth belly growing rock hard under Judith's very eyes. She saw the thick veins of the neck bulge out against the distended skin and the mouth contract in an ultimate twist before the cry of joy came out, loud and sensual, tearing at Judith's loins.

The body shook several times, first in a rapid succession of spasms, then progressively subsiding as she took her hand away from the retracted clitoris. Without a word, Doctor Marshall stood up and untied the limp body before taking the woman in his arms to then gently deposit her on the floor. He turned to Judith.

'Get dressed and go home,' his tone turned authoritative and almost cruel. 'I want to see you in my office first thing tomorrow morning. In the meantime, not a word to anyone.'

Judith began to tremble uncontrollably, suddenly worried by the change in his attitude. Had she gone too far? She picked her clothes off the floor and ran out of the room, her naked feet barely touching the ground as she passed the endless row of beds.

Chapter Seventeen

Judith took a deep breath, trying to slow the pounding beat of her heart. She had been impatiently waiting in Doctor Marshall's office for over 20 minutes now, even though he had made a point of saying he would be back shortly.

All this time her nerves had been constantly on edge, the anticipation growing more intense with every passing moment. She was eager to talk to him, to finally have confirmation of what kind of treatment the Clinic also offered in addition to medical care.

It was just a formality at this stage, for she already knew what he was probably going to say, yet she needed to finally hear it from him, to clear up all the confusion in her mind. But she had been waiting for what seemed hours now, and she wasn't any closer to finding out the truth. Besides, she was late for her shift now.

She could hear him speak in the other room, Mrs Cox's office. However she couldn't identify the voice of the person he was talking to. Now and again there were loud bursts of laughter, with a predominant woman's voice, but on the whole it was all reduced to a confused rumbling of conversations and it was impossible to make out more than an occasional word. She knew Mrs Cox wasn't in today, it was her day off. So who was in her office with Doctor Marshall?

Sitting legs crossed in a swivelling armchair, Judith fidgeted and pushed against the floor with her foot to make the chair turn. She quickly examined the room as it revolved around her. In the bright light the director's office looked different, the contrast between the black furniture and the white walls much more pronounced than what she had seen the previous evening.

In a corner stood a large television set, high up on a support cabinet, with a video recorder underneath. Strangely enough, there weren't any videocassettes to be seen anywhere in the office, so presumably the video recorder was hardly ever used.

She heard a door close in the next offfice and a third voice joined the first two. She expected Doctor Marshall would now come back, but each passing second made her realise she would still have to wait a little while longer. This only added to her curiosity. Who was this woman he had been talking to? And who had just walked in to join them?

Although she still couldn't make out their words, it was clear there were now three different voices, three people engaged in a lively conversation, but their words were inaudible. One of the voices belonged to Doctor Marshall; that was easy to figure out. As for the others, there seemed to be one male and one female voice, but Judith definitely couldn't tell who they were.

The voices died suddenly and she heard the sound of another door closing. A second later, the adjoining door to Mrs Cox's office opened and Doctor Marshall returned.

'Sorry to have kept you waiting,' he announced as he came to sit behind his desk. 'I had some rather important matters to attend to.' He pulled out a thin file from one of the drawers of his desk and opened it, taking out a few sheets of papers through which he quickly browsed.

'Miss Judith Stanton ...' he said, as if speaking to himself. His eyes moved fast, seemingly taking in all the information they glanced over but without really pausing to read every detail.

Superficially, it almost looked like they were about to discuss some business matter, and Judith was stunned by his attitude. Considering what had happened the previous evening, he should have looked embarrassed right now, yet he didn't seem to be. His face was relaxed, his hands steady. He sat back in his chair and picked up a sheet of paper. Every now and again he would quickly glance at Judith then resume his reading again.

She was starting to get nervous. She knew she had nothing to fear, yet she had hoped he would have been a little more friendly and welcoming. She still hadn't forgotten the tone of his voice the previous night when he had told her to go home. And right now his attitude was similar. He was utterly cold, obviously not the least bit embarrassed by what she knew, just as if last night had never happened.

'You've been with us for nearly three months now,' he said after a while. 'Usually, this is Mrs Cox's domain, but in view of what happened yesterday we felt we had no option than to have this conversation with you as soon as possible . . .'

This sounded bad. Was it his way of telling her she was about to get fired? Judith's mind worked fast, her thoughts connecting and all ending up at the same result. She shouldn't have been in that room yesterday. They had not protested when she had come in, but obviously they were not happy with her crashing their private party.

She had felt the same way when she had been summoned to the disciplinary hearing. When she had seen them in the Board Room, she had thought they were about to fire her because she had given in to her desires and she had felt betrayed because they had encouraged her to express her sensuality just a few days beforehand.

Of course, she had been wrong that day, the disciplinary hearing had nothing to do with her, but her frame of mind had been similar. Would she be wrong this time again?

He pulled up a pale pink sheet from the thin pile, which Judith recognised as her work contract. She closed her eyes for a few seconds and took a deep breath. The last image on her mind was that of his fingers holding the thin piece of paper as if he were about to tear it up. A sob rose in her throat but she managed to swallow it.

'You have not yet completed your probation,' he stated, 'you still have about two weeks to go. So far we are very pleased with your work. However, what I am about to reveal to you is usually not discussed until after at least three months have been completed ...' He stopped and cleared his throat several times, his eyes quickly travelling over the sheet of paper he held in his hands and never quite looking at Judith.

The young nurse suddenly felt strangely calm. Her palms were slightly moist and gently cupped the edge of the armrests. Judith was more curious than worried by now. If they were happy with her performance, there might still be hope. Perhaps her discovery of the previous night would only result in suspension or some other minor disciplinary action...

'As you may already know,' Doctor Marshall began, 'I founded this clinic almost 12 years ago. At first I set out to offer mainly cosmetic and orthopaedic surgery, but soon it became clear that ...' He stopped abruptly and looked up at Judith, his eyes suddenly alight with an inquisitive sparkle. 'Have you heard about the Special Care Programme? Has anybody discussed it with you?'

Judith was taken aback by his question and took a few seconds to reply. 'N ... No ...' she stammered. She didn't dare confess that Ray had already told her, feeling it could only make matters worse. However, should he ask her how she found the secret room, she would have to think fast. She remained silent and forced herself to concentrate, to come up with a credible explanation should the need arise. Silence and obedience were probably the best strategy right now.

Doctor Marshall cleared his throat once again. 'I was hoping you would have,' he stated. 'This would have made things much easier for me.' He paused for what seemed to be an eternity and just strangely stared at her.

Staring back, Judith started to wonder if this was the same man she had seen the previous night, standing completely naked before her, engaged in such naughty activities that now seemed unreal in the light of day. Maybe she had imagined everything, maybe that secret room only existed in her mind.

She couldn't help thinking how cold he was, and she also remembered how cruel he had been just a few hours ago when he had submitted Mrs Cox to that wicked ordeal.

But now that he was sitting behind his desk, with his clothes and his white coat on, he seemed even worse. The whole office seemed cold and impersonal as well. This man had power, and she couldn't help feeling that he was in fact dangerous. She felt an icy chill pierce her and her heart began pounding furiously, this time in apprehension.

'As I was saying,' he continued, 'we have been pleased with your performance as far as your professional duties are concerned. But now the time has come to reveal what else our patients can expect when they come here. I suspect you might have a pretty good idea by now. Oh, it is not something we advertise. Most people only find out through word of mouth. But it is a fact that we do require our staff to dispense special care if such is the patients' desire.'

He continued to talk but Judith wasn't listening anymore. Although he was merely confirming what Ray had already told her, she couldn't help being surprised. Happily surprised, in fact. It was all true, and this realisation sent a shiver down her spine, a delicious thrill that coupled with her imagination to form a vivid image of what her life would be like now that she didn't have to fear her patients' unusual requests.

Judith felt immense relief. Once again she had overreacted. Chances were he wouldn't even mention the previous evening, or else he would already have done so. Now she could concentrate on what he had to say. Now that she had officially been told, things would be much easier. She wouldn't have to fight her impulses anymore, there would be no hesitation, no remorse...

'I must admit you gave us a bit of a scare when you went to see Edouard with your story about being hypnotised,' Doctor Marshall continued. 'We knew you were having difficulties accepting this sudden blossoming of your desires but were still unable to resist advances. But I can assure you, everything you did was solely through your own will, although I must confess we did help matters a bit...'

The last trace of worry and fear vanished to leave Judith feeling angry instead. What exactly did he mean by that? What did he know about what she had been doing? She shifted in her chair uneasily but continued to stare at him defiantly. This time, it was too much for her to take without protesting. She didn't mind him discussing what had happened the previous night, but the rest didn't concern him, that was personal.

'What gives you the right to bring this up?' she finally asked. 'What I have done, even if it was my choice, is not something open to discussion.'

Doctor Marshall stood up and looked at her. 'As Director of this Clinic, anything that goes on between these walls becomes my business.' This time his tone had turned arrogant, almost dictatorial. He walked around the desk slowly, never taking his eyes off her.

Judith held his gaze and kept staring at him. For a moment she thought he was coming towards her but instead he continued to walk to the far end of the room. He stopped by the large black filing cabinet which he unlocked with a key he pulled from the pocket of his white coat. 'I see you might still have some problems coming to terms with the unusual nature of our clinic,' he said, turning his back to Judith. 'But I can assure you we'd be quite happy if you accepted to join our staff permanently.'

'I do not wish to be employed in a place where my every move becomes common knowledge,' Judith replied. She knew that opposing him like this might have severe repercussions, but she really meant what she had said. Maybe working at the Dorchester Clinic wasn't such an enviable job after all. Not if it meant that people would be watching and squealing on her all the time!

'Don't spoil everything, Judith,' Doctor Marshall said placatingly, as if talking to a difficult child. 'We have invested a lot of time and effort in you. We sincerely believed you would enjoy working here.' As he spoke he casually rummaged through the drawer, pulling out a series of videocassettes and looking at their tags before replacing them.

Finally he picked one out, closed the drawer and locked it again. Then he silently walked to the opposite corner of the room and switched on the television set and the video recorder. 'We screen our new members of staff very carefully,' he explained whilst inserting the cassette in the video. 'I must confess that from the start you have given us nothing but hope ...' He turned around and smiled complacently at a fuming Judith, then used the remote control to dim the lights and start the cassette.

Judith turned her chair around to look at the television set. But as her anger grew she decided she wanted to leave instead. She wanted to leave not only this office but the Clinic altogether. It wasn't worth staying anymore. From the very start her time here had been a whirl of confusion. She had spent the best part of her days wondering what would happen next, in addition to having to cope with the stress of her first job.

The rare nights she had managed to find some sleep had been haunted by strange dreams. This suspense had been eating at her long enough. What else lay ahead for her? Somehow she sensed it could only be more confusion and more troubles. Just like it was right now.

She made a move to get up and leave but Doctor

Marshall, now standing behind her, put a firm hand on her shoulder and indicated that she remain seated. She elected to stay just a little longer, her curiosity slowly erasing her fear. What was she about to see? Some informative programme about the services offered by the clinic? She wrung her fingers nervously, her eyes quickly glancing at the door, which she knew wasn't locked. If this video turned out to be some form of brainwashing exercise, she would make a dash for the door so quickly that Marshall wouldn't have time to stop her. She forced herself to remain calm and looked at the screen.

At first she couldn't make out the image, some kind of recording from a security camera, black and white and rather blurred. Then she recognised a naked figure, the back of a woman with a blonde head, standing in the middle of what looked like an office. Then she noticed a man kneeling at the woman's feet. This office looked familiar, but all she could see was the back of those two people and she couldn't make out who they were.

Then there was a switch to a second camera, showing the same scene but from another angle. A similar image appeared, the same man, the same woman, but this time the woman's face was plainly visible. Judith almost choked and stopped breathing, feeling her blood freezing in horror and her life draining out of her when she recognised herself on the video.

Yes, it was her who was standing naked in the middle of the office, with Edouard crawling on the floor around her, covering her thighs with long licks. She saw her own face twisted in a grin of pleasure, her head tilted back and her lips slightly parted.

Judith breathed deeply, trying to calm the disturbing feeling that was slowly creeping up within her. To see herself like this was horrifying, yet fascinating, and although she clearly recognised herself, somehow she also felt she couldn't be this woman, this sensuous creature that stood on her feet whilst being pleasured.

She felt curiously aroused at the sight of herself,

especially by the expression of delight she could read on her face. Of course, she could still remember how good she had felt that morning, but seeing herself being bathed by Edouard's tongue was even better.

'I'm sorry about the poor quality of the image,' Doctor Marshall announced from behind her, 'but I'm afraid the cameras in Edouard's office are getting a bit old.'

But just as he spoke the image changed and turned dark. For a second Judith thought there was nothing else to be seen, but then some adjustment took place and the picture suddenly appeared clearer. She held her breath once again as the same blond woman appeared, standing next to a bed on which lay a naked man.

The first thing she recognised this time was the white patch of the plaster cast over the man's left leg. Then she saw his thick cock, stiff and upright. Suddenly it all fitted in her mind. That blond woman was also her, and although she couldn't see his face, she immediately knew the man on the bed could only be Mike Randall.

She watched silently as the blond woman slowly walked around the bed whilst pulling on the curtain, each of her steps sending her hips swaying lasciviously, and then climb on the bed before falling all over the luscious reclining body. Then the image cut and she saw herself at the head of the bed, straddling his face, her hips sensually gyrating onto his mouth, her hands clasped over her own breasts.

She saw her head was also tilted back in this scene, but then it came up and she looked straight at the camera.

Judith shifted again in her chair. The memory of this evening, coupled with the weird thrill of seeing herself naked and moving so sensuously on the video sent a heat wave building up between her legs, her dew gathering and wetting her panties.

Yet she couldn't understand how she could have looked straight at the camera and not remember anything about it. All she did remember was looking at herself in a large mirror, a rather common-looking mirror . . .

'The mirror . . .' she whispered. Doctor Marshall's

hands rested on her shoulders and she felt his head descending towards hers to speak in her ear.

'It was only a mirror from where you were,' he said smugly. 'We could see you from the other side . . .'

Judith kept watching the television set, mesmerised by this vision of herself, this luscious creature now bending down towards the erect phallus to take it in her mouth.

'Look at yourself,' Doctor Marshall continued. 'You enjoyed every moment of it. You still do, even now.'

Judith remained silent. On the television set she could see her own face now looking up and her mouth contracting in an expression of utter delight; she could almost hear her own screams of pleasure. She saw her body tense under the strength of her orgasm then fall, lifeless, over the taut body.

She remembered she had watched herself in the mirror that night, but to see it on video was perhaps even more arousing. Her hand dropped on her knee and she felt its heat through the cotton of her uniform. It didn't take much to trigger her arousal nowadays . . .

But at the same time she felt Doctor Marshall's hands getting heavy on her shoulders. What had he just said? That 'they' had been watching from the other side of the mirror . . . Who were 'they'? And what right did they have to watch her? Even worse, how dare they film her on video?

Before she could ask he let go of her shoulders and seized the remote control. In a matter of seconds the television set was switched off and the bright light came back. Judith blinked a few times, as if awakening from a dream.

'I could show you more,' he said walking back to sit behind his desk. 'But not right now. Suffice to say we know what you've been doing, and that's exactly what we were hoping for. Now all we need is to confirm that you agree to become a permanent member of our staff and then we can fill you in on all the details . . .'

'I don't know,' Judith interrupted. 'I need to think about this.' She felt weak and baffled once again. But this time at least she was thinking clearly. They had watched her, they had filmed her, been with her in her most intimate moments...

Curiously, although she was angry she couldn't help a strange feeling of satisfaction emerging slowly in her mind. If she had known she was being watched, perhaps her pleasure would have been even more intense...

Yet at the same time she didn't agree to this, and she couldn't let them get away with it.

Doctor Marshall looked up, slightly irritated. 'Think about it?' he said. 'What is there to think about? From what I can see, you have already agreed.'

'I have never agreed to anything,' she protested angrily. 'What happened with Edouard and Mike Randall was a private matter, you have no right to blackmail me like this.'

Doctor Marshall sighed and closed the folder. 'My dear,' he said in his regular business-like tone. 'It is not our intent to blackmail you. All we have done was give you the opportunity to express your sensuality, and it is clear to us that you enjoy physical pleasure tremendously.'

'Give me the opportunity?' she interrupted. 'What do you mean?'

He looked at her in disbelief. 'I thought you understood,' he replied slowly, resting his elbows on his desk. 'Surely, now that you know what we expect from our staff you cannot continue to think that all the encounters you have had in this clinic were fortuitous? It was all meant to happen.'

Judith was baffled, not really knowing what to make of his words. 'It was all planned?' she asked in a whisper. 'What do you mean?'

'From the first day you worked here, we tested your sensuality. Didn't you ever wonder why Robert Harvey had been so, shall we say, "familiar" with you? It was no coincidence. He was instructed to try seducing you, to test your sensuality and your experience with sexual matters. Then you came to us, or rather to Mrs Cox, to seek advice on how to deal with your lustful impulses. We were very proud of you that day; the way you obeyed and displayed yourself for us. I must admit that this wasn't planned at all; you were the one who, voluntarily or not, gave us the opportunity to learn more about your sensuality.'

He paused for a second, his fingers now casually shuffling through the papers on his desk, then resumed his talk without looking at Judith, as if he were talking to himself once again.

'Of course, there were set-backs,' he continued. 'Lady Austin was rather disappointed with you, but since she's a regular patient she was also very understanding. Yet we knew it was only a matter of time before you came to give in to your desires. You did yourself an enormous favour when you went to Edouard's office with your wild accusations about being hypnotised. Thankfully, he was able to make you see that you were wrong and there was nothing to worry about. That's when we decided to set up some sort of "test" for you, to see how far you were ready to go.'

Judith looked up at him in amazement. 'A test?' she asked. 'What sort of test?'

Doctor Marshall took a while before answering her question. He looked at her and shook his head. 'I didn't think I'd have to spell it out for you...' he said. 'After what I've just told you I thought you'd be able to figure it out for yourself.'

He stood up again and walked towards her. By now Judith was beyond fear, anger or even surprise. All she knew was that she despised him, she despised the whole lot of them.

'If you must know,' he began, 'we arranged for you to find yourself alone with Mike Randall. We knew he would probably proposition you and we wanted to know if you would give in. Mrs Cox and I were in the next room, watching you through a one-way mirror.'

Judith was filled with dread. Her encounter with Mike Randall had all been staged, she had been set up. Now it all made sense: Ray's story about having to leave, it was all a lie! It had all been planned, a neatly set trap for her to fall into! Until now, Ray was about the only person she had thought she could trust in this place, yet he had betrayed her from the start.

She looked up at Doctor Marshall again.

'So the attendant lied to me?' she asked in a trembling voice. 'You had instructed him to con me into taking the patient out of the bath tub...'

Marshall looked surprised. 'The attendant?' he interrupted. 'No, you're wrong there. He was merely a pawn in our plan. We just made sure he would be kept busy on another floor so that he would ask you for your help. We knew he had a tendency to ask nurses for similar favours and we assumed he would ask you that evening. We were lucky it worked on the first attempt.'

'What about Mike Randall?' she asked. 'How much did he know about what was going on.'

'Mister Randall has a friend who had been a patient of ours some time ago. He already knew the staff were allowed to comply as per the patients' requests and when he mentioned it to us we assumed he would probably try something with you that evening. That is when we made sure to discontinue his daily dose of Desquel...'

Judith remained silent. She had to admit they were clever, very clever. Doctor Marshall rested his buttocks against his desk and bent down slightly towards her.

'There is no reason for you to be upset,' he said. 'You may feel that we set you up, which we did, in a way, but everything you did was entirely up to you.' His tone became harder, his voice cruel.

'Do you think we were unfair to you? We didn't arrange for you to seduce Nurse Stevens in the store room on the night you were working with her... Nor did we arrange for you to pay a visit to Desmond in Physiotherapy... And what can I say about young Lisa Baxter? That wasn't planned either, you know...'

He bent down further until his hands came resting on

her shoulders and forcefully gripped them, forcing her head up to look at him.

'All we did was wake your senses,' he said slowly. 'And judging from your reaction on these videos we can only assume that you enjoyed every moment of it. Now, you can hardly blame us for that, can you?' He let go of her and sighed.

'Obviously, it's up to you if you wish to remain part of our staff. If you don't, we'll even help you find work elsewhere. But I will ask you to consider this very carefully. You would have nothing to lose, and everything to gain, by staying here.'

He went back to sit behind his desk one more time. Judith didn't have the strength to reply. He was right, of course, but she was so confused by now that she didn't really know what to say.

'I want to think about it,' she whispered. 'I need time.'

Doctor Marshall lay both his hands flat on the desk and looked at her. 'Very well,' he said. 'Mrs Cox will be back tomorrow, she can answer any questions you may have. You'll be dealing with her from now on.'

Judith stood up slowly, feeling this was his way of telling her that he had said all he had to stay and that the matter was closed. 'Thank you,' she whispered one more time before turning around to leave his office.

As she opened the door she heard him get up behind her but she wasn't paying any attention to him anymore. She took only a few steps in the corridor before stopping to lean against the wall.

She was still shaking from what she had just been told, and her flesh was still throbbing from having watched herself on the video. His words were still haunting her as well... Nothing to lose, everything to gain... She would be dealing with Mrs Cox from now on... Indeed there were many advantages to staying here permanently, many wickedly sweet reasons. There was endless pleasure to be discovered, experienced. And there was also Mrs Cox...

Although Doctor Marshall hadn't mentioned the previous night, Judith was now keenly aware of what to do to get to the woman. She was so close to her goal, how could she give up now? All she had to do was to accept their conditions, which was not so bad in itself, was it?

She pondered it for a few minutes. What did she have to lose? Surely, signing a contract didn't mean she would have to remain here forever, did it? The least she could do was to give it a try. There would always be time to back out, right?

She resolutely walked back to Doctor Marshall's office. He was right: what was there to think about? All that mattered was how she felt. How true. She laughed.

She barged into his office. 'I've decided to...' she began. Her words echoed into the empty room and she stopped talking as she realised he was gone. But where could he be? Thinking fast, she knew he hadn't followed her into the corridor, so there was only one way he could have gone.

She opened the door to Mrs Cox's office and let herself in. Her eyes immediately searched the wall where she had found the door to the secret room the previous night. A thin crack was all that betrayed the existence of the secret panel. She walked toward it and pressed her ear against the white surface.

All she could hear were faint noises, objects being shuffled, furniture being moved. To her surprise and disappointment, there were no moans or sighs. If Doctor Marshall was in there, chances were he was alone.

She stood back a few feet and looked at the wall again. For anyone who didn't already know, there was nothing to reveal that the wall was in fact a secret panel, not even now in broad daylight. Judith could barely see the thin crack from where she was standing. Otherwise, it was just a blank wall like any other.

Then she heard sounds, loud laughter, but as she returned to press her ear to the door again she was surprised to realise that those sounds were not coming from there at all. She looked around. The office was the same as it had always been, of course, except for one small detail: a large crack in the wall on the other side of Mrs Cox's desk.

Judith nervously walked across the room towards it. She never would have seen this door if it hadn't been left slightly ajar. Obviously, it could only lead to yet another secret room. But just how many of those secret panels were there? And what did this one conceal?

As she approached, she heard noises coming from the other side. So, this was the place where all the laughter was coming from! Coming closer, she tilted her head slightly and was about to peep through the crack when she felt a presence behind her. A hand came pressing against her mouth and a familiar voice whispered in her ear.

'Do not make any noise,' Doctor Marshall warned. 'These people wouldn't appreciate having spectators.' His other hand came resting on the back of her head and pushed it forward slightly, as if he was forcing her to look inside this secret room.

First she heard another loud laugh and she finally realised this was the voice of the woman to whom Doctor Marshall had been talking earlier. She carefully looked in the room and saw part of a woman's face, and she recognised Marina Stone. Other then that, all she could see was part of the wall hehind the actress, which was covered in red, thick velvet-like wallpaper.

Silently, Doctor Marshall reached forward and grabbed the door to open it a little more. At that moment Judith was grateful that he still had his hand on her mouth, for nothing else could have muffled the cry of surprise that rose in her throat.

It was but a small room, not much bigger than a large closet and without any windows, but with one amazing peculiarity: the floor was completely buried under a thick pile of bank notes, forming a mattress about waist high. There was an incredible amount in there, layers upon layers of freshly minted notes.

Judith then remembered the satchel full of money that

Marina had brought with her. No doubt this was meant as the actress's personal contribution to this set-up.

The woman was laying completely naked on top of the notes, the weight of her body causing the thick pile to sink in like a soft cushion. Laying on her back, her hips were writhing sensually and her arms endlessly digging and disappearing underneath the crisp layers of money. Soon she began grabbing handfuls of notes and covering her body with them. Then she parted and closed her legs a few times until they disappeared under the money as well.

Judith watched silently, suddenly feeling a warm sensation invading her loins. The sight of Marina's white naked flesh moving amidst this sea of money was compelling, as was the expression of pleasure on the woman's face. She tried to imagine what it would feel like to simply lay on top of this fortune, to feel the rough paper brush against her naked flesh, to slowly be engulfed by thousands of bank notes. Yet even her wild imagination couldn't conceive of such a thing. She would have to experience it for herself.

At this moment she realised that Marina wasn't alone in there. Next to the actress an enormous pile started to move. The woman turned onto her side to face it, bank notes sensually slipping off her naked body. She laughed again and her hands dug deep into the pile, as if frantically searching for something.

Soon an arm appeared, then a leg, and finally a head. A man slowly came out from underneath the bank notes, a man Judith immediately recognised as Robert Harvey. He laughed in turn and his naked body emerged some more. Soon he shook himself out completely and came to cover Marina.

Together they writhed in this sea of money, their limbs tangling and their hips pressing against the other's. They laughed endlessly, kissing and caressing each other, their hands still gathering bundles of notes and digging until they both disappeared.

At that moment Doctor Marshall reached out once

again and closed the door in front of Judith's face. She turned to look at him, aroused and puzzled. He smiled smugly.

'As I already told you,' he whispered, 'you have nothing to lose and everything to gain.'

He put one hand on her back and swiftly ushered her back towards his office. As they reached the door Judith stopped and turned around one more time, staring at the empty wall, unable to erase from her mind the image of what she knew it concealed. She turned to Doctor Marshall once again.

'We have to cater to every taste,' he said simply.

Chapter Eighteen

The squeaky noise from the door of Judith's locker seemed louder than usual this morning. Since there wasn't anybody else in the room at this early hour, it sounded even worse. Judith opened and closed the door a few times, examining the hinges and trying to figure out which one needed to be oiled. This noise had been getting on her nerves for a little while now, but there wasn't anything she could do about it, was there? She opened the door one more time and shrugged as she sat on the long bench in front of her locker.

She was alone in the large room, alone with her thoughts. She had to see Mrs Cox before starting her shift, and she still didn't know what she was going to say to the woman.

When she had left to go home the previous night she had already decided that she wanted to stay on at the Dorchester Clinic permanently. But now, deep within her, something was holding her back; some nagging doubt persisting in her mind.

What would Mrs Cox say to her? Yesterday, Doctor Marshall had said that the supervisor would answer any questions Judith might have, and in the young nurse's mind there were hundreds of questions still without answers. And she felt she needed to know more before she could reach a final decision.

It was now clear to her that intimate contact between the staff and the patients was definitely not frowned upon; it was quite the opposite, really. The same was true of members of staff themselves. But how were the patients told about this particular aspect of the Clinic's care? And how did they go about asking for it? Did they simply have to ask for a nurse to pleasure them, the same way others would ask for a sleeping pill?

And so far Judith knew about the unusual set-up down in physiotherapy, and the two secret rooms adjoining Mrs Cox's office. But were there other rooms that also served similar purposes? Rooms made especially for the pursuit of pleasure? If so, where were they, and what were they like? Perhaps she would be told this very morning? The thought of finding out more sent a thrilling shiver down her spine.

When Doctor Marshall had finally confirmed the true nature of the Special Care Programme, Judith had thought she knew everything. But now she realised she hardly knew anything! Surely there was more to learn about, to experience; other sources of sweet pleasure to discover...

And soon she would find herself in Mrs Cox's office again. The last time she had seen her superior was in the secret room, a couple of nights ago. The woman had been in a rather embarrassing position. Would she mention it to Judith today or act like it had never happened? Would she be embarrassed? Maybe; maybe not. Doctor Marshall hadn't been embarrassed at all...

Yet Judith was herself somewhat embarrassed, although she was also eager to talk about it. What she wanted especially was to return to the secret room and possibly get to see what else there was that she might not have noticed the other night; perhaps even convince Mrs Cox to give her some kind of demonstration. This time Judith knew exactly what to do to get to the woman. This time she wouldn't let her walk out.

She finished doing up her shoelaces and checked her watch. Another forty-five minutes before going on duty. She decided to go up to the seventh floor and wait by Mrs Cox's office if the woman wasn't in already.

'Good morning!' said a cheerful voice behind her. 'Are you just coming in or are you finishing?'

Judith looked at her colleague. 'Just coming in,' she said. This was a girl she had never seen before, a pretty nurse with shoulder-length brown locks, a round face and a broad smile.

'I'm on my way home myself!' the girl continued in a loud voice, holding out her hand. 'I'm Susan. I just started working here. Last night was my first shift. Fancy starting a new job and being assigned to a night shift right away! Mind you, I don't think it can get any worse than that!'

She shook Judith's hand enthusiastically, her head shaking as well and sending her brown locks bouncing up and down at the same time. Then she opened a locker diagonally opposite from Judith's and sat on the bench to untie her shoes.

'We were ever so busy last night!' she continued. 'I couldn't leave the station to go for my break so my colleague said I could go home early this morning instead. Isn't that nice of her? Everybody here is very nice, I find. Anyway, we had this patient in room 427, right? She had an operation yesterday and initially she was fine, but then something went wrong and we ended up having to send her back for surgery in the middle of the night! Poor darling! Do you help out in the operating theatre? I used to, a long time ago, but I haven't done it in a couple of years now. What's it like in this place? Are the surgeons nice or are they rude bastards like the ones I used to work with? Mind you, at the end of the day all that really matters is that they do good work, right? Doesn't really make a difference how they treat the nurses...'

The girl talked constantly, asking questions and answering them right away without even looking at

Judith, seemingly never having to stop to catch her breath.

Still sitting on the other side of the bench, Judith just stared at her without really paying attention to what she was saying, but feeling out of breath just listening to her!

Susan was extremely friendly, perhaps even too friendly. She spoke in a loud voice, grinning all the time and giggling at everything she said. As she kept on speaking she stood up and began to undress, quickly rolling her white uniform into a ball and carelessly stuffing it into a large canvas bag.

She went on and on as she peeled her panties off, babbling about the place she used to work, her car, her family, and all sorts of other things Judith didn't really want to hear about. Yet there was something about this new nurse that compelled her to keep listening and looking at her; something about this mindless chatter that was strangely appealing.

As Susan took off her bra, Judith noticed her breasts were rather small but very round and firm, the nipples small and pink and looking delicious. In fact, the slender silhouette was quite attractive. The limbs were sinewy and slightly more muscular than average, but the skin was very pale and dotted with freckles. Indeed there was something youthful and rather refreshing about this new member of staff.

At this moment Judith began to wonder whether Susan knew about the Special Care Programme yet. That was unlikely. If indeed she had only started work the previous night, chances were she hadn't even had her "test" yet.

Judith's imagination started running wild once again and she wondered who would be assigned to try seducing Susan. Robert Harvey? That was unlikely. Somehow Judith could sense he would not be her type. She couldn't picture them together.

Obviously, the directors would choose carefully and decide what type of person a girl like Susan would preferably fancy before assigning anyone to this delicate task. Perhaps their plan was already in motion... Someone who had worked with her during the night shift might have tried to make a pass at her or began to flirt. Maybe nothing had happened yet, especially if they had been very busy through the night. However, sooner or later, Susan would be in for a rude, albeit delicious, awakening.

And in light of what she knew, Judith couldn't help being amused at the thought that the poor girl probably didn't have a clue as to what was expected of her now that she was working at the Dorchester Clinic. She was an attractive nurse, very friendly, even if a bit loud, and Judith couldn't help but think that the Clinic had made a good choice. This was a nice addition to the staff. Certain people might be put off by her constant chatter, but as Doctor Marshall had said, they needed to cater to every taste and some people might find her mindless talk quite attractive.

Right now the new nurse was standing naked just a few feet from Judith; having fished a bath towel out of a large plastic bag she was now searching for something in yet another bag.

'Now where's my soap?' she asked aloud. 'Ah! Here it is... Well, as I was saying, the salary they offered here was much better and I was looking forward to moving to London...'

As she kept on talking, a wicked thought rose in Judith's mind. In a way, Susan was not unlike herself when she had started to work at the Dorchester Clinic: trusting and innocent and probably not suspecting anything. And right now, Judith could remember a certain morning when she had been cornered by Tania and Jo in the very same shower room Susan was about to enter...

The memory of that morning almost made her laugh. She remembered how scared she had been, but now that she knew better, things looked very different indeed. She could even understand why Tania and Jo had set out to seduce her that morning.

Susan continued her mindless babble as she pushed

the last strands of her untamed hair underneath a shocking pink shower cap. She didn't seem shy at all, standing completely naked and talking to Judith as if they were long-time friends. The monologue continued for a while, then her naked figure slowly made its way to the shower room.

Judith stood up and followed a few paces behind her, pretending to be interested in everything the new girl had to say, when in fact her attention was focused on something completely different.

Her heartbeat accelerated with the excitement of what she was about to do. She felt a weird exhilaration, unlike how she had felt the night she had pounced on Jo in the store room. Today she meant to seduce, to give the new recruit a taste of what was yet to come but without necessarily scaring her. She wasn't seeking revenge this time.

Or was she? Was this her way of getting back at everyone for everything they had put her through? Did she want to inflict on poor Susan the same ordeal she had lived? Not really. All she knew was that there was a weird satisfaction to be gained out of giving the new nurse a taste of things to come. She didn't mean any harm, she just wanted to get to know her new colleague a little better. Who knew, maybe Susan would enjoy it?

Right now Susan had stopped talking whilst she adjusted the temperature of the water, seemingly unaware that Judith wasn't very far behind her. Soon the shower room was filled with steam and Judith stood immobile by the entrance, wondering if the girl knew she was being watched.

The constant chatter had changed to loud, grossly out-of-tune singing, slaughtering a song Judith couldn't recognise. Already the fruity aroma of Susan's soap floated in the air. This scene wasn't very different from that fateful morning.

That's when Judith decided to step forward. She walked up to Susan and stood by her for a few seconds before the new nurse even noticed her presence.

'Oh! You're here!' the girl said loudly. 'Be careful, you might get wet!'

Judith sensed Susan was just about to resume her tedious monologue and immediately pressed her hand against the girl's mouth. Her other arm snaked around the naked waist and grabbed it tightly.

In Susan's eyes she read surprise but didn't feel the wet body trying to wriggle out of her grasp. This disconcerted her somewhat. She would have expected her victim to protest violently but it seemed Susan was too surprised to even think of it.

She let her hand slip and uncovered a gaping mouth. The lips twitched a few times but no sound came out. Her other hand simultaneously slid along the rounded buttocks and caressed them lightly.

'What are you doing?' Susan asked after a while. 'This is a bit cheeky . . .'

Judith put her hand back on the girl's mouth. 'Shut up!' she ordered. 'Enough with all this nonsense!' She pushed the girl back against the wall and pressed her clothed body against her, placing both hands flat on either side of the girl's waist to stop her from going anywhere.

This time Susan didn't say anything, but Judith could see that the look of surprise had been replaced by one of fear. She burst out laughing. This was wickedly exciting.

'What's wrong, love? You're not used to sharing a shower with somebody else?' But before Susan could reply Judith had taken hold of her mouth and invaded it with her tongue.

She tried to imagine what could be going through the new nurse's head at that very moment, thinking it would most probably be worry or even fear. Yet she knew it wouldn't be entirely fair to scare the poor girl unduly so she let her hands wander over the wet skin to see how Susan would react.

Cupping the small breasts with both hands, she caressed them gently, toying with the nipples which readily grew stiff between her thumb and forefinger.

Susan let out a small cry and looked down at her breasts as if surprised to see that they would react to Judith's touch.

'What are you doing?' she asked again, her voice now a trembling whisper.

'What does it look like I'm doing?' Judith replied softly. She bowed her head and took one of the nipples in her mouth, sucking it greedily.

Susan started trembling and sobbed loudly. 'I'm not sure I like this,' she said as Judith switched to the other nipple. 'This isn't very proper, you know... Are you one of those lesbians? I don't know any lesbians... What are you going to do to me? Why won't you let me go? I promise I won't tell anybody! I really don't like this...'

'Shut up!' Judith repeated wearily. 'Just shut that big mouth of yours OK?' She was getting somewhat angry that Susan wasn't struggling but didn't seem to be aroused either. And most of all, she didn't want her to start talking again!

Her hand strayed and came down to fondle the girl's thighs. She heard Susan gasp a few times but she didn't say anything. By now the terrorised nurse was pushing back against the wall, her hands flat against the ceramic tiles, seemingly trying to push back further still in a vain effort to escape.

Judith was rapidly growing excited, her mouth discovering the slightly bitter taste of the warm, wet skin, her hands and her cheeks smoothly gliding along each slender curve. She lightly brushed the soft vulva and felt it getting hot and moist under her fingertips. Soon its heady aroma floated to her nostrils and only served to enhance her desire.

'Oh!' Susan whined. 'Why are you doing this! Please stop!' Judith slowly slid down until her knees came to touch the wet ceramic floor. By now her uniform was soaked but she didn't mind. Above her, Susan was shaking with fear, yet Judith knew this would change soon. Once she began toying with the tiny bud that was still hiding among the sinewy folds, once she took it in her mouth and gently sucked on it, then Susan wouldn't mind so much anymore . . .

Already she could feel the little shaft rearing under her fingers, growing stiff and swollen, and she let her mouth slide towards it, her tongue coming out in anticipation of the moment . . .

'Get up! Now!' a voice shouted behind her.

Judith froze and slowly turned her head towards the entrance of the shower room. A feeling of panic seized her as she recognised Mrs Cox. Curiously, she also felt like laughing at the irony of the situation, thinking how amazing it was that the same scene should repeat itself almost identically. Yet at the same time she knew she would be in big trouble.

She felt tempted to continue what she was doing, just to see what the supervisor would do, but she decided it was too risky at this point and slowly stood up. Once again she felt shameful, keenly aware that she had stepped over the line. Quickly glancing towards Susan, she still read the same surprised look in the brown eyes. Then she turned towards Mrs Cox.

'Dry yourself and meet me in my office right away!' the supervisor ordered dryly, handing her a towel.

Judith swiftly made her way out of the shower room, her uniform soaking. She felt betrayed by Mrs Cox who had walked in on her just as she was about to get Susan to react to her caresses. Although she had been looking forward to seeing her again, this wasn't exactly what she had in mind. And, of course, she knew Mrs Cox would now probably go to the new nurse and offer to release her . . .

This wasn't fair at all. She should be the one about to be pleasured right now, she had earned it. How much longer would she have to wait for her reward, how many schemes would she have to come up with to finally be allowed feel her supervisor's slim fingers torturing her tender flesh into submission?

She held on to the frame around the entrance of the shower room before stepping out, afraid of slipping once her wet shoe touched the tile floor. This was yet another set back, she would probably have to wait even longer now.

But then she heard Mrs Cox talking to Susan.

'I'm really sorry about this,' the woman said to the new girl. 'She will be severely punished . . .'

Judith smiled, knowing she had already won.

Want more sexy fiction?

September 2012 saw the re-launch of the iconic erotic fiction series *Black Lace* with a brand new look and even steamier fiction. We're also re-visiting some of our most popular titles in our *Black Lace Classics* series.

First launched in 1993, *Black Lace* was the first erotic fiction imprint written by women for women and quickly became the most popular erotica imprint in the world.

To find out more, visit us at:
www.blacklace.co.uk

And join the *Black Lace* community:

@blacklacebooks

BlackLaceBooks

BLACK LACE

The leading imprint of women's sexy fiction is back – and it's better than ever!

Also available from Black Lace:

On Demand
Justine Elyot

*I have always been drawn to hotels.
I love their anonymity. The hotel does not care
what you do, or with whom.*

The Hotel Luxe Noir is a haven for hedonistic liaisons. From brief encounters in the bar to ménages in the elevator, young Sophie Martin has seen it all since she started on reception. But as she witnesses the dark erotic secrets of the staff and guests can she also master her own desires...?

Welcome to the Hotel Luxe Noir – discretion assured, satisfaction guaranteed.

Praise for On Demand

'Indulgent and titillating, On Demand is like a tonic for your imagination. The writing is witty, the personal and sexual quirks of the characters entertaining'
Lara Kairos

'Did I mention that every chapter is highly charged with eroticism, BDSM, D/S, and almost every fantasy you can imagine? If you don't get turned on by at least one of these fantasies, there is no hope for you'
Manic Readers

Also available from Black Lace:

Wedding Games
Karen S Smith

Emma is not looking forward to her cousin's wedding: the usual awkward guests, the endless small talk, the bad dancing... But a chance encounter with Kit, a very sexy stranger, leaves her breathless.

Without a chance to say goodbye, Emma resigns herself to the fact their incredibly hot encounter will be just a sexy memory, but then she meets Kit at another wedding...

Black Lace Books: the leading imprint of
erotic fiction by women for women

Also available from Black Lace:

All You Can Eat
Emma Holly

Sex, lies and murder…

Frankie Smith is having a bad day: her boyfriend has just dumped her and she's just found a dead body behind her café.

Still, things look up when sexy local detective, Jack West, turns up to investigate. And when stranger turns up at the diner looking for work, Frankie soon finds herself juggling two men and an increasingly kinky sex life…

***Explicit, erotic fiction from the bestselling author of* Ménage**

Also available from Black Lace:

The Stranger
Portia Da Costa

Once she had got over the initial shock of the young man's nudity, Claudia allowed herself to breathe properly again...

When Claudia finds a sexy stranger on the beach near her home she discovers that he has lost his memory along with his clothes.

Having turned her back on relationships since the death of her husband, Claudia finds herself scandalising her friends by inviting the stranger into her home and into her bed...

Black Lace Classics – **our best erotic fiction ever from our leading authors**

Also available from Black Lace:

I Kissed a Girl
Edited by Regina Perry

Everyone's heard the Katy Perry song, but have you ever been tempted...?

If so, you're not alone: most heterosexual women have had same-sex fantasies, and this diverse collection of short erotic fiction takes us way beyond kissing.

An anthology featuring kinky girl stories from around the globe and women from every walk of life and culture who are curious and eager to explore their full sexuality...with each other.

***Black Lace Books*: the leading imprint of erotic fiction by women for women**

And available digitally, a brand new collection in our best-selling **'Quickies'** series: short erotic fiction anthologies

QUICKIES: GIRLS ON TOP
Emma Hawthorne

This new collection of sensational, sexy stories will arouse and, occasionally, even shock you. This volume contains brand new stories from women who ignore the rules unleash their sexual fantasies and find out just how wildly delicious sex can be when you take it to the limit – and sometimes, beyond….

Includes:

Darkroom – Jen and her boyfriend explore group sex

Doctor in the house – Debbie's visit to A&E results in a romp with a doctor which gives a whole new meaning to the term 'bedside manner'….

Mistress Millie – when Millie meets fit farmhand Jake she knows exactly how to put him in his place…

Juicy – Samantha is about to discover her husband and his best friend are hiding a sexy secret…

Festival Fever – Leanna shares a tent with her friends Dee and Mar. And they get up close and very personal…

Top Brass – She's the boss's wife and Cindy knows she shouldn't say no to any of her demands…

And available digitally, a brand new collection in our best-selling **'Quickies'** series: short erotic fiction anthologies

QUICKIES: SEX TOYS
Edited by Lori Perkins

***Because sometimes a hot partner
just isn't enough...***

Think of this Quickies collection as your erotic toy chest packed with twelve indulgent tales about wonderful devices to be used by good girls and bad boys.

Featuring bedroom staples such as dildos, strap-ons, vibrating panties and leather cockrings to more inventive toys such as sex machines and even futuristic playthings, this collection has everything you need to have a devilish time. Surprisingly romantic and wickedly tempting, you'll find stories from your favourite erotic authors such as Liz Coldwell and Rebecca Leigh.

9 780753 541005

Printed by Libri Plureos GmbH in Hamburg
Germany